From the Ice to the Fire

A Sicilian Immigrant's Death
struggle with Pittsburgh politics,
The Teamsters, and Mafia.

James John Lomeo

Bagheria Publishing House

Copyright © 2014 by James John Lomeo. All rights reserved. Printed in the United States of America. No part of this book may be used or reproduced in any manner whatsoever without written permission except in the case of brief quotations embodied in critical articles and reviews.

For information:
Bagheria Publishing House
4232 Northern Pike
Suite 203, Monroeville, PA 15146.

jameslomeo.com

Publisher's Note

This is a work of historical fiction. Some names, characters, places and incidents are either the product of the author's imagination or are used fictitiously, and any resemblance to actual persons, living or dead, business establishments, events or locales is entirely coincidental.

ISBN 978-0-9915117-0-9

PERSONAL DEDICATION

This book is dedicated to my four wonderful girls, my wife Sue, and three daughters, Natalie, Lucia and Juliet. Without them I would not be alive.

"I love our family"

Dashiell (Dash) Parr, a character in The Incredibles (2004), a Pixar picture presented by Disney

DEDICATION

To all the women and men that provide
and protect their families every day out of love.

IT WORKED ONCE when Mr. Lomeo walked into the office of J. C. Hetherington, general manager of the Federal company, armed with a court order. He removed several baskets of his plums and other produce. When he returned, he says, the warehousemen refused to allow him to load.

Photo courtesy of Pittsburgh Post-Gazette

Table of Contents

Prologue 7

Chapter 1: Why are beginnings so difficult? 10

Chapter 2: How do you know if you are moving forward? 22

Chapter 3: Does a beacon have to be seen? 41

Chapter 4: The land of milk and honey? 52

Chapter 5: Arrival? 65

Chapter 6: Meriwether Lewis started from Pittsburgh? 87

Chapter 7: The next Rockefeller? 103

Chapter 8: The American Way? 142

Chapter 9: Due process? 154

Chapter 10: Pickets and plums? 175

Chapter 11: Prophet in the Wilderness? 197

Chapter 12: What price faith? 202

Chapter 13: Is it ever over? 204

Notes 227

Afterword 235

Author Bio 237

PROLOGUE

This is an account of one of the many immigrants who arrived in America during the great immigration wave of the late nineteenth and early twentieth centuries.

As with most immigrants from Sicily, Paolo Lomeo made the decision to leave his place of birth to escape the harsh poverty common to this area. He also emigrated from Sicily to America to experience the civil liberties guaranteed by the U.S. Constitution.

Sicily has a tortured history of struggling for individual freedom against numerous oppressors and conquerors over the centuries. Revolts, insurrections, and the formation of vigilante groups are manifestations of Sicily's desire to govern itself without interference from others. This history has ingrained a fierce streak of independence behavior in the Sicilian population toward established government laws. Some Sicilians recognize that this innate trait of objecting to rules and laws can lead to an undesirable result if there is no regard for the individual liberties of everyone. The Mafia is the most known example of a positive idea of self-governance turned legally and morally corrupt.

Paolo had received no formal education, which was not uncommon for Sicilians of Paolo's generation. However, Paolo was fortunate to have a father of thought, and a caring grandfather, both of whom taught him how to live as a man of dignity and to recognize the difference between a demagogue and a true man of respect.

Paolo was born in 1896 and emigrated from Sicily to America shortly after the First World War. Once in America, he encountered some of the evil forces his father and grandfather had to deal with in Sicily. He also dealt with employee discrimination, governmental negative bias against immigrants, and the intimidation and expectations the Mafia used on newly minted immigrants from Sicily.

Paolo's story reaches its conclusion as he starts his own business, only to have its existence challenged by the political corruption in Pittsburgh, Pennsylvania. This story shows the marriage of politicians with the Teamsters and Mafia reaching its pinnacle of corrupt influence in Pittsburgh during the labor strikes of 1945.

Soon after the end of the Second World War, America was in the grip of labor strife due to the wage and price restrictions imposed during the war. Once the restrictions were lifted, large business owners and unions were demanding higher prices and wages. Unfortunately, this demand directly affected Paolo, the owner of a small fruit market in McKeesport, Pennsylvania, which had no employees.

The tensions were intense because the Pittsburgh area was the birthplace of the American union movement, which became part of the family and social fabric of southwestern Pennsylvania. Paolo challenged the Teamsters' demand that he join them since he drove a truck to retrieve his goods from Pittsburgh's warehouse district. His challenge took him to court and eventually into a physical battle to save his life. In the end this challenge caused his death and the death of his son, John.

I began the research of this book to explain and reflect on the true experience of America's immigrants trying to become Americans, in name and spirit. Paolo's experience may have been different from other immigrants, but only in degrees rather than a completely opposite experience.

Researching the facts in this book was more difficult than I had initially imagined. Written records, diaries, letters, and newspaper articles were limited in a generation that did not know how to read or write in their native language, let alone in English. Therefore, I decided only to use relevant facts that I could independently verify. Most of the other information I used was based on oral history I learned through my relatives, enhanced by articles, books, and websites discussing the immigrant experience of early twentieth-century America.

In addition, I changed the names of certain people to protect their families from embarrassment when I could not verify their actual roles. Some of the characters in this book are composites of people my relatives discussed over Sunday meals. I used these composite characters to add flavor to the story, not to change its meaning.

For example, Paolo had told my father about his experience when crossing the Atlantic coming to America and the people he had met. It was possible for me to verify the name of his ship and where he arrived, but I could not verify the actual people he met. So, I based his voyage on this hearsay evidence bolstered by the voyage stories of my maternal grandfather, given that he also was an immigrant from Sicily in the same time period. Even though I could not verify the actual names and occupations of the people who befriended Paolo on his trip to America, I believe I captured the portrait of Paolo's first step.

I verified the important events through primary sources, mainly newspaper articles from the former The Pittsburgh Press, Pittsburgh Post-Gazette, and The Daily News, McKeesport, PA. Additionally, I used two books on Italian history as primary sources, La Storia by Jerre Mangione and Ben Morreale, and Italy from Revolution to Republic by Spencer M. DiScala. I used the actual names and circumstances for all the relevant events, regardless of the level of embarrassment it may cause, even for my own family. The characterization of these events and people were how Paolo perceived them. However, if Paolo's perception was harsh or negative of any person, I used their actual name only if such person had purposefully put himself in the public light. My thought is that these people should expect that their statements or politics might cause others to criticize them in written words, speeches, or stories.

For most of the descriptive facts of buildings, well-known businesses, and other general information, I used the Internet as primary and secondary sources. I believe it is sound to use these websites to describe physical structures and common areas, for these attributions are not significant to this story. Would it change the spirit of the injustice Paolo experienced in the Allegheny County Courthouse if it was constructed out of brown sandstone or wood? I do not believe so.

Paolo's life story is a vehicle the reader can use to navigate the tension between ordinary Americans' ideals with the reality of everyday life.

Chapter 1
Why are beginnings so difficult?

Coughing, crowded hospitals, and death from this generation's plague, were all consuming to Caporale Maggiore Paolo Lomeo as he headed to the army hospital, located off the Piave River, to visit his sick friend.

Paolo, born in 1896 in Bagheria, Sicily, was the oldest of eight boys and one girl. His father, Giuseppe, labored on a speck of a rock and barren earth that he called his farm, while his mother, Agatina, desperately cared for her farm hands: her nine children. Schooling in early 1900 Sicily was as sporadic as the fruit growing on Giuseppe's farm. As the oldest child and son, Paolo's obligation was to till the land with his father. Since the age of five, his arms and back grew stronger while aching every day from the meager and consistent diet of citrus fruits and fish. Only on special days when his father scrambled enough money from his nightly card game would Agatina bake scacciata to serve with braciole meant for King Victor Emmanuel III of Italy. A cannoli was given to the child who expounded the wildest fantasy about obtaining wealth fit for a king. Paolo, at age ten, smiled and held his hands in prayer when Mama awarded him the cannoli for his story about hopping a sailboat to France to take an ocean liner departing from Cherbourg, France, to America to work for the Standard Fruit Company.

The words "Standard Fruit Company" were always whispered in the Lomeo household the same way other families normally spoke of a relative's mistress. The Standard Fruit Company was founded in New Orleans by Sicilian immigrants, one of whom was a childhood mentor of Giuseppe's. His Sicilian name was Salvador D'Antoni, but he changed his name to Samuel Daniel when he settled in America to better assimilate in his new homeland.

Mr. Daniel founded Standard Fruit in 1898. He had asked Paolo's father to leave Sicily to help with managing his growing business's fruit farms. Giuseppe refused the offer as he did not want to abandon his children and have them become part of the fatherless epidemic infecting late nineteenth-century Sicily. The children of Sicily either lost their fathers to the Italian wars in Northern Africa or to the attraction of America's golden streets.

However, throughout the years of his childhood Paolo could feel his father's regret in not risking it all, as others such as Salvador had, to rise above the deep poverty of Sicily like the hot air balloons that Paolo saw rise above Palermo during the springtime. Success of one so close to Giuseppe only highlighted his lack of courage to fight and figure his way to America.

He once confided to a thirteen-year-old Paolo, "I feel no better than the many dead fish on ice in the expensive stores of Palermo."

Paolo felt his father's pain. Somehow he knew that it was not his father's fault. Life in Sicily with its unspoken class system, and Mafiusu corruption was the opponent of a free-thinking man such as his father. Paolo and his father made a compact that only a father could make with a son: Paolo would fulfill the broken dreams of success that tortured Giuseppe. In return, Giuseppe would explain to Agatina why Paolo had to leave Bagheria and move forward to America.

"Patri, don't worry! I will go to America, start a canning business, and have enough money to move the whole family to America," Paolo reassured Giuseppe.

Giuseppe, knowing his son's emotions controlled his thoughts prior to true reflection, told his son, "Traveling to a new country and learning a new language and customs will be difficult enough without you worrying about me. I don't want to diminish your enthusiasm. Your passion will take you far, but try to act and react reasonably and calmly. Patience will bring you success quicker than moving fast without thinking."

Lowering his head, not really understanding why his father always popped his bubble when he had an exciting new idea, Paolo said, "OK, Patri."

Then, on May 23, 1915, their compact was compressed to nothing more than another piece of the shattered dreams of Giuseppe. The government of Italy declared war on the Empire of Austria-Hungry.

The men of Italy, including Sicily, involuntarily prepared for war with a call of arms for all males from the ages of eighteen through twenty-five years. The ironic twist was that no true Sicilian believed Sicily was a part of Italy. Their participation in a unified Italy was by force, preventing a truly self-governing Sicily. So, now the actions of their Italian oppressor dissected Giuseppe's battle plan for success, just as the Italian armies were traversing the Isonzo River in Northern Italy, cutting the defensives of the Austrian Army.

Paolo reluctantly joined the Italian Army and through his natural way and attrition of the competition, he was eventually promoted to caporale maggiore, which loosely translates in English as "corporal major." This was an accomplishment for a poor, uneducated kid from Sicily.

After three years of muddy, wet, cold weather with the constant fear of dying, Paolo was ready to go home. Before he was to depart for the last battle of the war in October 1918, he desperately wanted to see his paisan, Vincenzo Orlando, who had mysteriously contracted a terrible cough and cold sweats. What Paolo did not know was that his friend, similar to many other souls, had contracted what today is called the Spanish influenza. As Paolo approached the hospital tent housing the sick, he noticed a doctor in a French uniform, Jacques Petit, treating Vincenzo without success. The French doctor was only a doctor in name; he had no formal training. Vincenzo's doctor obtained his title because his father was a government official in Nice, who arranged for a medical certificate for Dr. Petit after only a six-month stint in an army hospital in Paris. Unfortunately, Jacques treated Vincenzo by "bleeding" Vincenzo's veins, contrary to the treatment that Vincenzo needed. As Vincenzo gazed at the fear-stricken face of his friend, he struggled with all the strength he could muster and screamed with his dying breath, "Moranu li Francisi!" Death to the French!

Sicilian history is full of tragedy, but no tragedy is greater than the French occupation of Sicily throughout the different stages played over centuries.

Even as a child Paolo had always been emotional, reacting without thinking. His father constantly instructed and scolded him that his quick reaction under the stress of his emotions would reduce his ability to act reasonably. Three years of marching, taking orders from army officers, and avoiding death in battle did nothing to strengthen his self-control.

As Dr. Petit took a dismissive glance at the face staring in horror through him, Paolo reached for his sidearm, a Beretta 7.65 mm automatic pistol, which an Italian officer had given him as an award—or more of a bribe—to stay quiet about the officer's amorous affair with a local Italian official's wife. The Beretta was known as an inaccurate weapon, which would have serious consequences for Paolo. Paolo wanted to maim the uncaring doctor, wanted the Frenchman to live the rest of his life in pain, even though the doctor's pain would never equal the heart-heavy pain that Paolo felt at seeing his friend die at such a young age for seemingly no good reason. Paolo repeated his friend's words while firing the pistol toward the doctor, "Moranu li Francisi!"

The Beretta, true to its reputation, inaccurately placed the screaming bullet in the doctor's heart instead of into the leg that Paolo wanted to injure. Consequently, the gun changed the trajectory of not only the bullet, but also Paolo's life, foreshadowing his future life obstacles, while simultaneously ending Dr. Petit's life.

The doctors, nurses, and patients stopped and stared in disbelief as Dr. Petit stumbled backward, knocking down a tray of medicine and sprawling on the wooden floor of the tent hospital, spilling a river of blood. In a weird twist of logic, Paolo believed that he was only applying the same medical treatment that the incompetent doctor had applied to Vincenzo, "bleeding the veins."

An American diplomat of Sicilian descent, observing the war on instructions from the U.S. Secretary of War, Newton Diehl Baker, Jr., happened to be visiting the hospital at the time of Paolo's act of revenge. He slowly walked toward Paolo with an outreached hand, and in a kind but firm manner said, "It is over now. Please give me the pistol before someone else gets hurt!"

Paolo, holding the pistol to his side, slowly raised the gun-wielding hand, offered the weapon as demanded, and introduced himself as Paolo Lomeo of Bagheria.

The diplomat, responding in the Sicilian language, which was reassuring to Paolo, introduced himself, "I am James Tomasello from America. You look confused, Paolo."

"You have an American first name with an American uniform but a Sicilian last name and you speak our language."

Ambassador Tomasello explained, "I am now an American, and Anglicized my first name so the Americans could have an easier time pronouncing it."

Ambassador Tomasello in a gentle manner continued, "As a young boy I followed my father and mother from Palermo to America. We settled in a community very similar to Palermo. The city is called Washington, D.C. It has a working community with a diverse population where my friends have different customs. I like how I am able to move freely and speak to whomever I please. It is a thrilling place. My parents have never been happier."

It was amazing; this was the life Paolo wanted to live. He had many questions for the Ambassador, but those questions would have to wait. As Paolo hesitantly handed his Beretta to his new American friend, he truly believed in these three short minutes he had forged a friendship.

The nurses had alerted the military police of the shooting. By time the police arrived, Paolo was sitting with Ambassador Tomasello waiting to be taken into custody.

The military guard demanded, "Caporale Maggiore Lomeo, stand at attention while he shackles your feet."

Another guard shackled his hands, then connected the two shackles with a long chain that ran the length of Paolo's body. These chains, a manifestation of his recklessness that his father warned him to avoid, made it difficult for Paolo to march to the military prison. The prison was only a few yards from the scene of the untimely death of Dr. Petit, but to Paolo it seemed longer than the marches he had experienced in the last three years. The difficulty in traversing this short physical distance probably had more to do with the emotional strain of thinking of the years he would spend in jail and the thought of his beautiful mother's worried face. His feelings of guilt for ignoring his father's advice to think before acting only added to his emotional torment.

Ambassador Tomasello watched as Paolo slowly marched toward the jail, and Paolo glanced at Mr. Tomasello with an expression of friendship mixed with a taint of regret.

As the American headed toward the wagon that had brought him to this army camp, Dr. Luigi Boselli, another doctor at the hospital, hesitantly approached Ambassador Tomasello, speaking in very crude English, not realizing that the American understood Italian.

Dr. Boselli explained, "Dr. Petit was a cruel man. He was purposefully experimenting with the Italian patients, not the Austrian enemy, to test his theories of sadistic punishment on human beings. He confided his dislike for Italians to me, especially the peasant class from Sicily. Once the Frenchman realized that Vincenzo Orlando was a peasant from Sicily, he wanted to use his most devious methods to prove that the lower class could withstand the pain of a brutal remediation that one would not give to a wounded animal."

Tomasello, who became suspicious of this seemingly self-serving statement from Boselli, asked, "Why would Petit confide in you to such barbaric acts? He basically confessed to you he was a criminal."

"For some reason, he thought I was French. Though I don't know why. Even though I was wearing the uniform of an Italian officer with the insignia of the medical corps," Boselli said, pointing to the shoulder patch attached to the top of the left sleeve of his shirt.

Tomasello could understand why Petit had mistaken the Italian for a Frenchman. Boselli was taller than most Italians, had a thin, angular frame, and spoke with the air of an educated person, or at least someone who thought he was educated.

Tomasello's perception of Boselli was close to the mark. Dr. Boselli was born in the Tuscany region of Italy, one of the wealthier regions of Italy. He was the son of a successful merchant who had sent him to Bologna to attend the oldest university in the world, Alma Mater Studiorum. Boselli learned his medical trade at the university, but he also learned that his standing in society carried an obligation to help and protect those less able to protect themselves.

Boselli confided to Ambassador Tomasello, "I did not live up to my duty. I should have objected to Petit's treatment. I physically should have prevented Petit from treating Orlando."

With sadness he continued, "Petit is probably the only one I could physically stop. But I didn't even try. I always thought I had the inner courage to do the right thing. How hard would it have been for me to report him? If I had, Paolo's friend would be alive, and Paolo would be heading south for home."

The guilt from his lack of courage was Boselli's motivation to report this conversation to Tomasello, because he knew that reporting this information through the Italian army chain of command was no better than telling his dead brother about the problem. He had confidence in the American. Tomasello had made an immediate impression on him. Boselli, who prided himself on being able to size up a person, believed Tomasello was a man of action with integrity. Tomasello did not let him down.

The ambassador inquired, "Doctor, would you be willing to testify for Paolo's defense?"

Answering meekly, Boselli said, "Yes."

"You understand that you will probably lose your medical license and, more importantly, probably your reputation."

Boselli nodded. "Yes, I will testify or do anything you ask to free Paolo. I know I will lose my medical license. I have already lost my reputation, but this is a smaller price than Paolo just paid."

Regardless of the outcome of the court martial proceedings, Paolo would have the knowledge that he had killed another person. Killing in war is different psychologically from killing a person you can see and smell. Paolo would never know who or how many people his war actions caused to die, but he would always know his rage was responsible for the death of Petit.

Paolo was sitting quietly in his jail cell when the guards approached and asked him to follow them. They did not put any shackles on him and did not brandish their arms in a menacing way, as they had done when they first brought him into custody. Paolo was taken to a board of inquiry, which was quite different from a court martial proceeding. The board was constituted for the sole purpose of determining if there was probable cause to officially charge Paolo with any crime. This was a highly unusual procedure for an enlisted soldier, especially one from Sicily.

The board typically consisted of five junior army officers who were appointed by the commanding officer. The commanding officer in this case really had no say in this board of inquiry. This board was suggested and constituted by the powerful hero of Italy, Gabriele D'Annuzio. D'Annuzio had personally involved himself in this case for many reasons, stretching from the political to the personal.

Tomasello had contacted one of his childhood friends from Sicily, who he thought would have the influence to extract Paolo from this mess. Tomasello knew that Italy was a rule of men, and not of law, unlike his new country. This was the main reason Tomasello had promised his father—it was a custom for Sicilian sons to make promises to their fathers about their future plans—that he would never leave America and return to Sicily to live.

Sicilians had an ironic pride in being able to manipulate any system, at the same time complaining that it was not fair how people used their friends to influence the outcome of any transaction or proceeding. Tomasello's friend was Carlo Di Rudini, the son of the former Italian prime minister and Sicilian leader, Antonio Di Rudini. Carlo was not as visible as his father in the workings of Italy; he had seen the political and personal abuse his father had taken to better Italy. He had decided early in life to develop friendships to benefit his friends if it brought him financial reward without regard as to whether the outcome bettered Italy. Carlo's actions portrayed him as an uncaring person who would never fulfill a request for assistance without an exchange.

However, in this case, Carlo had always counted Tomasello as his true friend, even though they had not seen each other for at least ten years. Friendships forged in the streets of Palermo as children were hard to break regardless of the types of adults those children became.

Tomasello called Carlo prior to the hearing. "Hello, Carlo? This is Selli. I need your help."

A young Carlo gave out nicknames to his childhood friends though no one would ever dare call Carlo anything but Carlo. Carlo had given the Selli nickname to Tomasello as soon as they met at five years old, and Carlo had never thereafter addressed Tomasello any other way.

"Well, old friend, how long has it been? How is America?" "I am here in Italy with your army at the Po."

Carlo quickly retorted, "It isn't my army. How can I help you, Selli?"

"I am representing a young soldier, a Sicilian, Paolo Lomeo from Bagheria. He is being unfairly accused of killing a French officer."

"Didn't know it was illegal to kill any French," Carlo said with a laugh although he was serious about his hatred of the French. "What do you need me to do?" Carlo asked after realizing he was ignoring his friend's request.

Knowing the answer, Tomasello asked, "Are you able to speak to D'Annuzio to help my client, Lomeo?"

"Consider it done, Selli." They chatted for a few minutes until finally Carlo said, "You take care of yourself, my dear friend," as he hung up the telephone.

Carlo immediately started the wheels of influence moving with a telephone call to D'Annuzio. Fortunately for Paolo, Gabriele D'Annuzio was in love with Carlo's sister, Alexandra, even though Alexandra was torn between her religious beliefs and her feelings for D'Annuzio.

Carlo also knew that D'Annuzio was planning to challenge Benito Mussolini for control of the Socialist Party after the war and would need to have the assistance of Carlo's Sicilian connections to provide Socialistic legitimacy to his candidacy. Calculating the motivation and actions of people is a natural gift possessed by few, and one of those few was Carlo Di Rudini.

D'Annuzio had appointed a three-person board of inquiry, all political friends of D'Annuzio. Paolo arrived at a large tent some thirty yards from the hospital tent. The sight of the tent of his killing caused Paolo to become panic-stricken. He carefully strolled through the large tent and sat on a wooden stool on the other side of a table from the three political friends of D'Annuzio. Paolo glanced at the empty stool next to him and stared in disbelief when Boselli was escorted to it. He knew that Boselli had seen the whole terrifying scene and would gladly testify against a peasant in defense of another physician. Dr. Boselli had the look of a frightened caged bird when he was asked to address the board.

One of the members of the board of inquiry asked Boselli, "Doctor, please tell this board what you witnessed regarding the shooting and death of Dr. Petit."

Responding slowly, Boselli explained, "Dr. Petit was an evil man. He purposefully withheld treatment from any soldier he felt was ethnically inferior to his ideals. He had a deep hatred for Southern Italians, especially people from Sicily."

"How do you know this? Couldn't he have just been an incompetent physician?"

"You are right, sir, he was an incompetent physician. But that had nothing to do with his actions and orders to the nurses. He thought I was a Frenchman and confessed to me one evening while we were having drinks in his tent."

"Didn't he see your uniform? Are we to believe he didn't know you were an Italian doctor? Maybe he spoke to you about his evilness because you told him you didn't like Sicilians either."

"That is not true! I wouldn't have told Ambassador Tomasello about Petit if I agreed with Petit's actions. There would have been no way this board would have known about Petit without me telling the American Ambassador."

"Fine, but ..."

Boselli interrupted his examiner to prove his point. "I feel bad about not having the courage to speak sooner about the Frenchman. This is something I will have to live with. I am resigning my physician's license. I don't deserve to be addressed as 'doctor'; otherwise, I will be just a pretender.

"Petit for some reason thought I was French but joined the Italian army medical section for a higher salary. I was intimidated by Petit, so I didn't correct him. I came here today to make sure another innocent Italian doesn't die due to the actions of Petit."

The testimony lasted only fifteen minutes, and the verdict was announced thirty seconds afterward.

The chairman of the board, Colonello Nino Guttuso, a Sicilian protégé of D'Annuzio, pronounced, "Caporale Maggiore Lomeo, please stand at attention."

Paolo slowly rose from his chair facing Colonello Guttuso not knowing his fate, but the chairman's face reminded him of his parish priest's face. What only took seconds seemed to last for minutes, as Paolo's mind drifted, thinking Colonello Guttuso could be a relative of his priest. How Paolo wished he had noticed the resemblance prior to the hearing's start.

Guttuso continued, "Caporale Lomeo, this board of inquiry has determined that you were justified in killing of Dr. Petit. We believe that your actions were motivated by the intent to defend a soldier of Italy from the abuse of the French doctor."

Standing with his legs shaking from nervous exhaustion, Paolo could not believe this favorable verdict. Shaking his head in agreement, Paolo said, "Thank you, sir."

"You will be honorably discharged with no further obligation to this army," the colonello responded.

Paolo was happy with his good fortune, but he knew that in Italy it was more than luck that had freed him, though he was not sure what political strings had been pulled, how they were pulled, or why. His family did not have any political benefactor or protector; his grandfather and father were too independent to ask for protection from any benefactor. Years later in America under a similar situation Paolo would learn the truth. The old adage "time will tell" applied to Paolo in this scenario and with so many other events in his life.

He departed the tent without saying anything more and immediately returned to his army outfit, packed his belongings, and headed home for Bagheria.

Chapter 2

How do you know if you are moving forward?

The Piave River is almost as far north as one could go and still remain in Italy. Paolo had never left Sicily before his interment in the Italian army. His army experience had let him see other parts of his country that he only heard about from travelers vacationing in Bagheria. Northern Italy was indeed cold, but it was beautiful and fresh. The young Sicilian loved to wake up in the morning and see the cold mist of the wind running away from the harsh Austrians to the waiting arms of the willing Italian army. Paolo had never seen such spring water, which looked like a string of diamonds worn by the wealthy women of Palermo to the opera. In the springtime, the landscape became a carpet of green. Green trees, green grass, green flowers, and green buds—it seemed that the whole region became Ireland, the land of green. His buddies were surprised at his expression of love for the sunlit emerald landscape and would derisively call him Paolo O'Lomeo.

Paolo boarded the train heading to Rome so he could connect with the train running south toward Naples. Everyone in Italy knew that riding the trains was an exercise in patience and the ability to deal with unforeseen events. Never did the rails run according to the published train schedules; they seemed to live in another time zone. The army trains were no exception. Paolo could only hope that when the train arrived in Rome, he would not have to wait more than a day for the train to Naples.

Paolo actually would not have minded spending a day in Rome, for he had missed the opportunity on the reverse trip at the beginning of the war. His war-bound train had stopped in Rome, but his commanding officer had ordered all soldiers to remain on the train throughout the night. Of course the older men and the more educated soldiers did not listen to the officer and spent a wonderful night in the city—if their stories could be believed. Paolo was afraid to leave the train, sleeping in his seat without even the comfort of a pillow. Paolo thought this time he would partake in the life of a city that had more people living in it than lived in all of Sicily.

Rome's reputation for a lively and vibrant population was an exaggeration. Palermo was the largest city closest to Bagheria. It was the capital city of Sicily. Palermo and Bagheria had a rich history of science, literature, art, and music. Sure, it was a mixture of all the groups that had invaded Sicily over the centuries, which Paolo thought made

Palermo and Sicily, in general, an interesting place to live and learn. To him, Rome was a homogenous city, where all the residents had the same history, ideas, and beliefs, whereas Sicily was a place where people looked, acted, and thought differently. He had an olive complexion with blue eyes, whereas his cousins on his mother's side of the family had blond hair with dark eyes. Sicily, especially the Palermo area, was a true melting pot long before America had the reputation.

Paolo's venture into Rome was of a short duration. He quickly headed back to the train. Ladies with nothing to sell except themselves reinforced the stories told in Sicily about the debauchery of Rome and Northern Italy. Three years ago he had slept on the train on orders; a wiser and older Paolo slept on the train of his own volition. He was starting to understand that acting without thinking carried consequences that he could not control.

The train moved from the station early the next day, only twelve hours behind schedule. As the train moved slowly down the boot-shaped peninsula, Paolo could see the various terrain and architecture had no overriding theme. It was a book with different chapters that did not relate to the previous or subsequent chapters. There was no wonder why Italy had such a hard time coming together as a nation.

Paolo thought Italy was doomed to repeatedly reinvent itself as a country as the great powers of Europe played chess, moving their pieces to gain an advantage for the elite class. He could not see how this war and previous wars throughout time had improved the life of families in Italy. Without traveling to the other countries of Europe, he thought that those people suffered like him with every power play of the wealthy and political class.

However, the stories of America were different. In America there was no ruling class, political class, or wealth class; all the people had an equal vote in the actions of their country. Ambassador Tomasello was the only American Paolo had personally met, and Don Tomasello confirmed his belief that America was a special place. How could Paolo know about Standard Oil, J.P. Morgan, and demagogues such as Theodore Roosevelt and Woodrow Wilson? He saw America through the prism of his ideal of freedom. His desire to settle in America would not be hindered by stories that imperfection existed there. To do otherwise would place a mental hurdle to his dream of living a life from want with freedom of action and thought. It would be difficult enough to start the journey to America—he did not need to have his buoyancy of hope deflated by thoughts of an imperfect America.

Slowly the train came to rest inside the Naples train station, and Paolo was startled awake by the lack of motion. He waited to exit the train, not because he did not want to begin his new life, but because he was afraid. The unknown and the possibility that he would not attain his dream of success in America paralyzed him physically and mentally for more than a moment. How could he do what his idol, mentor, father, could not—leave his family for the riches and comfort of America?

Then he recalled that his father had made him promise that he would try, and Giuseppe specifically told him that failing and falling were not the same as defeat. Giuseppe gave the same speech that fathers have been telling their sons since the beginning of time: trying and failing is better than never trying out of fear. Paolo wondered why his grandfather had not encouraged his father, and why his father did not listen to his own good advice. Was Giuseppe a good coach but a bad player? These thoughts were too difficult, complicated, and painful for Paolo to consciously entertain when he had a more immediate concern: he had to find a way to Palermo.

For some reason unknown to Paolo, the government would pay a soldier's fare only as far south as Naples. This was just another small discrimination that Southern Italians, and Sicilians, had to endure, even when they risked physical harm and death for the fatherland.

Sicilians were never short on sensitivities and perceived slights. Another reason for the lack of government assistance for the travel south beyond Naples was the condition of the rail system below Naples. Calling it primitive was exaggerating its efficiency. Paolo learned from the station master that he could take a ferry from Naples to Palermo, a ten-hour trip, and the fare would be waived for returning soldiers. The ferry owner had lost a son in the recent war and wanted to honor him by easing the hardship of sons returning to their families. Paolo boarded the ferry along with a family of three and two nuns, all heading to Sicily.

The passengers disembarked from the ferry ten hours later at a small wooden wharf in the Bay of Palermo. An escort from their convent, Mother Superior Tarsila, was waiting for the two nuns. She was a pious person who looked upon Paolo with a loving but concerned glance. It frightened Paolo. Why would such a caring person look at him with such an expression? Sicilians were famous for their superstition, even though most Sicilians believed that fate determined life's outcomes. Was her glance an omen of bad things to come? Did this mean he would not make it to America? Did it mean that he would fail? He now understood some of his father's feelings about leaving the known for the unknown. He was full of fear. It sounds odd that a person who had faced enemy attacks and a possible death sentence for a justified killing was afraid of the unknown.

His father had told him that physical courage was easier than inner courage. Giuseppe's most repeated phrase to Paolo was, "Have inner strength; most people don't have it."

Paolo was never sure what he meant; at such a young age he did not understand the philosopher's concept of moral conflict or moral courage. Because Paolo loved his father very much, he would never reveal or discuss his one damning thought: for all Giuseppe's talk about inner strength, Giuseppe did not seem to have it. Paolo knew that all human beings have strengths and weakness, and he could accept that his father was not perfect, but he subconsciously wished his father had moral courage. Immaturity has a way of making one believe he understands overt and covert actions of individuals, which tends to lead to judgments that are wrong. Maybe if Paolo had been a better student of his mother's religion, he would have learned and understood Luke 6:37: "Judge not and you will not be judged." Over time Paolo, would learn and truly understand Jesus's admonishment. Some just understand it earlier in life and those people are the successful ones.

Paolo stepped off the ferry to start his walk from Palermo to Bagheria, an hour and a half walk. He was excited to see his mother for the first time in three years and to sit in the lemon orchard splitting a loaf of bread and slices of cheese with his father. Some of the best times of his childhood were spent in the orchard with his father just talking and thinking about living in America. The slices of bread became American Midwestern beef and the slices of cheese became slices of apple pie— neither in much supply in Sicily, and never eaten by the Lomeo family. These thoughts of America during this lonely walk home were the first thoughts Paolo had in which he believed America and its riches were only a ferry journey away.

Paolo entered his family home a little before dawn, about the time his father should have risen from bed. The sight of the small rooms reflected by sunrays slowly and lightly touching the interior of the house made the home float in an air of serenity. This day, the fifth of

November, 1918, was beginning as an unusual day in Sicily, and for Paolo. There was no rain, and the sun was set higher in the sky than normal, as Paolo looked east to the town of Santa Flavia, the hometown of his dead friend, Vincenzo Orlando. Paolo interpreted this as a sign that Vincenzo was home and happy.

In Sicily, natural occurrences were omens or interpretations of their Lord's way. Sicilians never understood that scientific laws explained the physical nature of our earthly environment. Otherwise, their prayers and superstitious rites would have no meaning. It was the best way for an uneducated populace to have hope and take away the randomness of nature.

Knowing his friend was happy lifted Paolo's melancholy toward the sun's rays for a ride somewhere high and unseen above the Mediterranean Sea.

The young Sicilian arrived home satisfied and anticipating long walks with his father. Paolo's long, scary adventure had ended with him alive and home unlike so many other young Italian men. Truly, a generation of good men had died for the stated goal of the power elite to possess a deep-water port on the Adriatic Sea at the City of Fiume, a city in the Austro-Hungarian Empire.

It all began with the Congress of Vienna, 1815, which ended Napoleonic rule on the Apennine Peninsula and the catalyst of uniting the different regional sovereignties of Italy into one country. This unification process came to completion in 1870 with the creation of the Kingdom of Italy, with Rome being declared its capital city. An unspoken vision of the political class for their new country was to regain the power and adulation of the ancient Roman Empire. Italy's desire to play a role in world politics coincided with the formation of Germany as the major political power on continental Europe. Germany, concerned with protecting itself from invasion from the two other European powers, France and Russia, formed a military alliance with the Austria-Hungary Empire and Italy by treaty on May 20, 1882. This alliance was called the Triple Alliance.

When the First World War began in 1914 between Germany and Austria-Hungary against France and Great Britain, Italy did not immediately honor the May 20, 1882, treaty that formed the Triple Alliance. She withheld her declaration of war against Great Britain and France. The Italian government used legalistic arguments to justify staying out of the war. Their position was that the Triple Alliance Treaty was a defensive treaty and that Italy had no obligation to enter a war as Germany's partner if Germany was the aggressor. Historians and lawyers may have agreed with the government's position, except for Italy's subsequent treaty with Great Britain and France in 1915 to enter the war directly against Austria-Hungary and indirectly against Germany in exchange for Austria-Hungary territory, including the port City of Fiume.

The Treaty of London was supposedly a secret pact between Italy and its new allies, but Giuseppe had understood why Italy switched alliances and explained it to Paolo before his son departed for the war. Giuseppe, without the knowledge of the treaty, knew that the politicians of Italy were trying to relive the so-called glory days of the Roman Empire.

"Paolo, for some reason, the Northern Italians, the people who control so much of our destiny, always want to conjure up the lost glory of Rome," Giuseppe told Paolo before Paolo's departure for the war.

Giuseppe continued, "I am not sure Rome was ever a great and glorious empire. Didn't they kill Christ? Don't be manipulated by northern glory. They will never give a Sicilian any time on the stage of glory."

The Italian elite always spoke of their heritage connection with Ancient Rome, even though the true Roman Empire had disappeared from the globe two thousand years ago. Italians wanted to be respected as a world power, like the Britons and Germans; however, Italy was nothing more than a group of city-states trying to act like a country. It was a confederation of states with each region jealous and suspicious of the others. Plus, Italy lacked a strong and decisive leader. Government decisions and policies were made on the basis of the exchange of favors instead of the objective standard of the rule of law. This difference between Italy and the other Great Powers held Italy at such a disadvantage that it would never be able to compete with Britain or Germany.

Giuseppe thought Italy would overplay its slight momentary advantage by betraying Germany at its time of need and this duplicity would cause Britain and France to betray Italy after the war. Of course, history proved Giuseppe right.

Giuseppe advised his son, "Avoid giving promises of enduring loyalty and never believe in promises to be paid in the future without collateral."

He used this international situation to show Paolo how to behave as an adult. Italy should have never promised to aid Germany in time of war for an infinite period of time. Nor should the politicians have agreed to aid Britain for promises of Austrian territories without the means to collect or enforce such promises. Giuseppe's main concern was that Paolo, as a young Sicilian man without means, would be encouraged to follow the local Mafioso on the basis of promises of future riches and respect. He could only pray and hope that Paolo understood the analogy. It was hard for Paolo to focus his fatigued eyes in the early sunlight, but for a moment he thought he saw his father walking away from him toward the backdoor and out into the orchard. He called out, "Pa, I am home."

Giuseppe glanced over his shoulder and winked his right eye toward Paolo, his sign of approval or happiness. Then he disappeared behind the closing door. As Paolo's eyes encountered reality, his heart rate increased to such a high degree that the pressure in his head caused him to hit the half dirt, half-stone floor headfirst. The noise was loud enough to awake his brother Eugico. Eugico was seven years younger than Paolo and was the second eldest son of Giuseppe and Agatina. His innate nature was different from Paolo's, even though they had the same parents. Every parent wonders how their children develop different moral codes while being raised under the same situation. Maybe it is physical differences in the brains or subtle messages that parents send by assigning different degrees of responsibility to their children. Regardless of the reasons, Eugico caused a lot of trouble for Giuseppe and Agatina.

Eugico rushed to Paolo, screaming his name and shaking Paolo not in a medically safe way. "Paolo! Paolo! Wake up! Mama can't have both of you dead."

Paolo's mother woke slowly from her depressed slumber and yelled, "Eugico, please son, be good today. Respect your father on this day."

"Mama, it is Paolo! Come quick. I think he is dead," Eugico sobbingly implored his mother.

Seeing her eldest son unconscious on the floor caused her innate motherly instincts to control her behavior and ignore her emotional pain, as a mother can easily set her own needs and wants aside for the care of her children. Agatina slowly bent down and gently rubbed Paolo's head with a wet towel and watched his capillaries carry a normal flow of blood to his face. As Paolo regained his senses, he was thrilled to see the angelic face of his mother. It was nice to feel her loving hands again.

She whispered, "Your father was so proud of you. He loved you." Paolo asked, "Where is Patri?"

Agatina, startled, looked at Paolo in confusion. "What? Didn't you see your father laid out in his funeral dress?"

Giuseppe was supine in the backroom of the small house on a long, ornamented table belonging to the local funeral director. Giuseppe had died suddenly the day before on November 4, 1918.

Giuseppe was born in Bagheria on April 14, 1865. His parents, Alberto and Giuseppa, were typical Sicilian parents. They were peasants, leasing the land they called their farm. Giuseppe grew up handling the heavy work on the farm as his father had been permanently disabled when he took part in the unification revolution of Giuseppe Garibaldi and his followers, known as the Redshirts.

Garibaldi's army wore red shirts, the eponym for the "Redshirts." Giuseppe Garibaldi headed south in April 1860 to assist in the revolution that had erupted in Palermo. The insurrection against the hated Bourbon rulers would have failed without outside help, and Garibaldi was the man to exploit the revolution for his political benefit. Alberto was passionate and a romantic. He believed in Garibaldi and in the democratic ideas then spreading throughout Europe. After the battles, the unification's flow and ebb finally formed a unified Italy—at least in name—by 1870. Garibaldi and the other northern politicians forgot about the peasants of Sicily who made unification possible. The power elite of the unification partnered with the landowners of Sicily to continue the oppression that Sicilians had endured for centuries.

During the fighting in Palermo, Alberto was struck with a bullet that shattered the lower portion of his left leg. His leg never healed properly due to the poor medical treatment he received on the battlefield and afterward. The poor medical care had nothing to do with the lack of resources during the revolution—it was the standard of care in Sicily. Sicilian peasants could never rely on effective medical care, as their doctors were not scientifically trained but learned their trade through apprenticeships.

Alberto received no assistance from any of the power players of unification. He could not obtain a government job or pension. He had given his limb and almost his life to benefit Italy while his family suffered for his foolish belief in Italian democracy and Garibaldi. Giuseppe could always sense his father's bitterness toward the whole episode, even though Alberto and Giuseppe did not discuss such sentiments the way Giuseppe did with his son. Alberto stressed to his children to stay out of public affairs and concentrate on providing for their families.

As a Redshirt, Alberto had met an American, John Patterson, who had been one of the many foreign soldiers thrilled to assist Garibaldi in spreading democracy first to Sicily and then, hopefully, to the remainder of Europe.

John told Alberto about where he lived. "I live in a place called Birmingham. It is across the river from Pittsburgh, Pennsylvania." Alberto, barely able to understand John's Italian, shrugged his shoulders, saying, "I never heard of Pittsburgh. Is it a city like Palermo or more like Bagheria?"

"It is like neither city," John replied.

John described how two large rivers merged in Pittsburgh to form a formidable river, the Ohio River. He told him about the shop owners and industries that used these three rivers to transport supplies and goods to and from every part of America.

"Jobs are plentiful. Any person with a little ambition and a lot of heart could start a small little shop of any sort," explained John. "When I get back home, I am marrying my sweetheart, Almira, and starting a gun repair shop in Birmingham."

Alberto listened with interest but thought his stories were tall tales, as no place he ever heard of could have so much commerce and people. Alberto played along, saying, "Your hometown sounds wonderful. Maybe someday I will take the long journey to America and visit with you." Chuckling, Alberto continued, "And bring this old rifle for repair," while pointing to his gun beside him.

Patterson made Alberto promise that he would come to America with his family to visit him. "Now shake on it, my friend," John said as he extended his hand to Alberto. Sensing Alberto's confusion, John clarified, "This is what we say in America. Shake on it means we agree or we promise. It is similar to your Sicilian custom of acting with honor. You make a promise and do your best to keep it."

Taken back by such a generous offer, Alberto hesitantly but eagerly said, "Yes." He shook on it.

John Patterson and Alberto Lomeo would never meet again.

John died in the Battle of the Wilderness during the American Civil War on May 5, 1864, a day after his twenty-ninth birthday. His widowed wife would have to suffer the loss of her husband and raise their children alone while dealing with the financial ruin John's death caused. Mrs. Patterson knew that her husband believed in democracy and was willing to die for it, but she wished he had thought more about his own family instead of the families of the nation. In fact, as administrator of his estate, she was ordered by the Orphan's Court of Allegheny County, Pennsylvania, to sell their family home to pay John's debts. The notice in the Pittsburgh Daily Gazette stated that the sale was to take place on March 2, 1865, at the courthouse in the City of Pittsburgh. So, whereas most of the citizens of Pittsburgh and other northern cities were celebrating the continual Union Civil War battle victories, Almira had nothing to celebrate but her faith in God that the future would be kinder to her children.

Alberto had the same feeling. He wished he had been intelligent enough to avoid the insurrection, so he would not be physically unable to provide for his family.

Alberto could not hide his desire to visit and even live in America. If there was a story Giuseppe could remember his father telling him, it was the meeting of John Patterson. Giuseppe had learned from the dockworkers at the Port of Palermo that America was a place of vast opportunities where large American companies were seeking hard-working immigrants to perform the unpleasant jobs that Native Americans would not perform. The only problem was that if Giuseppe departed for America, there would be no one to manage the farm that sustained his family. Giuseppe had always been a sensitive, dutiful child, and this did not change as he grew into manhood. He would not leave his mother as the only able person to provide for the family.

Alberto was a man who reflected backward with many regrets of "what could have been." This is why he had difficulty overcoming his disability and adapting to his new reality. He was not an uncaring or selfish man; he loved his family and wanted his children to improve their lot in life. Alberto unselfishly encouraged Giuseppe to follow his dream of being an American and to live a life of luxury like the

Americans in the dockworkers' tales. If a father's love is not enough, then his duty should compel him to encourage his children to achieve a greater kingdom than he has. Alberto had a sense of duty, or he would have avoided the insurrection like the other young men in Sicily, but he also had a deep love for his son. Giuseppe had Alberto's permission and blessing to leave Sicily for America. Alberto would do what was necessary to manage the farm; Giuseppe had done enough. It was time for Giuseppe to move forward.

Slowly, reality was being absorbed into Paolo's body, and his body was trying to reject this infusion. The only idea that kept Paolo sane throughout the terrible war was the knowledge that he would eventually see his mother and father again. Even though he had been involved in difficult skirmishes and battles, he had tried his best to avoid danger. He did not want his parents to spend the remaining years of their life mourning the death of their eldest son from a senseless war.

Paolo could not know that his father would die on the day the Southern Front went quiet. November 4, 1918, was the day the war ended on the war front between Italy and Austria, called by the military strategist and press the Southern Front.

Italy rejoiced with joy and relief that the war was finally over. The news did not come to the Lomeo household until the next day, the day of Paolo's arrival home. Giuseppe had previously received Paolo's telegraph that Paolo was heading home and anxiously awaited his son's homecoming, but never learned Italy's participation in the war had ended. He had not seen his son in three years and missed the fatherly advice that he gave Paolo and that Paolo seemed to love to hear. He thought how nice it would be to finally have Paolo home. Managing the farm had become physically draining over the last three years with fewer chores being completed each day than the day before. Giuseppe's other sons were too young to assist with the hard labor required on a small Sicilian farm.

Giuseppe had recently complained of peripheral vision deficits and loss of balance.

"I got dizzy again and had to rest on the big stone," Giuseppe told Agatina a couple of days before Paolo's arrival.

"Love, I am concerned for you. You're slurring your words again. I think you need to rest tomorrow," suggested Giuseppe's caring wife.

Agatina had witnessed speech complications and noticed that Giuseppe was fatigued after only a few hours of work. This was atypical for Giuseppe; physical work never seemed to fatigue him.

Rising early as usual, Giuseppe slowly moved out of bed and barely ate enough to nurture a small child. His severe headache sapped his appetite. Watching Agatina walk from their bedroom toward him sitting at the kitchen table, Giuseppe wondered how this scene would have played if they lived in America. Giuseppe felt fortunate to have her as a wife and wished life's hurdles had not prevented them from immigrating to America. As she sat next to him with a caring and concerned look, Giuseppe glanced out the kitchen window viewing his farm and wondering how he could do his job feeling so sick.

Turning to the beautiful face looking at him, he worriedly said, "Agatina, my age is finally catching up with me. I feel terrible. I am going back to bed now and will try to finish my work tomorrow. Maybe Paolo will help me."

Agatina, always the caring wife and a thoughtful person, said to Giuseppe, "You don't look well. Go to bed and I will bring a plate of cheese and bread for you. You probably are anxious to see Paolo, and it is causing you too much stress."

Giuseppe responded, "You are probably right. Maybe a good rest and night of sleep will do me well."

Waking early on November 4, Giuseppe woke up his wife, complaining, "It feels like a little man is tapping a small hammer inside of my head, and each hour the little man is using a larger hammer than the hour before. I didn't sleep at all."

"Giuseppe stay in bed and I will see if one of our neighbors' sons wants to earn a few extra coins by helping you."

"No, everyone is celebrating. Work and money is the last thing on their minds. I will just do the minimal and rest until Paolo comes home tomorrow."

"Fine, but please take it easy," Agatina pleaded.

Giuseppe slowly made his way to his favorite part of the farm hoping the quiet atmosphere would ease his pain. The pain became disabling and Giuseppe collapsed in a final fit of agony, dying alone in his lemon orchard. When Agatina found him, he had a peaceful and pleasant smile on his face. He held his good luck charm in his right hand, a U.S. coin, the 1870 Liberty Seated Half Dime, which he had found years before while strolling on the docks of Palermo. He felt finding the coin was an omen that his legacy belonged in America.

The doctor surmised that Giuseppe died of a brain aneurysm.

The family, friends, and neighbors would not have a lengthy time to show the Lomeo family their respect for Giuseppe. Agatina was stricken and was unable to tolerate or endure the niceties of the viewing and funeral rituals. She loved Giuseppe and appreciated his devotion to her. Giuseppe had agreed to forestall his desire to travel to America to appease Agatina's father.

In Sicily, the bride's father had undue influence on the marriage contract, especially when the father had connections with the Mafia. Antonio Maggiore, Agatina's father, was a government clerk in the Treasury Office, Port of Palermo Chief Inspector. Though he was not a "made" member of the Mafia, he assisted the criminal enterprise by overlooking the graft at the Port of Palermo. Antonio was a petty and jealous man who believed that his children owed him an unfailing willingness to serve him. Agatina had to remain in Sicily to care for Antonio's household, for there were no other females in Antonio's home. Agatina had lost her mother when she was a young girl and had no sisters to share the burden. In nineteenth-century Sicily, women were expected to manage the household of their husbands and, if not married, their fathers' home.

The only parent she had ever known was Antonio. If she had not met Giuseppe, she would never have experienced the feeling of true love, for her father was one of the most uncaring and selfish men in Sicily. Giuseppe decided to lay aside his personal wants to have Agatina as his wife. The young suitor performed the ritual of asking Antonio for terms in exchange for Antonio's consent to his daughter's marriage.

Antonio demanded, "If you want to marry my daughter, you have to promise to stay in Sicily until my death. Yes, that is right. I heard from Agatina that you want to take her to America and raise your family. You can go to America, but it will be without Agatina."

Even though as the wife of Giuseppe, Agatina would care for the Lomeo household, Antonio knew he could manipulate Agatina to manage his household as well. However, he would not be able to work his magic if Agatina lived four thousand miles away in America.

"Why would you make your daughter stay in a place with no future? Don't you want a better life for your grandchildren and daughter than what Sicily can provide?" Giuseppe asked Agatina's father.

"Young man, don't patronize me. It is not my fault that you have no future in Sicily. I was able to provide a comfortable life for my family. Maybe you should listen to me and follow my career," Antonio smugly told Giuseppe.

"I am not interested in being a criminal," Giuseppe angrily told Antonio.

Antonio's face cringed with anger preventing him to rebut Giuseppe's insult. He thought he could physically intimidate Giuseppe by moving toward him in a threatening way; however, Antonio did not have an intimidating physical presence. He was barely five feet four inches tall, with a body weight over 180 pounds and no muscle development. Giuseppe laughed to himself. How did this small little man with a slippery character think he could intimidate Giuseppe? Maybe he really did have a self-inflated picture of himself to think Giuseppe would not violently respond to any attack by his nemesis.

"Short, fat, slow, bald man, you make a move toward me, it will be your last move. I have to abide by your wishes because of Agatina, but don't push me. You disgust me."

Antonio knew he had the advantage and did his best to make Giuseppe submit to his will. The father-in-law could make the son-in-law stay in Sicily, but he could not bend Giuseppe's character to his criminal ways. The stare from Giuseppe's enlarged pupils set in the middle of his crystal blue eyes frightened Antonio with the thought that one day his rage could prematurely end Antonio's life. Giuseppe never acted upon his rage, for his anger was not caused by Antonio's deprivation of character but by being shackled and imprisoned in Sicily against his will. Though Bagheria was not a large enough city to hide from a local devil, Giuseppe was able to, in subtle ways, prohibit his children from developing a familial relationship with their grandfather. So, when the Lord took the physical Antonio from this earth and sent his soul to the inferno below, the Lomeo family barely interrupted their daily routine to attend the funeral mass.

Salvador D'Antoni, Giuseppe's childhood friend and mentor and owner of the Standard Fruit Company in America, was in Bagheria to visit his family at the time of Giuseppe's death. Of course, he came to the Lomeo home to pay his respect to Giuseppe, dressed in a blue silk suit with a three-pointed white handkerchief showing from the left pocket of his suit coat. His gold tie with a diamond jewel pin in the middle was sending the message to those visiting the Lomeo household that he was a business success in America. At least he hoped that was the message being conveyed.

The funeral parlor turned purple and hazy as Paolo approached his father for the first time. Large steps seemed small, two feet was now ten feet, light-weighted shoes weighed five pounds each, dry eyes became wet, and the laws of gravity were declared void as Paolo's head floated from his body. Paolo kneeled by the foot of the death table with the outward appearance of praying to his mother's God, when in reality he was damning the gods or power that killed his father.

"If you watch over the blessed people, why did you take my father prematurely?" Paolo silently prayed to his mother's God.

Continuing his harbinger against God, "You play your little games with us, the little people of Sicily. Why didn't you prematurely strike dead the arrogant Northern Italians that abuse their friends and neighbors for material gain? Are you on their side?"

Maybe his father was not an inventor of machines that saved lives, a great politician fighting for reform, or a savvy businessperson who created wealth for his family and community, but he was his father. Salvador wanted to comfort and start the healing of his friend's son. Placing his right hand on the kneeling Paolo startled Paolo and caused Salvador to help Paolo return to standing next to the table. Quietly, Salvador began talking about his childhood in Bagheria and how Giuseppe and he became friends, more like brothers.

Salvador, looking down at Paolo, since he was tall for a Sicilian, five feet and eleven inches high, told Paolo, "Any spare time away from our family farms, we spent together and dreamt about leaving Sicily for the freedom of the American continent."

Both were serious about moving forward, heading to the country where gold coins lined the streets and where food and drink were plentiful. Salvador emphasized to Paolo, "Your father was the most encouraging, courageous, and intelligent person I have ever known, and I have dealt with many different people during my fifty-eight years of life."

Grief, like alcohol, has a way of lowering inhibitions to ask questions that in normal situations would not be asked. Paolo challenged his elder, "I don't want to hear exaggerated stories of my father at this depressing time."

He loved and respected his father even though he believed his father never had the courage or the character to risk failure by striking out for America. Forgetting where he was and who was standing close by, Salvador laughed out loud while gently placing his arm on Paolo's shoulders. He then proceeded to scold the young man as a color-blind man who cannot see all the colors. Friends and relatives in the funeral parlor stopped in disbelief but did not object or come to the protection of Paolo. An unseen force of nature made the funeral visitors cease talking and listen to Salvador. Years later Paolo's younger sister, Maria, revealed to her children that she thought the Lord wanted silence in the funeral parlor in order for Paolo to listen to Salvador without distraction.

"I used all of Giuseppe's ideas to succeed in America. The only reason your father did not leave Sicily was because of his promise to Agatina's father," explained Salvador. "He was an honorable man, a person of dignity, and he will now receive all that is due him from the only one that matters, God."

Salvador would gladly have handed over his worldly goods if he knew he would have the degree of respect and love equal to Giuseppe's. A young man could not understand that a man of dignity does not complain, tout his honor, or behave like a spoiled child. Grief also has a way of clarifying past events, and Paolo began his mindful journey that would take a generation to complete.

"Don D'Antoni, I am sorry," Paolo said as he started to cry. Agatina slowly reached for her son's hand in an effort to comfort him in his time of need.

"Paolo, you don't have to say you are sorry. Just try your best to live your life as your father would have wanted. No one could ever be as great as him, but you probably are the only person in this world who could come close. I know your father loved to hear stories of the great American president, Abraham Lincoln. I have read a lot about Lincoln while in America and have met a few people who knew him. Indeed, Mr. Lincoln was a great man. But, in my opinion, Mr. Lincoln was half of the man of my friend, Giuseppe Lomeo."

Chapter 3

Does a beacon have to be seen?

After World War I, Italy's different geographical regions were moving parts of a once great ancient machine that now were turning in contradictory ways from each other. Southern Italy, and more so Sicily, suffered the most from this disorganization. Rising food prices, decreasing wages, and scarcity of natural resources led Sicilians to lose their inherent optimistic attitude. Sicily's location in the Mediterranean Sea had attracted invading and conquering peoples throughout history. Controlling Sicily meant controlling the western half of the Mediterranean Sea, which equaled to controlling the commerce trade throughout the Mediterranean Sea. However, for some reason the inhabitants of Sicily never benefitted from this geographical advantage. Sicilians were able to adapt and assimilate with the different invading cultures, but they seemed unable to gain financial or governmental independence. Through all these adversities, Sicilians held the belief that their redemption was soon to come due to the severity and length of their suffering. In short, they had hope. Hope provides humans with the ability to forgive and forget the deprivation of the present for the security and peace of the future. Early 1919 Sicily had no hope. Collectively, Sicilians strolled through a hazy mixture of depression and defeatism as they tried to endure their unfair lot on this earth.

Paolo's optimism deflated more and more as the days crept along after his father's funeral. Being the oldest male in the family was more than a chronological fact in Sicily—it meant new obligations and duties for Paolo. Managing the farm was only part of these new duties; this new honor included responsibility for the well-being of his brothers, sister, and mother. Working the farm was not new to Paolo, as he had assisted his father for years. He knew exactly what needed to be done and how to do it. However, the stress of knowing that his every decision would affect not only him but also nine other individuals compounded the level of stress experienced only by an eye surgeon trying to save a person's sight. Stress can lead to pity, especially after the death of your mentor, friend, counselor, and father.

Alberto, Paolo's grandfather, saw how the random changes of life were affecting his beloved grandson. The emotional pain experienced by a seventy-eight-year-old father witnessing his son's funeral is as intense but different from the grieving of a twenty-two-year-old son losing a father. Alberto had always felt that his self-pity led Giuseppe not to respect him as a man, and for some time he wanted to prove to his son and his grandson that he was a man of respect. Paolo loved his grandfather. He was proud of Alberto's integrity and sense of duty to his family and neighbors. Giuseppe told Paolo countless times how he did not believe there was another man in this worldly kingdom that could compare to Alberto's fortitude of character.

Paolo informed his grandfather, "Nonno, Patri always told me that you were a man of honor. He said if you hadn't been injured in the insurrection, you would have been prime minister of Italy."

Alberto never knew that his son held him in such a high light. Giuseppe and Alberto had never had the frank conversations or relationship that Paolo shared with his father. Crying from the release of years of perceived shame and pain, Alberto hugged and kissed his grandson for such a tremendous gift.

"Paolo, I would have never been elected prime minister. You have to be willing to compromise your morals and convictions, and I just for some reason could never get past that hurdle. My disability made me sad, but I don't regret getting involved in the political process.

"When the insurrection started, I was willing and excited to participate. I wanted to be part of the New Italy! I thought Garibaldi was the messiah for Italy. I believed his every word. Oh, I was so wrong.

He had a smooth way with words. His appearance was elegant. He was refined. He also was a liar. He was a corrupt individual who used Sicily for his own material benefit. People of this island still think he was a great man. Fools, plain fools," Alberto animatedly told Paolo.

Paolo implored his grandfather, "Nonno, you have to leave the past in the past. You can't keep getting angry over events that happened so long ago. It is not good for you. We know, especially my father, that you are a true Sicilian patriot."

Alberto began crying again and said, "Thank you! You saying this means so much to me."

Alberto asked Paolo to walk with him to his farm, only two miles from Paolo's home. Grandfather and grandson talked like they had never done before. They learned in those short twenty minutes that grandfather, son, and grandson had similar thoughts about family, religion, Sicily, and America. The only thing they did not solve in those twenty minutes was if these ideas were learned and passed along through the generations, or inherent in the genetic framework of the Lomeos. Knowing his grandfather was not a stranger gave Paolo a new surge of energy, and he began to drop his suit of depression for a suit of action.

Alberto reached his front door and asked Paolo to wait outside. "I have a present for you."

Paolo waited impatiently on the porch. This character flaw of impatience always grabbed hold of his thoughts in times of anxiety. Paolo had been through so much in the last few days, losing a father and finding a grandfather, he did not want to be disappointed in Alberto's gift. The selfishness of a twenty-two-year-old man is hard to explain. Throughout the trials and tribulations of his remaining life Paolo would always reflect on this lonely and silent moment on his grandfather's porch. How could he have been so selfish and disrespectful to the memory of his father by worrying about the kind of present a poor Sicilian would give? Wasn't any present from his grandfather good enough?

Alberto came through the door onto the porch with a wide smile and holding a small wooden box. He handed the box to Paolo and said, "I was saving this for your father to have upon my death. Now that he has passed and never realized his dream of living in America, I did not want to wait a minute to give you the chance."

Opening the box, Paolo saw numerous gold coins, enough to pay Giuseppe's farm debt and hire a working hand for a year.

Paolo confusedly looked at Alberto and initially refused the gift. "Nonno, I can't take this from you. How would you support yourself in your old age without this money?"

He did not want to take an old man's life savings. How would Alberto provide for himself in his old age without this money?

Alberto protested and sternly admonished Paolo, "What gives you the right to refuse a gift from your grandfather? Why do you think you know more than me? I have lived and experienced life more than you will ever know. Maybe when you are a grandfather and feel the joy of being wiser than when you were a father, you will understand me.

Never show a friend such disrespect. It is not gentlemanly."

Alberto taught Paolo he should always accept a true gift given from the heart. Alberto warned Paolo, "People will try to manipulate you with so-called gifts and favors."

"I know, Nonno. I will be careful," Paolo said, not really understanding or appreciating what his grandfather was saying.

Alberto sensed a youth's lack of experience and tried again. "Paolo, a true gift means there is no expected return or exchange. A true gift does not require a returned favor. In Sicily, accepting a gift from the wrong type of person is dangerous. I think the same would be true in America."

"I understand," an exasperated Paolo assured his grandfather. "Paolo, knowing the difference between a manipulator and friend is the secret. Making sure a friend is not a manipulator is a hard thing to do," Alberto warned his grandson.

Trying to change the direction of their conversation, Paolo reluctantly accepted the gift, with the condition that his mother had to approve. Hesitantly, Paolo said, "I appreciate the gift. But Mama may be disappointed in me. She will think I took advantage of you while you were grieving. She will tell me that a man of honor doesn't need to have gifts. A man of honor bestows gifts."

Alberto's smile returned to his face. "Paolo, I have already spoken to your mother. I explained to her that I wanted Giuseppe to have this gift upon my death. And I realized now that I should have given it to him a long time ago. He could have used the gift to move you, your mother, and the rest of your family to America.

"Maybe somewhere in my soul, I was afraid that he would leave and I would never see him again. Now, I see that was selfish on my part. He is gone and I will never see him again anyhow. I wanted him to be happy, and I know if you become an American, he will be happy wherever he is."

Alberto had stopped believing in the Roman Catholic Church teachings years ago, but had more love and empathy for his family and neighbors than most of the Sicilians that religiously attended Mass every Sunday. Alberto only wanted the best for his son. He just did not how to accomplish this goal.

"Patri would have never thought you were selfish. He loved you, Nonno," Paolo reassured his grandfather.

"I hope that is true."

Agatina had listened and understood Alberto's reason for giving such a generous gift. Alberto wanted Giuseppe to be an American, but circumstances stopped this from happening. Giuseppe wanted Paolo to be an American to fulfill Giuseppe's dream, and Alberto did not want life's circumstances to prevent the completion of his son's dream. Both fathers wanted their sons to be Americans. Now, Paolo would fulfill the dreams of his grandfather and father.

Alberto and Giuseppe knew being an American meant more than just living in America, it meant living in a country that respected the individual without paying deference to a king or emperor. Paolo would learn in a very personal way in future years that America's system of government does not always protect an individual's right against the politically connected individuals and groups. Alberto and Giuseppe would have been astounded to learn that corruption existed in America also.

Paolo would use the money to pay the corrupt Palermo bankers and hire a competent farm manager to help his mother and brothers maintain the farm during this year of transition. This would give Paolo's brothers enough time to learn the trade and manage the farm for the benefit of the family. The only stipulation on Alberto's gift was Paolo's timely departure for America.

Another impetus for a timely departure to America was Benito Mussolini and the growth of his new Fascist Party. Ironically, this new totalitarian-minded, right-wing extremist party combining the interest of the nationalists, landowners, and wealthy elite took its name from the group of Sicilians who, in the early 1890s, formed a people-oriented workers' league called Fasci Siciliani. Fasci Siciliani expounded a program of land reform, the true wealth in Sicily, and workers' rights not practiced or protected in the other industrial nations. This concept of workers' rights was just beginning to take root in the souls of the working poor in Paolo's future American hometown, McKeesport, Pennsylvania.

Alberto had persuaded a young Giuseppe not to participate in the riots that followed the island-wide workers' strikes that were instigated by the Fasci Siciliani. Giuseppe's comprehension of the dynamics of a political and cultural revolt did not equal Alberto's understanding.

Alberto had suffered physically and psychologically from Garibaldi's promises of personal and economic freedom. Garibaldi used simplistic slogans and ideas of freedom to attract and retain the loyalty of the peasant class, especially in Sicily. The Redshirts still were heroes to Sicilians fifty years later. However, Alberto was keen enough to know that Garibaldi had used the young men of Sicily for his own fame and grab for power. Alberto vowed never to worship or speak of the Redshirts or Garibaldi in a positive way. He understood to the core of his soul after fifty years of brooding what Garibaldi meant when he said, "You have to force liberty on people for their own good."

It meant Sicily's status as a subservient region to the power elite of Northern Italy had not changed. Every conquering and tyrannical culture from the Ancient Romans to the Moors and then the French used Sicily's natural resources to benefit their own people. These conquerors oppressed and repressed the Sicilian desire to live as equal children of God, while outwardly encouraging Sicilians to accept these dictatorships as the best way to bring social and economic reforms to Sicily. These foreign powers believed Sicilians were unintelligent and backward and could not govern themselves. It never seemed to occur to these other societies that Sicily had neither the natural barriers to protect itself from invasion by a great force nor the population to develop and sustain an actual effective fighting force for protection. If Sicily had this natural mix, it may have been a Sicilian eagle devouring pies consisting of French, Moors, and Romans.

Alberto knew Fasci Siciliani would end like all the other Sicilian attempts to free itself of imperialistic chains: in failure. The leaders of the movement would either be arrested, emigrate, or be seduced by the lure of power and collude with the northern regions to take advantage of their own family, friends, and neighbors. Giuseppe realized by the time Paolo was born that Alberto's knowledge of politics surpassed that of other Sicilians, even its political leaders. Fasci Siciliani ended in a brutal assault by the Italian army, which led to the arrest of some of its leaders. The other leaders escaped to America in time to participate, and in some cases lead, the growth of workers' unions in the United States.

Paolo knew of his grandfather's reputation within the family for analyzing the Byzantine puzzle of Italian politics and listened attentively to Alberto's opinion of Mussolini. Mussolini was another Northern Italian, with simple slogans and the skills of a Shakespearian actor to convince a war-fatigued population that his way was the path to glory once held by Caesar. A former Socialist who avoided military service during his youth, thus escaping physical danger, and now a newspaper editor and political leader of the Fascist Party, he advocated military adventures abroad to stir nationalistic pride and economic programs that the robber barons of America could only pray for. Mussolini's brigade of enforcers, known as Blackshirts, harassed the peasant populace into accepting this new great leader through intimidation and outright violence. In future years, these tactics were copied and used in a more lethal way by a man just as evil but more cunning: Adolf Hitler.

Alberto reached for and held Paolo's arm as they walked off his porch toward Paolo's farm while Paolo clung to his box of fortunate. It was not a fortune, but he was fortunate that he had such an understanding and loving grandfather. The old man advised him to leave Sicily as soon as he could, for once Mussolini became the new prime minister of Italy, he surely would restrict emigration of the young working men of Southern Italy.

"Paolo, you must not wait a minute to start your journey to America. Mussolini has to distract the populace from the misery of the post-war inflation and food shortages. The only way he can do this is to start a foreign war to rally the populace. The recent war veterans, like you, will be the first drafted due to your war experience. He doesn't want a long war, but something quick, so he will not have time to train the inexperienced youth of Italy," Alberto advised his grandson.

Paolo responded, "Nonno, he isn't even prime minister yet. I have time to make the proper arrangements to America. I want to make sure I have a job contract before setting sail across the Atlantic. Otherwise, I will starve in a strange land without my family."

Responding with the frustration of an old wise person explaining a situation to a know-it-all youth, Alberto said, "Paolo, have you listened to the young man's speeches? He is setting the stage for his rise to the top spot.

"The talk is all about how our allies, Britain and France, are taking all the spoils of war at the costs of the Italians. The northern newspapers are blaming Prime Minister Orlando for the bad terms of the peace treaty. When Mr. Orlando's government falters, the Northern Italians will blame Sicily for its misfortune, because Orlando is a Sicilian."

Alberto, too excited with emotions to stop talking to determine if Paolo understood his point, continued his political venting. "Mussolini needs to have a 'fall guy' to rally the rest of Italy. He will blame Sicily, and then our Sicilian politicians will offer our young men as draftees into Mussolini's army to show that Sicilians are loyal Italians. Sicily should never have agreed to become a part of unified Italy after Garibaldi's treachery against us."

"I understand now. Sicilians will be the first ones drafted to restore Italy's honor. We will die, so the industrialists can have a few more lira," Paolo told his grandfather while nodding his head in agreement.

"Of course our politicians' sons won't be drafted. Just dumb people like us," Alberto retorted with resignation.

Mussolini was unlike any other politician in Alberto's lifetime. The previous prime ministers and kings were power-hungry men eager and willing to speak of personal liberty while participating in actions that were contrary to a true republic. However, Mussolini did not hide his belief that the uneducated and poor of Sicily did not have the character or intellect to govern themselves.

"Paolo, you are right for sure. I can't figure out why the Sicilians are not offended and ready to revolt, as we have done so many times in the past," Alberto wondered aloud to Paolo.

Paolo leaned down to whisper hesitantly, as he did not want to act as though he comprehended the matter better than the "all-knowing" grandfather. "It had to do with the lack of hope."

Sicily had lost many resources over the years: sulfur mines were shuttered, twenty percent of the people who emigrated from Italy in the great immigration wave of the early twentieth century were from Sicily, and the physical and psychological hurt of the Great War also played a part in the economic depression of Sicily. However, the most valuable resource, hope, was in low supply. Paolo, being young, did not know if the lack of the other resources caused this scarcity of hope or if the lack of hope caused the other resources to be in short supply. He did know that the future of Sicily had to fight the vultures of northern progressive and economic programs circling its almost dead carcass if Sicily was to have a chance at prosperity.

As they were crossing the neighbors' rows of lemon trees, Alberto leaped his old, thin skeleton frame off the ground in sheer enjoyment that his grandson had such thoughts of politics.

"You are right. You are right, Paolo!" Alberto exclaimed.

Alberto wondered if Paolo understood the difference between having a government dictate the actions of its citizenry, as opposed to a government that respected and honored the governed enough to let them enjoy life as God had intended. Alberto was an uneducated farmer in faraway Sicily, but somehow he had grasped the meaning of the Enlightenment. He wished Paolo would eventually understand the difference. Alberto thought as Paolo experienced life's ups and downs in future years, the difference would become clear.

As they reached Paolo's farm, Agatina reflected the famous painting by Leonardo Da Vinci, Lady with an Ermine, half smiling and half wondering what the future would bring to this young man who had introduced her to motherhood. With all the analysis over the centuries of this famous painting and Da Vinci's message, maybe the meaning is nothing more than a mother watching her son leave her home to become a man. A mother's wish to have her son grow to be a man of respect is paramount, though somewhere in the deep regions of a mother's heart there is a section that wants her son to remain dependent on her. A mother is so dependent on a child's love.

Paolo slowly bent over to kiss his grandfather good-bye. "Nonno, good-bye. Thank you for everything. I will make you proud," Paolo assured his grandfather.

As tears started to slowly stream from the old man's eyes, Alberto said, "I know."

He turned away and slowly headed home knowing he made a difference in Paolo's life. His job as a grandfather was complete.

Before saying anything to his mother, Paolo quickly approached her and hugged Agatina until she thought she would crumble to the ground in sheer pain.

Chapter 4

The land of milk and honey?

Being asked by your parents to carry out a task or to follow a demand under the threat of arrest by the government is different from taking a course of action of your own volition. Thousands of Sicilians had departed the island for America searching for a better quality of life. However, some returned with stories of horror about living in America's largest cities. They told about the raw sewage flowing in the gutters of the street, the brutal northeast winters without home heat, and demeaning jobs being the only employment offered. Others returned with stories of success. They did not live the life of rich men, but they were able to provide for themselves and enjoy the amenities of life that most in Sicily could only dream about.

Paolo loved to hear these stories. He also listened to his father's stories and advice, his grandfather's theories, and the Palermo dockworkers' tales of adventure across the Atlantic. Understanding that descriptions of events come from the perspective of the speaker was a lesson Paolo had learned listening to the men discuss current events issues or tell tall tales in the piazza. Exaggeration was the main ingredient that made the discussions more exciting and lively. The more exaggerated the story, the more it seemed to brighten the faces of the other men and ladies. Some told stories of their success and others told stories of their failures, but all the storytellers acted with such energy and excitement that the only response was wonderment.

At an early age, he understood that most times the truth lay somewhere on the bridge from bragging to understatement. Paolo concluded from piecing together all the stories he heard that America's spirit and ideal of self-reliance helped a person, regardless of place of birth, reach his financial and moral potential. He was concerned with reaching his potential as a person of God, as his father repeatedly told him was the true path to happiness. Paolo realized too late that his father was not bitter about giving up his American dream, only sad that his potential was unrealized. This Sicilian was determined to reach his potential.

Not talking to his father before heading to Palermo to start his journey held his excitement and enjoyment in check. He most definitely could not discuss the killing of the French officer with his mother or grandfather. Along with his sack of clothes he packed this episode deep in his soul to be taken to America with his worldly possessions. America may inspect his person or sack, but its instruments of physical prodding and questions to uncover a lack of intellect had the inability to find this deep, dark secret.

As he awoke on the morning of his new life, Agatina prepared a hearty breakfast of bread, cheese, and fruit and packed a lunch for his trip. A worried Sicilian mother only had so many ways in early 1900s Sicily to comfort her son in times of stress. Unlike women of twenty-first-century America, Sicilian women had no separate means to provide for their families and would not be able to solve family financial problems or assist a child with financial help. She could tender an edible and sometimes delicious meal for nutriment and delight. The most important thing she could give was unconditional love, and no mother gave more love to her children than Agatina. Paolo graciously accepted the meals, and hugged and kissed his mother just like he did a thousand times as a boy. He held her tightly and whispered into her right ear, bedda. Tears from both faces merged together to form a larger droplet before hitting the half stone, half dirt floor of the farmhouse. Paolo assured her he would return next year with enough money to pay for the family to settle with him in America.

Paolo told her, "Mama, please don't worry. It will all work out as Patri had planned. I will see you next year when the American work slows down. Patri told me it will take me about two years of hard work to save enough money to bring the family to America. But I still can visit. It shouldn't cost that much."

Birds of passage were common in Sicily. These "birds" would return on an annual or biannual basis to visit with family. Most traveled to Sicily during the winter months, as manual labor jobs diminished in America during the coldest months of the year. A very high percentage of Sicilians immigrated to the northeast of America, where the winter months could be very severe. Also, the cost of Atlantic Ocean travel after the First World War was becoming financially cheaper. So, Paolo's sincere words fell on a believing heart, since they both knew fathers and sons who were birds. How could they know this would be the last time they would see each other?

Agatina slowly reached into her apron pocket and withdrew Giuseppe's 1870 Liberty Seated Half Dime and tenderly placed it in Paolo's right hand.

Agatina quietly said, "Paolo this was your father's most prized possession. It had always brought him luck. He planned on giving it to you when you left for America. Always carry it with you, that I way I know you will be safe."

Paolo raised his right hand and stared at the coin in cold silence. Paolo thought Giuseppe's most treasured possession should belong to Agatina or the other children.

"Mama, I can't take this. You have given me enough. You will need it to help you care for the farm. Both Patri and you have given me enough; the courage, encouragement, and means to immigrate to America, while the other children may never have the opportunity."

A slight giggle came from his mother, a sound she made when someone was being obtuse to the situation. He needed to have a good luck charm to succeed in America and thereby the money to finance the rest of the Lomeos' journey to America.

Agatina instructed Paolo, "Your success in America means we all will be successful."

Superstition is part of Sicilian life, even if it conflicts with the Church's teachings. The Lomeo men never practiced in the Sicilian superstition rituals and charms for practical reasons, though in reality they were superstitious because of their fatalistic view that luck only came to the lucky.

Paolo turned away and dragged his feet through the front door, over the porch, and onto the soil heading for Palermo. When his home was barely visible in the distance, Agatina, standing on her toes, waved her red handkerchief good-bye to a son she knew to be a man of faith and love. He turned to wave, thinking she could see him, but her worn eyes lost the ability to focus on an object so far away. Life would never be the same for either.

Paolo made it to Palermo by midafternoon, when all businesses closed for siesta. This gave him the time to locate a ship departing to the different Northern European ports without interference from other passengers and shipping vendors. Ships departing from Northern European ports to America had lower fares than ships whose debarkation were elsewhere in Europe. Paolo could not afford a direct voyage to an American port from Palermo.

Fortunately, Paolo knew to avoid dealing with a pardone. A pardone was a middleman that arranged passage from Sicily to America. Most of these middlemen targeted unsuspecting and naive men who had no idea how to get to America. Usually, the pardone contracted with an American employer who wanted a large quantity of unskilled laborers for its business. The pardone first approached men from his own village and pumped them up with stories of gold in the streets and milk and honey on the dinner table. With no guarantee of a job when they arrived in America, these less sophisticated Sicilians were overcharged for their passage and sometimes ended up abandoned in America heading for a life of crime to support themselves.

Paolo had been taught by his father to talk to the Palermo dockworkers and locate a ship hauling Sicilian produce to either

France or England and to hire on as a temporary worker until the ship reached its destination port. Giuseppe explained to him that it would be easier and cheaper this way and Paolo would not have to rely on the trustworthiness of a pardone. Trusting an unknown individual with one's money contradicted the mores of the Lomeo family.

In addition, America had recently passed laws restricting the number of immigrants from Southern Europe, a quota system was established, and the immigrants accepted from Northern Europe greatly exceeded those from Southern Europe. Therefore, if Paolo could claim citizenship of a Northern European country, there was a better chance that he would be permitted to immigrate to America. If the immigration laws discriminated against Sicilians, then Paolo could enter America as an Englishman or, for goodness' sake, a Frenchman. How ironic would it be for a Sicilian to start his American life known as a Frenchman? Determination has a way of rationalizing almost anything. One qualifying trait of Sicily was the ability to adapt. How else could Sicily maintain its own separate identity from its multiple oppressors?

Though Giuseppe may not have been able to leave Sicily, he still paid attention and listened to the returning Americanos—native-born Sicilians who were now visiting as American citizens—talk about how the American Congress passed laws of discrimination against Sicilians. Giuseppe wondered with a young Paolo as to the nature of discrimination that the expatriates experienced, since the Americanos seemed well fed and finely dressed, and had money to spend.

"I wonder what type of discrimination these new Americans are talking about?" Giuseppe rhetorically asked Paolo. He continued, "Why do they keep going back to America if these laws are so unfair to them?" Paolo agreed. "They just want us to know that they are not stinking rich only because the American laws hold them back. They are looking for excuses. When I get to America, I will succeed regardless of the bad laws!"

Giuseppe nodded his head in agreement. "Paolo, you will succeed, no matter of the circumstances."

The faith a father has for a son knows no limit.

The only produce ship hiring temporary workers was the ship heading to Cherbourg, France. Paolo's uncle, Simone Maggiore, had worked as the hiring agent for the Port of Palermo for many years and felt duty bound to help his sister's son. Simone's father had used his Mafia connections to exempt Simone from the First World War draft and to arrange his selection as a hiring agent. Simone and Paolo were about the same age, although Paolo was the oldest in his family and Simone was the youngest in his family. Seemingly unusual to today's Americans, people in Sicily married as teenagers and the women gave birth to their last child while in their thirties. Therefore, it was not unusual for the parents' oldest child to have their own newborn when the parents were having their last child. This was the case with Agatina's family. Simone was born five years prior to Paolo, so that Paolo and Simone treated each other more as close cousins than uncle and nephew. This is why it was not disrespectful for Paolo to address Simone by his first name, even though he was Paolo's uncle. Approaching Simone, Paolo asked, "Simone, are you able to get me a job on the ship heading to Cherbourg? My friend told me that it is the only ship hiring temporary workers."

Even though Sicilians believe in destiny, nothing randomly happens in Sicily. Paolo knew his uncle had connections with the ship owners' representatives and would assist him in finding a job on a departing ship.

"Paolo, the ship to Cherbourg is only looking for young men who will commit to work for six months," Simone told Paolo.

"Simone that is unacceptable, I only need the ship to take me to France. Once in France, I will find a ship to America," Paolo informed Simone. Simone knew Paolo's intention without being told, since Paolo had been talking about his planned escape for years.

Simone said, "The only way you can do it that way is if you agree to no pay. Though you still can eat in the worker's galley for free."

This was fine with Paolo.

Paolo's new job consisted of carrying and stacking the produce baskets from the dock to the deck. The deck crew consisted of three men native to different countries throughout Europe and one from the United States. Each worked on the ship for various reasons. They all spoke French except Paolo. The Sicilian language has words with French roots, so Paolo could somewhat understand their conversations.

Heinz Schmidt ran from the Dusseldorf authorities after he committed a petty crime and hid away on this French ship when it had docked in Duisberg. After the Treaty of Versailles, the German authorities would not dare inspect a French ship. Once the other crew members found Heinz, he involuntarily became a member of the crew, though Heinz did receive wages like all the other deckhands. Jean Luc Rabideaux, the only actual Frenchman on the deck crew, joined the ship's crew to escape an abusive father and to settle in America. He and Paolo became fast friends, even though he was French. They both had grown up on a small farm with a large family and could easily relate to each other. Joseph Kane, a son of an American banker, signed up for a year's work to experience different cultures and other jobs.

Even though the deckhands had different backgrounds, their common idea of leaving home to find something new bound them together. The two-and-a-half-day trip to Cherbourg went smoothly with no unusual or memorable events, except four young men becoming friends. As the ship floated into the dock, Paolo watched the people hustling about the wharf, some workers, some shoppers, and others relatives waiting for their family members to disembark from the incoming ships.

Paolo was excited and anxious to leave the ship. Though it was a pleasant maritime experience, he realized he was more suitable to the land. Also, he could not wait to eat a hearty meal, and Jean Luc knew just the place. Jean Luc took them to his home. He knew his father would not be home and wanted his mother to meet his new friends. They spent the evening at Jean Luc's, his mother prepared dinner, and for the first time in a couple of days they slept in an actual bed that did not move with every motion of the ocean. In the morning, after another delicious meal from Jean Luc's mother, the friends separated from each other, each going his separate way. Paolo started walking back to the harbor to find a ship heading to America. However, he would need to have help to determine which ship was America bound and how to pay for the voyage.

Taking his mother's advice, Paolo grabbed his father's lucky coin from his front right pants pocket, wishing he knew how to find the America-bound ship. Confusedly searching the dock, he let the coin slip from his fingers while looking for a ship with an American flag at its stern. As he reached down to retrieve his coin, he suddenly saw flapping in the wind a rectangular cloth with thirteen stripes alternating between the color white and red with a blue field of forty-eight stars in the left hand corner. Paolo immediately knew his father was right to hold onto the coin for all these years—an American coin would innately find a ship heading toward America.

The writing on the ship identified it as the Olympic. The Olympic was one of a trio of ships built by White Star Line, a British company. The other two ships were the Titanic and Britannia. Olympic's keel was laid in Ireland in 1908 and the ship was launched in 1911. It was the first ship of its class to be built. His Majesty's ship had a length of 850 feet with a width of 92 feet 6 inches. Its gross tonnage was 46,400 British tons with a capability to carry 1600 passengers. Olympic was a passenger ship until the First World War started. The Allies, short of troop transport ships, commandeered Olympic into the Royal Navy. Ramming and sinking the German submarine U-103 on May 12, 1918, is considered Olympic's most important contribution to the war effort. Her two sister ships did not last as long. Of course the story of the Titanic is well known, and the Britannia was sunk by the German Navy two days prior to the Armistice. Refitted and converted back to a passenger ship in July, 1920, Olympic was ready for sea travel in time for Paolo's trip to America.

Approaching the ship's gangplank in a hesitant manner, Paolo tried to think of a way to communicate to the first mate that he wanted to hire on as a temporary worker in exchange for free passage to America. The first words out of his mouth, an English "hello," only made the first mate start to move aggressively toward Paolo. Then a familiar voice called out to Paolo; it was his new American friend, Joe Kane.

Joe interceded with the first mate and then in French asked Paolo, "How do you plan to board without a ticket?"

Paolo understood enough of Kane's words to detail his idea to Kane.

Speaking in his half-Sicilian, half-French language, Paolo said to his friend, "Joe, I was planning to offer my services to the ship's captain for free passage to America. I don't have much money and definitely not enough to pay for a voyage across the Atlantic. I will do any type of work for the free passage. I am willing to work without wages for the free passage."

Kane, knowing that Atlantic Ocean passenger ships hired only full-time and experienced sailors, had to think fast to help his friend gain passage.

Joe Kane had been educated at Groton Preparatory School and then went on to graduate from Yale University with a degree in history. He had a privileged life as the son of a J.P. Morgan banker. Serving a year in the U.S. army during the war disillusioned him on the goodness of mankind, and he had difficulty understanding why so many young men had to die to determine the boundary lines of European countries. Connecting with, working together, and understanding working- class people, Joe thought, would relieve him of his sense of guilt for living through the war while so many died. Hopefully, his feelings of a meaningless and listless existence floating through earthly time would end soon. His travels across Europe and trying to blend into post-war European life revealed Europeans as pessimistic and resigned to their lot in life. He wondered why America had an almost opposite attitude toward the future, when most Americans traced their ancestry to the European continent.

Joe's grandfather had emigrated from Ireland in 1809 as a young boy of about nine years old. The Scottish-Irish family settled in Westmoreland County, Pennsylvania, not far from the frontier post called Pittsburgh. Eventually, the family moved westwardly toward Pittsburgh and settled on a farm in the vicinity of present-day Monroeville, Pennsylvania. Thomas Kane, Joe's grandfather, assisted his father and older brothers with the farm work, while sporadically attending Mr. Johnston's schoolhouse to shake off the chains of manual labor. Thomas's father, the first Joseph Kane, encouraged his son to learn and willingly paid Mr. Johnston for his son's attendance. Their new farm was about twelve miles from Pittsburgh, and an older Thomas decided to attend the Western University of Pennsylvania, now known as the University of Pittsburgh. Thomas left the farm, found a job in Pittsburgh, and eventually graduated from the university. Changing and expanding from a rural economy to an industrial city, the late 1830s and early 1840s Pittsburgh gave a young ambitious man many opportunities to change his financial and social standing. Taking advantage of these new opportunities, Thomas began his professional career as a messenger and clerk, along with Andrew Carnegie, for the Pennsylvania Railroad under the tutelage of J. Edgar Thomson. From this beginning, he introduced himself to the industrial elite of Pittsburgh's growing industrial businesses, such as Henry Phipps and Henry Clay Frick, and his fellow Scott-Irish friend, Thomas Mellon, became his mentor and business partner. Through these connections, his financial net worth increased substantially, and he was one of Carnegie's first investors in Carnegie, McCandless and Company, the first U.S. company to construct and operate a Bessemer steel plant.

Being an investor in a steel mill was the complete opposite of actually working in the mill. Of course the financial awards were different, as was the ability to raise a family in a clean and safe environment. The only similarity was that both the mill worker and stockholder used the mill to provide for their families, though at different degrees of dependence. In these times of horse-drawn carts or walking as transportation to work, a manual laborer had to live close to his place of work. Unfortunately, living close to a mill filled the body and home with pollutants that would cause the early deaths of many people in the Pittsburgh region, mostly immigrants who had no other living arrangement options. Thomas's hard work, intelligence, and most importantly, his connections to the financial elite gave him the means to make sure his children had a choice to live without worry of physical deprivations and discrimination.

The second Joseph Kane, Paolo's friend's father, as the son of a successful businessman attended the best schools, met the financial elite of America, and married a socialite from Boston. Brilliant and sly were two adjectives that described Mr. Kane and soon would lead to a public embarrassment that caused Joe Jr. to search the world for the true meaning of honesty. Joe Sr.'s public reputation suffered from advising his clients to invest in railroad stocks of regional railroads controlled by his business friends. Eventually, these regional companies went bankrupt from mismanagement or thievery. Either way the clients lost their family fortune, large and small, whereas Joe Sr. still received and retained substantial monetary fees.

Though Joe Sr. did not go to jail, the public circus surrounding his family was more than Joe Jr. could tolerate. He volunteered for the war and refused an offer to become an officer. Wanting to experience the life of everyday Americans raised on farms, mill workers, and small-town merchants, he hoped to become like them: self-reliant and proud of their heritage. His war experience only caused him more confusion and contemplation, since he could not understand why average Americans easily accepted the platitudes of the politicians that told them that it was their duty to travel across the ocean to risk life and limb to make the world safe for someone else's democracy. Whose or which type of democracy was Wilson talking about? Kane believed America should protect its citizens, land, and other countries unable to defend themselves from ruthless conquerors, but to fight to determine new borderlines in Europe was not an American ideal worthy of the thought let alone the loss of American blood.

Paolo stood silently listening to Joe speak to the first mate, though not understanding the English words, and slightly shaking his head up and down in agreement. The first mate shifted his eyes from Paolo to Joe, then back again, and repeated this absurd behavior until he extended his right hand to shake Joe's hand, then motioned to Paolo to follow. Paolo climbed the gangplank and closely walked or more like jogged behind the first mate snaking through the middle deck toward the lower deck and into the kitchen. Paolo replaced or substituted for the assistant chef, who had either skipped on his commitment to visit with a French lady or had taken sick with a severe stomach problem.

Paolo's understanding of Kane's French could start a war if they were diplomats.

The story Joe told the first mate exaggerated not only Paolo's culinary skills, but also his region of birth. Americans loved Italians from Northern Italy—the land of Da Vinci, Michelangelo, and Galileo— believing these Italians understood fine painting, opera, and cuisine. However, gossip by Northern Italians encouraged and enforced Americans' vision of Sicilians as criminals and as people of African descent, meaning black people like their former slaves, and believed a Sicilian or Southern Italian could never give America the culture that a growing young nation desired now that it had conquered its physical want.

Fortunately, for Paolo, the chef and other kitchen crew were not Italian or even European but were Americans serving and working for a British ship. Otherwise, they would have recognized that his Italian was not the Italian of the sophisticated or cultured Italian but rather the language and slang of an illiterate and uneducated Sicilian. Remembering his mother's recipes, Paolo started in silence to cook dishes that any good Sicilian would love to eat. His silence only gave extra mystique to his cooking, and the staff went about the ship bragging about the fine Italian cuisine orchestrated by a man so young. Ten days at sea, Paolo interacted with Joe Kane enough to recognized Joe's nonverbal communication of leaning forward and raising both eyebrows as saying, "My friend, you made it this far, keep up the journey."

Paolo anticipated with worry the problem he would face when he tried to enter America. He needed to have a job sponsor in America or else the U.S. immigration officer would send him back to Sicily wearing the cloak of failure. Returning to Bagheria without becoming an American was Paolo's greatest fear.

Chapter 5

Arrival?

The late morning summer sun highlighted the Manhattan skyline as the Olympic sailed into New York Harbor while the passengers viewed a massive sculpture of a woman with a crown holding a torch welcoming some to the land of opportunity and others to the land of exile. Sounds of excitement and words of "viva la America" soon whimpered out as the newly arrived immigrants' anxiety about being accepted into America by the inspectors on Ellis Island took over their thoughts and emotions. These "to-be" Americans stood on the deck staring at Lady Liberty, wondering and hoping that this tiresome journey across the Atlantic Ocean in a British ship meant that their American dream had come true. Paolo belonged to a generation with a common dream: success in America. Without a doubt, Paolo's anxiety level rose as he learned from another Italian passenger that France had given the Statute of Liberty to America as a gift for perseverance and defending liberty during the American Civil War. Ironically, Paolo admired this enormous granite inviting him to America given by a country that had oppressed his native land for centuries. Superstition learned at any early age is a hard habit to break even for one as optimistic as Paolo.

He had taken a ship from a French port and sailed to America and was greeted by a French gift to America on his entrance. He now thought that the oral and physical examinations with the U.S. marine physicians and immigrants on Ellis Island would not go well. All the road signs were pointing back toward Sicily. Was his father's coin magical enough to turn the negative omens toward a positive result?

Since Ellis Island could not accommodate large vessels such as the Olympic, all the immigrants, including Paolo, had to disembark at the

From the Ice to the Fire

Lower Bay of New York Harbor to barges ready to take them to the Island. Sardines in Agatina's favorite lunch recipe were not packed as tight as were the Europeans on the immigrant barges. The new arrivals shuffled down the gangplank to the Registry Room on Ellis Island, as none of them were eager to start the medical examinations. The Registry Room was dubbed Judgment Hall by the marine physicians, since they were the judges of who remained in America. Judgment Hall resembled a large herding facility used by American farmers to transport their animals to the slaughterhouses. Line ropes outlined twenty lines toward the examination rooms, usually divided according to nationality in order for the U.S. government to assign translators more efficiently. The Italian immigrants formed three lines this day with only one translator, which was a better ratio than normally given to the Italians.

It was the American government that classified people from the Apennine Peninsula as Italians, for the immigrants from the southern regions preferred to be known by their own distinct region. Sicily is not even connected to the peninsula, but Sicilians were still classified as Italian. No true Sicilian would ever consider himself an Italian; it is similar to calling a Belgian a Frenchman because of Belgium's proximity to France. Unknown to the new Southern Italian immigrants, some Americans believed people from the northern regions were superior to the Southern Italians and on equal footing with Americans' forebears. Therefore, classifying all of them as Italians probably lessened the discrimination and harsher treatment, as opposed if they had been further separated by regions on and off the Apennine Peninsula.

Paolo, holding his lucky coin in his pocket, entered the exam room facing a stern-looking U.S. marine captain, Dr. Alex Hilton.

Captain Hilton addressed Paolo in his best French, since he did not know Italian.

"Good day, sir, I am the doctor assigned to you by your new government."

For some reason, the military men with the least common sense and life experience believed that Europeans, regardless of country, spoke French. It may have had to do with their French ally's tall tales heard during the Great War about the importance of French culture to the growth of Europe and Western civilization. It was odd that an educated American would be captivated by these French stories after witnessing the ineptitude of the French government's conduct of the war.

Fortunately for Paolo, the Sicilian language had a French influence due to the years of French dominion in Sicily so Paolo could, by inference, determine that the marine captain was giving a salutation. Paolo responded in Sicilian, "Fine, Captain. Just a little excited to get started in America."

Alex Hilton believed he did not understand Paolo's French because of his self-awareness that his French and overall education were not on par with the universities in the eastern part of the United States.

Dr. Hilton had earned his medical degree from the University of Cincinnati, located in Cincinnati, Ohio, after having graduated from The University of Toledo in Toledo, Ohio, where he played left tackle for the football team. He could trace his family heritage to Colonial America and believed Southern European immigrants were inferior to people with Northern European roots. He believed it was his duty to sadistically examine any Southern European to ensure that only the best bred of the inferiors settled in America.

The exam room's black and white tiled floor evidenced signs of careless and unsanitary methods of examination. Disregarded tissues, medical swabs, and exam paraphernalia littered the floor. Between this litter, Paolo notice dried blood stains on the floor, as well as on the walls and exam table. The reputation that trachoma affected Southern Italians clouded the judgment of these doctors. Southern Italians feared eyes affected by the salt water spray of the Atlantic Ocean, smoke irritation, and other causes of red eyes, not only because the examiner lifted their eyelids with a buttonhook, but also because any indication of eye disease meant deportation or—at minimum—detention in crowded quarters. Adult immigrants with their families were in constant fear that they would be separated from their children and some unscrupulous examiner would then prey on the children. This dreadful anguish caused the Italian immigrants to call Ellis Island the Island of Tears.

Seeing Paolo facing him, and overhearing the previous immigrants discuss Paolo's silent confidence and Northern Italian heritage, made it easier for Hilton to perform a cursory examination.

Dr. Hilton, while holding the buttonhook with a perverse smile, said in French, "We don't need to use this today."

Slowly, he placed the buttonhook into the right-side pocket of his blood-spotted white medical jacket.

Hilton, similar to a lot of the examiners, preferred Northern Italians to Southern Italians, especially Sicilians, the Renaissance bias being a strong motivation. The nurse assisting Dr. Hilton in his examination of Paolo, Rita Kirkpatrick, informed the doctor, "Captain, this man is not speaking French to you but Italian."

With the conceit that a snobbish doctor would address a first-generation Irish-American lady with less education and social status, Hilton asked, "How do you know? If you had experienced the war instead of staying in America secretly wishing for the defeat of the English, you would know that different regions of France have different dialects. Do you even know what dialect means?"

"Yes, doctor, I do know what dialect means. I know he is speaking a form of Italian, since my neighborhood has plenty of dagos and I recognize the words," Kirkpatrick firmly informed Hilton.

Captain Hilton ended the conversation quickly, hating to be upstaged by an immigrant's daughter. "Regardless, nurse, being from the cultured northern part of Italy, he understands French and German along with his native Italian. Your dagos are from Southern Italy or Sicily, and their gutter Italian reflects poorly on the Romans."

Fortunately for Paolo, Dr. Hilton and Miss Kirkpatrick had no understanding of languages and did not detect that Paolo's elocution, in addition to the actual language Paolo used, originated from Sicily and not Rome. It was all Italian to the doctor and nurse. Plus, the translator assigned this day to Paolo's line fluently spoke Spanish not Italian, so he could not detect the place of Paolo's birth through his language. It also seemed Paolo's look of anxiety translated into a face of confidence. Now that Paolo passed the medical inspection, he had to pass the interview with an U.S. Immigration Service employee to prove that he would not be a charge of his new government.

Paolo approached the gated teller window after a small man with a small brim hat called out in Italian, "Paolo Lomeo, come forward."

The small man was born Angelo DiCarlo in Naples, Italy, in 1885, and had arrived in the United States with his parents when he was fifteen. Growing up in Brooklyn, Angelo's family Americanized their name so that job opportunities Angelo's father, Enzio, would not be limited to the most dirty and unwanted jobs. Assimilation also would make life easier for the whole family. Avoiding discrimination from the general society of America was the goal. Enzio believed if his children could be raised and educated as Americans, his grandchildren would attain all the same rights and privileges of the Americans who rode the elevator he operated at the Park Row Building in New York City.

Angelo DiCarlo, now Andrew Davis, had more empathy for the immigrants than most Americans, especially the Italian immigrants, because of his family's experience assimilating into America society. Andrew always warned his new fellow citizens about the con artists at the pier that preyed on new immigrants.

"Paolo, you know there will be men outside on the pier promising you jobs or schemes for quick riches. Stay away from them. They are liars and will only take your money," Angelo explained to Paolo.

"I understand. We have the same type of predators at the docks in Palermo," Paolo told Andrew.

When Andrew heard Paolo was from Palermo, his face lit up. "Do you know my cousin through marriage, Frank Di Capra?" Andrew asked.

Paolo, shaking his head, said, "Palermo is a large city with a lot of people, and the people just rush from one part of the city to another part of the city. I am not sure anyone knows anyone in Palermo. Plus, I am from a small town outside of Palermo, Bagheria."

Andrew nodded. "It is just like New York City, I am sure. I need to have your sponsor information. You do have a job here in America?"

Reaching for the note in his pocket with Joe Kane's address, Paolo handed it to Andrew to answer the question of who hired him in America. Joe had only given Paolo his address so that Paolo knew where to mail the five dollars he had lent Paolo before they disembarked from the Olympic. Since Paolo did not have a sponsor or a job, Paolo knew he needed to behave as if he did or face defeat and a return to Sicily. Knowing he lacked an education and money, he used the one skill he did not know he had: the ability to say and do the right action at the right time. He quickly reached for his coin, pulled it out, and looked at it in the same manner his mother would stare at her rosary in times of stress, praying that Andrew would accept this handwritten note. Thinking the coin helped, not realizing that his innate intellect solved his problem, Paolo breathed a sigh of relief as Andrew signed the necessary papers that made Paolo a legal immigrant in America.

Andrew took a quick likening to Paolo and with a smile and in English he said, "Good luck, Paolo."

Paolo had learned enough from his time on the ship with other Americans to know what "good luck" meant. He responded with a typical American response in his broken English, "Thank you. You too, Andrew."

Paolo understood not to act like he was lost or had no place to go. Walking through the examination area toward the outside, Paolo strutted with the phony air of confidence that a high school freshman uses to avoid the more confident upperclassmen. He headed for the train station north of the pier and from there he could figure out where to go. There would be less chance of being taken advantage of far away from the pier.

Heading to the train station carrying his satchel without the ability to read English, Paolo realized that this adventure may be more difficult than he had imagined. Naively, he had assumed the foremen of the employers looking to hire him would be waiting for him, and that the foremen would find a place for him to stay. He assumed that it would be similar to his army experience: a group of young men in the same position without any knowledge, being told where to eat, sleep, and fight by an authority figure. His first three minutes away from the pier felt like the splash of cold water his mother used to entice him to wake up to help his father on the farm. How he missed the farm and his family now! Carefully, he watched the other people exchange their money for

U.S. dollars and watched the denominations of dollars given. Having relatives who worked for the Port of Palermo, Paolo had heard stories of how some merchants used the exchange of currency to take advantage of an unsuspecting customer. They taught Paolo not to trust the money exchangers. His mother's Savior and Lord had been right to overturn the money exchangers' tables in the temple. Paolo exchanged his lire and francs for American dollars and confidently walked toward the ticket purchasing windows, while his stomach turned upside down with anxiety. He noticed that the buyers of the tickets just screamed the city of their destination and pushed their money under the ticket window without ever looking at the ticket clerk. Imitating the other passengers, in his best mimic of Joe Kane, Paolo screamed out Pittsburgh at the same time as sliding his money under the ticket window toward the ticket clerk. The ticket clerk repeated the reverse action by pushing one passenger ticket for Pittsburgh back to Paolo while saying Pittsburgh.

From the Ice to the Fire

The young, new American immigrant chose Pittsburgh because of Joe Kane's story about Grandfather Kane beginning his American success story in Pittsburgh. Paolo assumed that Pittsburgh must be a city inviting to young ambitious immigrants. However, only an unknowing person would consider 1920s Pittsburgh inviting to immigrants. It was a city with many immigrants working in the different mills throughout the region, but inviting and accepting of immigrants, especially Sicilians, would be the opposite of what Paolo would encounter.

Boarding the Broadway Limited on track three heading south toward Philadelphia for the first leg of his journey to Pittsburgh, Paolo grabbed a window seat, took off his light coat, and went to sleep. It had been a long twelve days, and it felt good to be on land and sitting on a comfortable seat. The train started slowly out of the station, and Paolo's slumber was disturbed by the increasing speed. By time he oriented himself, New York City was in the distance. Fatigue and dread hung over him, and remembering his grandfather's advice that a good nap brings a new perspective to a bad situation, Paolo decided to revisit his slumber. He dreamt about returning to Bagheria as a man of respect with a fancy blue three-piece suit and a tiepin in the middle of his yellow tie. Broadway Limited chugged and pulled along uneventfully through Philadelphia continuing westwardly toward Harrisburg by rolling over the hills and dales of central Pennsylvania.

While transferring to a train heading toward Pittsburgh at the Harrisburg station, he spied a lunch counter inside the small train station and ordered the same item that the old man in front of him in line ordered, a grilled cheese sandwich. He ordered by pointing to the old man, for he was afraid that he could not describe the sandwich with his limited English.

The attractive young lady behind the counter, with flowing brunette hair and wearing a white with pink polka-dot waitress uniform that wrapped tightly around her small, thin frame, grabbed

Paolo's attention. For a moment, he forgot why he was trying to communicate with her. She had to guess Paolo's order.

She responded to Paolo, asking, "A grilled cheese sandwich?"

Not really understanding her and hoping she was asking about the sandwich, Paolo said "Sì," while using his head to sign the international meaning for yes.

She prepared the sandwich herself. Paolo noticed that she did not use the bread loaf on the counter but had reached below the counter to retrieve a fresh loaf. The waitress added four slices of cheese to the bread, whereas the other customers only received two slices of cheese. She then grilled the bread and cheese slices to make the traditional American grilled cheese sandwich.

In Sicilian she said, "I hope this meets your expectations. Do you have the six cents?"

"You're from Sicily? I am from Bagheria, Sicily. This is my first meal in America," Paolo excitedly told the young waitress while handing over a quarter, not really knowing what she meant by six cents.

The beautiful waitress replied, "Yes, I can tell you are new to America. You shouldn't act so scared. Try smiling a little more, they like that in America. My name is Rosalia."

Feeling embarrassed but not wanting to be told how to act by a lady, Paolo said, "Thank you for the advice. I didn't know American women were counselors of newly scared immigrants. My name is Paolo. Thank you for the change."

Paolo decided to leave her lunch counter and walked across to the other side of the train station to eat his sandwich in peace. As Paolo ate his lunch standing up, Rosalia Cali, feeling sorry for offending this scared but proud man, quickly approached Paolo with a broad smile, saying, "Bonu!"

She grabbed his hand to lead him to a little wooden table outside on the train platform where the other passengers had gathered to eat their lunches. Women in Sicily never approached unattended men, let alone suggestively held a man's hand in plain view of other people. Sicilian women followed the old custom of having their fathers arrange their lifetime partners contrary to the way Americans chose their casual or permanent love interest. In Sicily, a casual love interest could get a man killed, so only the dumb or influential men would risk a casual affair with anyone but a lady of disrepute. In 1908 Rosalia's family had arrived in America and settled in Harrisburg when she was six years old. Her family had also come from Bagheria, Sicily, and she could tell from Paolo's accent that he was from Sicily.

"What are your plans? Where are you headed?" Rosalia inquisitively asked.

Within minutes Paolo felt at ease with her, telling her, "I have no job prospect and only chose Pittsburgh as a destination because of a story I heard on the boat coming to America."

Rosalia worriedly asked, "How do you plan on supporting yourself? Do you have a place to stay?"

Showing her his lucky coin, Paolo confidently said, "I know upon arriving in Pittsburgh opportunity for income, wealth, and a successful life will present itself. My father's lucky coin has gotten me this far, so there is no reason to believe it will let me down now."

However, Paolo acted more confidently about his luck than he actually felt. He could not tell her of his fear of failure, the fear of not being able to provide for his family, and the fear of having his children live and die in Sicily with no hope of a better future.

"There are a lot of jobs here in Harrisburg," Rosalia informed Paolo.

Paolo told Rosalia about his family in Sicily. Youth's indiscretion reveals itself in more than one way. Both Paolo and Rosalia understood that under the old custom they should not be sitting alone discussing such feelings of wonder, fear, and hope without being chaperoned by the girl's family. Rituals, obligations, and ideas taught since childhood are not easily dispelled. Without notice, the train for Pittsburgh left the station absent Paolo. The train headed toward its intended destination while Paolo moved in the direction of an unknown future.

"I am sorry I kept you from your train. Maybe I can make up it up to you," Rosalia sincerely told Paolo.

"It was my pleasure and maybe I was supposed to miss the train," Paolo brashly told Rosalia while holding his coin.

Rosalia suggested that Paolo have dinner with her family and relax for a couple of days with other Sicilians. Walking together from the train station along a deer trail through the woods, for about a mile, Rosalia and Paolo arrived at the three-room apartment above the grocery store managed by her father. Rosalia introduced her family to her new friend. Mr. Cali, being a man of short stature but a large ego, immediately took a dislike to his daughter's new friend.

Giovonni Cali expected any suitor of his daughter to ask his permission prior to speaking or approaching his daughter. He did not find it necessary to adapt his convictions because he was in a different country. Any man without the respect for his customs should not be treated as a guest in his home and definitely should not think his daughter was available for a causal relationship.

Nineteenth-century Sicilians did not believe in dating or the love rituals of the typical American. If a man had a love interest in a young lady, then the young man's father had to approach the young lady's father prior to any contact between the young couple. One of the many Sicilian hurdles Paolo thought he could avoid in America.

In Sicilian, Paolo, with an extended hand, said, "Good afternoon, Mr. Cali. I appreciate your kindness in letting me enter your home."

Responding in a rude and curt manner, Giovonni, in their native tongue, said, "What do you want?"

Trying to reassure Rosalia's father, Paolo said, "I am also from Sicily."

Mr. Cali from a quick observation of Paolo knew from Paolo's dress and mannerism that he was from Southern Italy but did not guess that he was from Sicily.

Giovonni snapped back to Paolo, "Then you should have known better than to escort a young lady alone through the woods. You have called into question her virtue and shown disrespect for me, as her father."

Barely listening to Giovonni as he stared in the direction of Rosalia, Paolo retorted, "I just met your daughter. She nicely asked me to dinner, since I missed my train. I am new to this country, and I thought it would be fine to accept an invitation from another Sicilian. I am sorry. I didn't mean any disrespect."

Paolo had initially been attracted to Rosalia as a friendly face in a new, confusing land; he had no ill intentions or any thoughts of love or marriage. Though standing in the kitchen doorway watching Rosalia help her mother cook, barely hearing Mr. Cali lecture him on his American disrespectful behavior, he finally noticed her soft demeanor as she giggled while telling her mother about Paolo's lost look on the train platform. Giovonni angrily tugged on Paolo's front collar, pulling their faces together as he screamed Sicilian obscenities, including calling Paolo a son of a weak father for not teaching him better. "What type of man teaches his son to walk a young lady home without a chaperone? I will tell you, a donkey's ass, that is who," Giovonni screamed at Paolo.

"Father, stop! He has shown me nothing but respect and acted properly at all times," Rosalia angrily told her father.

Suddenly, a bright light blinded Paolo as his breathing become more rapid and blood flowed to his muscles. He wrapped his hands around Rosalia's father's chin, pushing his head backward until Giovonni fell to the rug-covered floor. The death of Giuseppe still brought great sadness to Paolo. The mention of his father in a negative way evidently lit a powder keg that was set barely underneath the fragile emotional structure of a still grieving young man.

As he came back to reality and realized what he did, slowly turning from the frightened face of the grocer, he apologized to Rosalia and her mother, Della. "I am sorry, Mrs. Cali. Rosalia, please forgive me. I had to protect the honor of my father. My father was a great man. I wouldn't be the person I am today without him. His encouragement and confidence in me gave me the confidence to come to America without any job or promises of success," Paolo sadly said to the two ladies.

Paolo excused himself and rushed out of the front door of the apartment in something less than a run, skipping every other step down the staircase onto the street. Now, the sunlight dimmed as Paolo started thinking where he could sleep until tomorrow morning. Noticing a detached garage across the street from Rosalia's apartment, Paolo entered through a side door, deciding to find a spot on the garage floor close to a window on the east side of the garage. Finding his spot, Paolo took a mechanic's pad from the shelf, laying it on the floor and using his rolled-up coat as a pillow. Paolo slowly drifted to sleep with a stomach asking for food, a feeling more familiar to Paolo than he would ever admit. His father had warned him constantly about his temper, but the admonishment never seemed to truly set with Paolo. Reacting without thinking caused the death of a French doctor, a horror he lived with every day. Now, his stupidity embarrassed him in front of a young lady who was only trying to help him adjust to his new homeland. Life moves too fast not to use every minute wisely. Paolo wondered if he would ever fulfill the high expectations of his father. He wanted his father's approval more than anything else, and being his father's best friend, he knew heaven was disappointed this evening.

The morning sunlight glistened through the garage window, casting upon Paolo's face a reminder that it was time to begin the journey anew. Hearing a slight tapping on the door, Paolo glanced over his right shoulder as the silhouette of an angel appeared, softly calling his name. His mind raced with thoughts of enjoyment at the pleasantness of it all, but at the same time wondered how he had died in his sleep.

Again, softly the angel said, "Paolo." As he came to his senses, he saw Rosalia standing in the doorway with a basket in her hand.

Jumping to his feet, brushing and patting his hair down, he raced over to Rosalia with a large grin and a hearty American "Good morning!"

As the mechanics would soon arrive to work, Rosalia suggested that they walk together back to the train station as she handed him the basket of bread and cheese.

Rosalia tried to apologize and explain her father's situation. "I am sorry my father treated you so harshly. He is frustrated with America, and Mother says his personality changed once he realized he had to work hard to be successful here. He is so bitter at times. He is a good man and just needs to understand that one's dreams are not always meant to come true."

Paolo looking slightly down out of embarrassment and said, "I understand about frustration. My father was also frustrated in his inability to come to America. I hope your mother and father can forgive me."

"My mother thinks you were right, and she will convince my father to accept your apology," she reassured Paolo.

Paolo now realized Rosalia expected him to apologize to her father, even though her father was so inconsiderate to mention Giuseppe in such a poor light. "My father unexpectedly died before I left for America, so I guess I am still a little emotional about his death," Paolo explained, trying to rationalize his overreaction.

"Paolo, I am so sorry. I am sure it is very hard for you to come to a new land while grieving for your father," Rosalia said to Paolo.

She again apologized for her father's behavior and his insensitive statement about Paolo's father. Paolo had told her in their brief conversation about his hero, Giuseppe Lomeo. Her mother also wanted to come and apologize, but did not think it was proper for a lady to approach a young man while sleeping.

As Rosalia was speaking Paolo began to wonder how Rosalia found him. He asked her, "How did you know where I was?"

Meekly Rosalia confessed, "I followed you after you ran out of the house last night. I was worried about you. I knew you were not familiar with the area and was afraid you would get lost. I thought you might try to head back through the woods to the train station and get lost in the woods.

Once I saw you go into the garage I knew you would be safe for the night. I wanted to make sure you were awake and out of here before the mechanics arrived for work. A lot of people in this area do not like Italians, especially the owners of this garage. They would have had the police arrest you for trespassing. Funny, without me, you may have been a criminal for sleeping," Rosalia giggled.

Paolo—not finding the humor in his predicament—sarcastically said, "Yes, it would have been really funny."

"Can I walk you to the train station? Maybe we can talk?" Rosalia shyly asked.

They strolled together through the woods as couples do in America, and Paolo with the brashness of a young man and again letting his emotions control his action, asked Rosalia, "I think I will stay in Harrisburg. Is that fine with you?"

Rosalia, being a woman of strong religious conviction and family loyalty, said, "Paolo, you have to ask my father for permission before asking me such a question. I am not that American."

Looking dejected and rejected, hanging his head low, he continued walking toward the train station, letting go of Rosalia's hand.

Reaching her hand under his chin, she brought his face to her level and said with a slight smile, "I didn't say I didn't want you to ask him."

Paolo never had a love interest in Sicily and felt that America must be a great place to give him the opportunity to court such a gracious lady. Then, with the bravado of a young man and a short memory of his recent depression from her noncommittal response, he retorted, "I will discuss this proposal with your father, man to man."

Rosalia, patting him on the back with a slight rub, said, "You know best," and giggled at her success.

Following Sicilian tradition, Paolo requested permission through Mrs. Cali to speak to Rosalia's father on an important matter.

Giovonni refused to meet with Paolo, still upset about the roughness with which Paolo had treated him at their last encounter. In reality, Giovonni feared Paolo and knew he would not be able to manipulate him as he hoped. Paolo approached the Cali home and had just started climbing the steps to the front door when Paolo was met by Giovonni screaming for him to leave his property or he would call the police.

Pointing his finger at Paolo, Giovonni said, "You sciccu. Leave my home or I will call the police."

Giovonni, believing his manhood was threatened by Paolo's harsh treatment the day before, decided to embarrass Paolo in front of his new love interest, Rosalia. Giovonni, noticing how Paolo hesitated when threatened with an arrest, figured he could push the limit by threatening Paolo with bodily injury.

Giovonni pulled what looked like a small Browning pistol from his back pocket, pointed it, and dared Paolo, "You coward. Now, tough Mafioso, let's see how fast you can run back to the train station."

Paolo observed how Rosalia's father looked slightly downward like a dog afraid of his master, instead of straight in the eyes as a man in control would have. Giuseppe had always instructed Paolo to look at a person's eyes to see inside their soul. A person's thoughts can be revealed through his eyes if one had the courage to stare into those eyes.

Most people do not look directly into a person's eyes for the innate human fear of facing an unknown challenge.

Knowing Giovonni was fearful, Paolo assumed that the gun was either not loaded or not a real gun. He decided to take the risk and challenge Giovonni in front of Mrs. Cali and Rosalia. If he guessed wrong, Giovonni surely would kill Paolo, since no Sicilian man could bear the indignity of being humiliated in the presence of his family.

Paolo, approaching Giovonni in a rushed fashion, said, "Mr. Cali, please put away the toy. We both know you don't want to shoot me for such a small scuffle. I want to stay in Harrisburg and court your daughter."

Realizing that Paolo called his bluff, Giovonni quickly put away his fake gun. He was not sure if Paolo used the word "toy" literally or figuratively. To avoid further embarrassment, he hid the toy gun in his sweater pocket and buttoned his sweater to secure its hiding place.

Stepping aside to let Paolo enter their home, Giovonni said, "Speak to Mrs. Cali. I have no use for such a brash young man."

The young Sicilian arrogantly told the older Sicilian, "A true man and Sicilian of any character has to refuse my offer in person and not through his wife."

Feeling the humiliation and shame of his wife, Giovonni agreed. "OK, wise guy. Follow me."

Leading him to the kitchen, Giovonni sat across from Paolo at the small wooden table in the kitchen—two pugilists facing each other ready to answer the bell.

"Paolo, would you like a cup of coffee?" Mrs. Cali asked.

"Yes, I could use a cup of your delicious coffee, Mrs. Cali," Paolo answered, knowing that it made sense to flatter his ally in this fight.

Mr. Cali stared at his wife in disbelief. How could she respect the man who had caused him to lose his title as the leader of the family?

Using the trading tactic that Giuseppe had used countless times to negotiate with Palermo fruit wholesalers, Paolo stated the outcome with confidence prior to starting the negotiation.

"Mr. Cali, I plan on staying in Harrisburg and courting Rosalia until she agrees to marry me," Paolo stated as he sniffed the sweet aroma of his coffee before taking a sip.

Giovonni could barely control his temper at Paolo assuming that a girl he just met would follow him without the approval of her father.

Giovonni emphasized to Paolo, "I haven't given my permission for Rosalia to see you. You need my permission first!"

Giovonni believed he had put Paolo in a trap. He thought Paolo would strictly follow the Sicilian custom of asking permission from the girl's father prior to approaching a girl for a date, let alone courting with the object of marriage. Under the custom, if the father refused, the suitor had two choices: the suitor could move on or entice the father to grant permission with some form of compensation. Giovonni was hoping for some form of compensation to pay for his unannounced intention to leave America for Sicily.

However, Giovonni, not being a man of great intelligence, did not realize that Paolo wanted to be an American and chose to ignore any old customs that interfered with his American ideas. Paolo's impression of America as a place where a person could do as he pleased showed his immaturity. However, his cocky sureness in this instant worked and only reinforced his misperception that he could live by his own rules in America. A perception that would be dispelled in the years to come.

Paolo explained that he was courting and marrying Rosalia regardless of Giovonni's permission, and Giovonni's objection would fall on deaf ears and set in motion his separation from his grandchildren and daughter.

"It is up to you, Mr. Cali. If you think Rosalia will agree with you and will follow the old country custom in America, then say no. But it may be better for you to agree with me and make it your decision."

Dr. John Von Neuman, the inventor of the game theory in 1944, could have learned its practical application watching a Lomeo negotiate. Giovonni weighted the seriousness of his nemesis's intention or ability to keep his daughter away from him. He realized if he chose incorrectly he would lose his daughter, grandchildren, and more importantly to him, his outsized perception of himself.

"I will agree to you courting Rosalia with two conditions. First, you have to agree to use Cali as the middle name of your first son.

Two, you cannot propose marriage for at least three months from today. Rosalia's mother and I have to make sure you are a good man," Giovonni quickly retorted in a desperate plea for peace.

Once again, not having the character or courage to challenge a threat to his authority, Giovonni covertly prayed Paolo would accept his compromise and not unmask his façade of courage.

Using another of Giuseppe's tactics, Paolo always gave his opponent a safe way out of harm once he reached his goal. "Mr. Cali, I agree to your terms."

This gracious hand of peace easily extended by the victor at no cost was eagerly accepted by the vanquished. Paolo's generosity and charity toward a morally weak man manifested his mother's love. The two men stood up and shook hands to evidence the end of their little feud. Heading for the front door with a sense of pride and excitement, Paolo felt a strong tug on his arm, pulling him back into the kitchen.

His mother-in-law began to hug him and whispered, "I knew from the first time we met that you were the right man for my daughter."

Paolo thought, isn't America a great place!

Paolo stayed in Harrisburg for three months working at any manual labor job he could find, including working in Giovonni's store when Giovonni needed the help. In those three months, Giovonni, Della, and Rosalia witnessed the man they all hoped would be part of their family. Paolo impressed them with his work ethic and his ability to resolve life's situations in a thoughtful way. Giovonni grew to love Paolo. Paolo slowly became the son Giovonni never had. Della had given birth to a boy prior to the birth of Rosalia, but the young child died soon after the birth since the medical knowledge in 1890 Sicily was not equal to the task of saving the child.

Paolo lived in a small room in the home of a widow, Mrs. Laughlin. She would rent her rooms only to men baptized in the Roman Catholic faith and who attended church regularly. Sicilian men had a reputation of attending church only on Christmas Eve and Easter Sunday. In Sicily, while the women are asking for forgiveness and trying to better their spiritual well-being, the men sit outside in the piazza discussing issues suitable and non-suitable for a Sunday discussion.

Paolo also knew attending church regularly would impress Rosalia and help convince her father that Paolo would be a good role model for Giovonni's grandchildren. Paolo went to Mass every Sunday with the Cali family. Though the Calis and Mrs. Laughlin went to different churches, Mrs. Laughlin saw the Calis and Paolo walk together toward the Italian Roman Catholic Church, two blocks from her home, dressed in their Sunday best. Harrisburg was like every other American town in the 1920s; the Roman Catholic churches were divided along ethnicity lines.

On the way home one Sunday, as Rosalia and her mother strolled ahead of Paolo and Giovonni, Paolo interrupted Giovonni's conversation on the upcoming presidential election between Republican William Harding and Democrat James Cox. "Excuse me, Mr. Cali, I have an important matter to discuss with you."

Giovonni lifted his head to say wait one minute. "Paolo, I know what you have to discuss, and I am not sure why you waited so long. But let me finish my thoughts about these two men running for office. It is important you understand the American political system so you can raise your children to be good Americans."

Paolo found Giovonni saying, "why you waited so long" odd because Giovonni had asked him to wait three months before proposing marriage. Maybe Giovonni had forgotten about their agreement or realized he had initially misjudged Paolo.

"My father and grandfather always encouraged me to listen to what the politicians say but never to trust their words. My grandfather fought with Garibaldi," Paolo tried to continue before Giovonni interrupted him.

"Oh my! Your grandfather actually knew Garibaldi? What a leader! My father loved Garibaldi and one of his dreams was to meet him."

Jokingly Giovonni continued, "If you had told me the first time we met that your family was with Garibaldi in liberating Sicily, I would have had you marry Rosalia that evening."

Looking disappointed, speaking slightly above a whisper, and wanting to tell the truth to his American father, Paolo meekly explained, "My grandfather said he knew Garibaldi. I am sure my grandfather, Alberto, exaggerated his time with Garibaldi, but he did fight for the liberation of Sicily. In fact, he was permanently disabled from his war wounds.

"He did not like Garibaldi. Nonno thought Garibaldi used the Sicilians to gain a reputation as a freedom fighter in order to gain political power in Rome. Once Garibaldi gained the esteem and political power of the elite of Northern Italy, he basically forgot about Sicily."

Giovonni looked at Paolo, shocked. He had the expression of an American father who lost a son in the Great War and belatedly came to the realization that President Woodrow Wilson had used the American middle class to fight a war that only benefitted the older European political structure and business mercenaries. Giovonni knew Alberto was correct. Sicily did not benefit from the new Italy. The Republic of Italy's lack of attention to Sicily was why so many young men and women left Sicily over the last few decades. But with all its disadvantages, Giovonni missed Sicily. He missed his family. He missed knowing the language and customs. Basically, Giovonni did not feel at home in America. It probably had more to do with his low self-esteem or high expectations than anything different from other Italian immigrants' American experience.

"Paolo, I guess it is never too late to learn something new. Your grandfather must have been a very smart man."

"He was," Paolo said.

The conversation fell silent as the two men reached the Calis' apartment. Giovonni did not now expect Paolo to formally request his permission to propose marriage to Rosalia because Paolo and he knew something had changed with this small conversation. Giovonni realized that he was living the dream of his father and had never really developed his own identity. It took hearing that his father's hero was nothing more than a mere politician to awaken him from his slumber.

Paolo may have thought Giovonni learned something new about Italian politics when Giovonni said, "It is never too late to learn something new." However, Giovonni was thinking about his own growth as a person. It may have taken him sixty years of life, but he finally knew he had to be his own person.

Paolo felt the familiar sadness from Giovonni that he felt from his own father. Paolo felt ashamed to have denigrated Giovonni's hero.

It served no purpose to talk about events from sixty years ago in a different country.

"I am sorry, Mr. Cali. I had no business contradicting your father with my grandfather's opinions," Paolo sincerely said to Giovonni.

"Paolo, you did me a favor. You helped me see that my assumptions about life may not be true. I truly don't know if your grandfather was right about Garibaldi, but with how our young men died in wars to benefit Northern Italy, Alberto may be right. I am a better man for knowing it and you."

With that, Paolo approached Rosalia, and in front of her parents, he asked her to be his wife. Rosalia, with a smile fit for a queen, said, "Yes. I love you!"

Chapter 6

Meriwether Lewis started from Pittsburgh?

After a small marriage ceremony in the Calis' front room, Paolo and Rosalia kissed Mr. and Mrs. Cali good-bye and promised to visit as soon as they were settled in Pittsburgh. Nervously, Giovonni told the young couple that Mrs. Cali and he had to talk to them before Paolo and Rosalia started their new journey as husband and wife.

"My children, I have some terrible news," Giovonni told the newlyweds.

"Father, what is it? Are you sick?" Rosalia inquired of her father while looking at her mother.

"No, Rosalia, nothing that serious. We are going home, back to Sicily," her father exclaimed.

Giovonni's experiment of being an American had failed miserably. Giovonni managed a local grocery store with the promise that after ten years he would be able to become an equal partner with the owner, David McGillis. McGillis owned three stores in the area and had agreed to share the profits of the Harrisburg store with Giovonni after ten years of employment. Twelve years later, McGillis changed his mind and told Giovonni that he was selling the store to one of McGillis's relatives. This relative did not want or need to have Giovonni as the manager.

Paolo asked, "Father, don't you have a contract with McGillis?" "I do, Paolo. But I really don't understand it and it wouldn't help anyway," Giovonni explained.

"Why? America has a court system unlike the Sicilian court system. Everyone is treated fairly," Paolo naively instructed his elder.

Giovonni, showing the patience of a father and realizing Paolo was trying to help even though his statements seemed patronizing, informed the new immigrant, "America's court system is better than our Sicilian courts. It is probably better than all the other Italian courts. But the American court system discriminates against immigrants, especially if a Sicilian tries to sue an Irishman."

"It is at least worth a try. Someone has to pay for your ten years of hard work!"

"Paolo, I would have to hire an attorney, which will not be cheap. Plus, finding an attorney in this town who would be willing to sue McGillis is unlikely. I made a bad business decision and just want to move on. People make bad decisions every day. It is how you respond or deal with the unexpected that separates the strong from the weak."

"Father you are probably right. It seems the odds are stacked against you," Paolo said, though not truly believing that Giovonni was correct.

Giovonni, sensing Paolo's disappointment in his judgment of not fighting because of the unfairness of American life, hoped life would be different for Paolo's family. "My son, maybe your family and you will become such a part of the American fabric that the court system will provide you protection from the McGillises of the world. But please remember something—sometimes you have to forgo the short-term reward for a long-term win. The long term is the lives of your family."

This was the first time in Giovonni's life that he made a decision based on thought and logic. His days of trying to impress people or live up to the mythical figure of the Sicilian "man of respect" were over. Giovonni's action this day helped set the standard that Paolo and Rosalia would use throughout their lives. Without knowing it, and just by being himself, Giovonni became a "man of respect."

"I understand," Paolo said, not realizing that a little less than twenty-five years from this day, he would be at the same crossroad, but in a different degree.

After hearing the shocking news of her parents' sudden departure, Rosalia started to cry with sadness once she realized she might not see her parents, especially her mother, for a very long time. Her mother hugged and kissed her tenderly and knew that God's goodness would bring them together again very soon.

"Rosalia, don't cry. Once Paolo gets settled in Pittsburgh, you can come home for a visit," Della whispered to her daughter.

Her mother may have thought of Sicily as home, but Sicily to Rosalia was a mythical place of great food, weather, and friends. Rosalia had emigrated from Sicily when she was too young to form her own memories. Her memories of Sicily were formed by the conversations of her parents and their friends. She had the same feelings of Sicily as Americans have of their childhood family trips to the beach. A six-year-old child's memory enhanced by others' feelings of the place made Sicily a fond memory for Rosalia more than reality would permit.

"Mother, Sicily is not our home anymore. This is our home. Please stay and come to Pittsburgh with Paolo and me," Rosalia implored her mother.

Della sadly said, "Your father is not happy here. He wants to go home. I do too. Sicily is our home, even though it is not your home."

In a youthful expression of naiveté Paolo promised both Rosalia and her parents, "Let's not worry about the future. My new American business will be successful enough that your father and mother can come live with us next year."

Looking at Rosalia, Paolo continued, "Your father taught me the produce business and I am sure in a busy city like Pittsburgh, we can solve our money worries." Paolo did not understand that Rosalia was not worried about money. She was concerned that she would not see her mother again—a scene they had seen repeatedly with other families and friends. A visit every so often is different from living close enough to be involved in each other's lives.

Before departing, Mrs. Cali gave Rosalia the address of her good friend from Sicily, Josephine Mangini, who operated a boarding home for Italian immigrants in McKeesport, Pennsylvania.

"Mama JoJo will take care of you, my love," Della told her daughter as Paolo and Rosalia departed.

Ostensibly to reassure her mother, but more to reassure herself, Rosalia said, "Mama, God knows we are meant to be together. We will see you soon."

Rosalia and her parents never saw each other again. Giovonni and Della died soon after arriving in Sicily. He had been in America too long and had forgotten that he could not challenge the local Mafia chieftain with impunity. Giovonni developed a successful wholesale produce export business by using his connection to Harrisburg to handle the American export part of the business. He refused to pay tribute to the Mafia. One Sunday evening, as Della and Giovonni were driving back from a family gathering, a vehicle of assassins approached the Calis from the opposite direction and opened fire with machine guns. Giovonni and Della were killed by the multiple bullets. The local Mafia instructed the area law enforcement officials not to retrieve the bodies for three days from the bullet-ridden car still stalled on the country road. The Mafia wanted to send a message to the Sicilian population—especially to the recently returning Sicilians from America—that in this country the rule of men still ruled the day. Rosalia and Paolo did not learn of her parents' death until a year after the incident, when a visiting Roman Catholic parish priest told Rosalia about it.

McKeesport is twelve miles southeast of Pittsburgh down the Monongahela River, which was about the same distance between Paolo's hometown of Bagheria and Palermo. Paolo thought it would be easy for him to live in McKeesport and work in Pittsburgh. Paolo wanted to work in Pittsburgh for he believed there would be more opportunities to make a fortune in a larger city. He had heard of Pittsburgh but had never heard of McKeesport, and the city's name sounded like it would be a town for the Irish. Paolo wanted a town where other Sicilians lived and planned only to stay in McKeesport until he was able to establish himself financially. Ignorance and confidence is a powerful combination for great success or great disappointment.

McKeesport was the fastest growing city in America in the 1920s. It was a mini-Pittsburgh. The Youghiogheny River merged with the Monongahela River at McKeesport, where the Monongahela continued to flow northwest to Pittsburgh. Mills of all sorts lined both banks of both rivers throughout McKeesport and all the other smaller communities that bordered McKeesport. Communities such as Glassport, Port Vue, Duquesne, Braddock, and Clairton had developed smoking and soot- making steel mills, but the hub of all this activity was McKeesport. These other communities depended on the success of McKeesport as much as McKeesport's success was tied to these other communities.

In fact, the whole Pittsburgh region up and down the Ohio, Allegheny, and Monongahela rivers was linked together with certain parts of the chain being more important links than others. The only other link more important than McKeesport was the city of Pittsburgh itself. McKeesport had the second largest population in Allegheny County, but it was still nine times smaller in population than Pittsburgh's 600,000 people. Many immigrants of different ethnicities settled in the McKeesport area, called the Mon-Yough Valley after the names of the rivers surrounding the area. The immigrants from Southern and Eastern Europe were the newest members of the labor force in the valley. Since most of the plants were mills or industries related to steel, the air and water pollutants were so dense and toxic that most immigrants wished they had never left the fresh air of their rural farms for America. However, not Paolo; to him, everything about America was great. He was living his father's dream.

Streets were filled with people, and transactions happened in all the stores along the streets of McKeesport as Paolo walked from the boarding house of Josephine Mangini on Shaw Avenue to work at the National Tube Works, a manufacturing plant that was part of the U.S. Steel Corporation empire. Paolo dreamt of being a proprietor of a store in Pittsburgh. However, first he had to earn enough money from the hot, hard, and bruising labor of a steelworker in the mill.

National Tube Works, as it was then known, had a rich but infamous history. The first plant built along the Monongahela River site was the Fulton Bolman Company of McKeesport. In 1872, the Flagler brothers, John and Harvey, built a plant to weld and make many different types of tubes used in industry. They had relocated their plant from Boston, Massachusetts, to McKeesport to be closer to the iron and ore regions of southwestern Pennsylvania and northern West Virginia. McKeesport's easy access via river transportation to the essential ingredients of iron and ore needed to manufacture industrial tubes made the city a more financially efficient place than Boston to conduct business. Over a few decades tube mills throughout the nation consolidated and merged into National Tube Works. In 1901 National Tube Works became part of the new U.S. Steel Corporation formed by J.P. Morgan.

Urban legend has it that when J.P. Morgan, the man, visited McKeesport in 1901 to inspect National Tube, he asked a local "down on his luck" real estate attorney, "How much would you charge to prepare the necessary paperwork for my daughter to purchase a home on Euclid Avenue?"

The attorney, thinking Mr. Morgan was a traveling salesman with his New York City dress coat, responded, "Sir, if you have to ask, you can't afford me."

McKeesport legend has it that J.P. laughed out loud and said, "Sir, I will have to remember that quip."

Morgan's daughter never did purchase a home in McKeesport. Sure enough, a few years later Henry Clay Frick of Pittsburgh inquired of Mr. Morgan how much would it cost to purchase Morgan's yacht, Corsair. Mr. Morgan responded with his best impression of the McKeesport attorney, "Sir, if you have to ask, you can't afford it."

Mr. Frick pondered for a moment, then said, "Sir, I will take it."

With that Henry Clay Frick was a yacht owner. The urban legend continued that these two men could be so cavalier about money given that it was the working-class people of McKeesport who made it possible. The activist trade organizations had a friend in the city of McKeesport, and National Tube workers participated in the steel strikes of 1909 and 1919. U.S. Steel Corporation dismantled the Dewees Wood plant section of the National Tube Works because, as one corporate official stated, "McKeesport... has a population that is largely in sympathy with lawlessness, and has a mayor who will not use his police to protect the property of manufacturers and will not permit a non-union man seeking work to enter the town."

Union activities did not bother Paolo; he was used to it growing up in Sicily and thought the union would protect the laborers from corporate abuses, although it did not work exactly that way in Sicily, where eventually the union leaders would collude with the owners and politicians to better their own personal financial station. Paolo thought the American unions would be different. Quickly, Paolo learned that American industrial unions favored certain workers and discriminated against other workers. Workers from Southern and Eastern Europe did not have the same influence as other workers. Southern and Eastern Europeans were assigned the worst jobs and received the lowest pay.

Some accepted this caste system, and others rebelled.

After only two months of working in the mill, Paolo told Rosalia, "I am quitting the mill job to start selling fruit to the mill workers with a pushcart."

"Paolo, how can you quit a paying job when we have a baby coming and have to find a new home?" a worried Rosalia asked her husband.

Hugging his new wife, Paolo said, "My dear, don't worry. The union boss said I could work any shift and as many hours as I want. As long as I am willing to do any task they assign me."

Paolo knew that this meant he would have to perform the worst and direst tasks at the mill.

"Rosalia, instead of working hard for the company's profits and in a dirty job, I may as well work in my own business and keep the money for us. I am sure I can make more on my own."

Rosalia worried about being a new wife in a new city, with a baby on the way. Rosalia was now pregnant with her first child. The pregnancy also caused another concern: where would their new young family live? Josephine had rented one room to the couple and had warned them that if they added to their family they would have to move. It was not in Josephine's nature to move a young couple with a new baby, but she could not have a crying baby in a home meant for immigrants transitioning to American life. She could not afford to lose paying customers because of a baby. With the numerous immigrants entering McKeesport to work in the mills, Josephine would not have a problem renting the Lomeos' room. However, she could lose all her tenants if she permitted children to board in her home.

Josephine's husband had abandoned the family some three months prior, and afraid of being the only provider for her children, she had to remove all emotions from her life and make decisions based on financial rewards. Feeling for her mother's friend and hoping she never had to change so much just to provide a meager existence for her family, Rosalia began to cry. "Mama JoJo, I am sorry I have to leave you," Rosalia sobbed.

Josephine tried to explain, "I told you before I agreed to board you, that if you have a baby you would have to leave. I don't have a husband, and I need to have money to buy food for my children and pay my mortgage to the bank."

Rosalia quickly responded, "I understand. I am not mad. I just feel bad that we will not see each other every day. I am afraid we will not stay friends."

Being judgmental was not a trait Rosalia had developed. She had empathy for her new friend, and understood Josephine's situation.

Realizing she had a new friend, Josephine told Rosalia, "I am also expecting, and I hope that our children will become lifelong friends."

Rosalia agreed. "Our two new Americans will become fast friends and successful business people."

The union hierarchy did not bother Paolo, having listened to stories from his grandfather and father about Fasci Siciliani. He knew how an idea or system initially intended to assist farmers and factory workers easily could be corrupted by the power and money of the financial power elite. After only two months of living in McKeesport, he realized instead of fighting with the union bosses for better job assignments, it made more sense to spend his energy and time learning how to operate a sole proprietor business in America. The land of the free and home of the brave encouraged individualism and self-reliance, and Paolo believed he had these qualities to succeed in America. Moreover, the protection of the common man's property from unfair confiscation by the political and financial classes was guaranteed under the American Constitution and its courts.

This was in stark contrast to the protection that the average citizen in Sicily received. In Sicily, one had either to pay for protection or have the means to protect one's property. The government officials not only ignored such confiscation but urged the elitists to confiscate as much property as possible to extract a higher ransom from the elitists. Everyone in Sicily was a hostage in some form, precisely for the lack of order and rules to regulate the conduct of private business. Paolo naively believed that America was different. He thought that the American ideal that a society should be governed by the people in laws passed by the governed would prevent the rule of men governance he had known in Sicily. Youth's excitement for a new adventure and a break from a parent's way of life sometimes fails to recognize the weakness of man. A superior legal system in America surpassed the Italian or Sicilian legal systems, but some men controlling America's legal system were just as corrupt as those managing the Sicilian system. The American system inherently was harder to corrupt, so justice did seep through the judicial robes, but not as often as Paolo would have imagined.

Paolo's first encounter with the American system occurred when he first tried to operate his pushcart on the streets of McKeesport.

Not fully understanding the local ordinance of the city of McKeesport, Paolo did not realize that he needed to have a permit to operate the pushcart. An officer of the law wearing his blue uniform with an impressive gold badge on his left shirt pocket and a gun holster around his oversized waist approached Paolo in a menacing way while Paolo was crying words of encouragement to people heading toward the corner of Sinclair and Sixth streets.

The police officer gruffly said, "Hey, Mr. Dago, you can't sell your rotten fruit on this corner. You are interfering with the pedestrian traffic on the sidewalks and blocking the entrance to a legitimate store."

On the corner of Sixth and Sinclair streets was a small fruit market owned by a native McKeesporter.

In reality, the city regulation of pushcarts permitted Paolo's location, but the owner of the fruit market, Sean McDonough, had asked his police officer friend to move Paolo from the front of his store. Paolo's low prices were diverting customers away from McDonough's store. Objecting mostly in Sicilian but with some English, Paolo confirmed, "I have a right to sell fruit on any street corner in the city. You have no power to tell me otherwise."

Searching for a response, the officer peered at Grocer McDonough, who looked confused and afraid that his existing customers would understand that he unfairly targeted Paolo; he just shrugged his shoulders and turned his back on the officer. Being humiliated by a foreigner and abandoned by a friend made the officer angry, so he proceeded to write out a citation to Paolo. Handing the citation to Paolo while other immigrants and working-class people were passing by focused on their own problems, the officer said, "Here, Garlic Eater.

I will see you in court in a few days."

Unable to comprehend the officer's English nor the scribble now in his hand, Paolo stuffed the citation in his pocket and took his cart up the steep hill of Sixth Street, turning right onto Shaw Avenue past the Mangini boarding home. Then after a few more yards, another right turn to his new small home on Fairview Avenue. It was less of home and more of a shed. It had one bathroom and two bedrooms with a small front room that served as a kitchen and living room. Rosalia was perplexed less by Paolo's early arrival home than by the look of angry frustration and hopelessness on his face.

"What's wrong, Paolo?" she asked.

Paolo, barely able to contain his anger, explained, "A custurinu was harassing me. I am not sure what he was saying but could tell he didn't like Italians. I think he would have arrested me or beat me up if there weren't so many people on the street."

Trying to be reassuring, Rosalia said, "Paolo, maybe you misunderstood what he was telling you. I have seen people, including Italians, in Harrisburg and here using pushcarts without any problems."

Handing her the citation, Paolo said, "Then why did he give me this? Can you read it?"

After hearing about his encounter with the police officer and reading the crumbled piece of paper from his pocket, Rosalia determined that Paolo had been cited for selling goods without a permit. The citation was signed by an Officer Guy Rodkey of the McKeesport Police Department. Officer Rodkey would soon have a well-deserved reputation as a police officer who used his police powers to intimidate immigrants and curry political favors from McKeesport's politicians. The two adversaries did not know that this day would foreshadow a greater clash between them some twenty years hence.

Paolo entered his appearance at the local magistrate office to adjudicate the citation. As Paolo sat in the reception area of the court, which was nothing more than the living room of the home of the justice of the peace, he noticed that most of the defendants waiting for a hearing were immigrants or poorer Americans. Clues such as manner of dress and grooming usually revealed the station of the man, regardless if one was in Bagheria or McKeesport. Paolo could tell that the clothes worn by the other defendants were no better than his. Paolo wondered to himself why only the poor in McKeesport had criminal citations. It never occurred to Paolo that these were not the only people to receive citations but the only the people who either could not afford the fine or didn't have the influence to resolve their problems behind closed doors.

Over time Paolo would learn that the appearance of a person or the overt observations hid more of the facts or even hindered a thoughtful analysis of the true situation. The justice of the peace quickly decided most of the cases in favor of the city, since his compensation was based on the amount of fines collected at his hearings. As the parties were called to the courtroom by the justice's wife, Rodkey and Paolo entered the small room at back of the house to begin round two of their encounter.

"Well, Mr. Lomeo, it seems you have had a run-in with Officer Rodkey," the justice said from his perched seat behind the trial bench.

Not knowing the proper protocol, Paolo responded, "Mr. Notary, I didn't do anything wrong. I have a right to sell my produce."

In Sicily, a notary public was a man of high intelligence and influence, contrary to American notaries public. Paolo thought any man important enough to decide his fate must be a notary public. When Paolo saw Rodkey shifting in his seat, Paolo reached in his pocket for his lucky coin. He figured to fight the American government, he would need to have something more than his own willingness. He would need to have a little divine intervention.

Rodkey was moving to stand up and address the court to respond to Paolo's defense, when the justice held his hand up signal to Rodkey to remain seated. The justice of the peace looked directly at Rodkey and said, "Mr. Lomeo, I believe you do have a right to sell your fruit in the city. I can tell you are new to our city and may have misunderstood our ordinances. You are required to have a permit to operate a pushcart in the city.

"However, I believe the officer was wrong in not explaining this to you. He should have known you were new to the city and given you a chance to get a permit. Therefore, I am dismissing the citation with the stipulation that you have a permit within thirty days."

The English words were too many and spoken so fast Paolo was not sure what the justice was saying. Paolo could tell from his demeanor that he was angry with Rodkey, but Paolo was not sure what this meant for him.

"Do you understand? Telli, come here," the justice yelled.

Telli was the justice's cook. She was nineteen and the daughter of Italian immigrants from Naples. Telli was born in Italy, but her parents emigrated when she was two years old, so her childhood was more American than Italian. She did not have an Italian accent when speaking English. Her spoken English was the typical form of English spoken by the lower middle-class people of McKeesport. She used the slang and improper pronunciations just like any other McKeesport teenager in the 1920s. Except for her dark complexion, long black hair, and dark eyes, she was as American as her Irish neighbors whose family came to America in the early 1870s. She also spoken the Italian of her parents, which also was the Italian spoken by the lower middle class of Naples. She always spoke to her parents in Italian, since her parents did not understand English very well.

"Telli, did you hear my verdict in this case?" "Yes."

"Please translate it to Mr. Lomeo. I am not sure he understood me."

Addressing Paolo in Italian while standing in between the justice and Paolo, Telli began, "Mr. Lomeo, the justice is waiving your fine if you are willing to get a city permit within thirty days. If you are willing, just say sì and I will tell the justice you agree."

"Sì."

The justice smiled and said, "Fine. Now that is resolved. Mr. Lomeo, good luck on your new venture."

Paolo thanked Telli and the justice and headed for the exit door as quickly as possible without running. His father told him never to stay around to wait for an explanation if the first news you receive is good. Paolo was surely glad he had his father's coin on this day; otherwise, his American dream would have ended before it started.

Paolo's not guilty verdict had more to do with the justice of the peace's dislike for Officer Rodkey than the merits of Paolo's defense.

It seemed Officer Rodkey had political ambitions and had told a few political hacks he planned to run against the justice at the next election. Regardless of the reason, Paolo's good fortune continued in America.

Another defendant, Antonio Grazie, assumed Paolo had influence with the authorities and introduced himself as a Sicilian in need of a little assistance. "Excuse me, paisan, I would like to talk to you," Antonio said as he approached Paolo from behind on the sidewalk outside of the justice's home.

Paolo and Antonio walked together, heading toward a local tavern close to the mill. They entered the dimly lighted tavern, most of whose patrons worked at the mill. Antonio ordered two beers from the male bartender. No woman of any standing would have worked in this tavern. Antonio explained, "Paisan, I am in a bad way. I have no money and will have to go back to Sicily if I can't make it here soon."

"Antonio, I understand, but I have the same problem. My pushcart is barely making enough to support my family. I am not sure I can help you," Paolo responded, thinking Antonio wanted to borrow money.

"I don't need to have your money. I need to have your political connections."

"What political connections? I am new to McKeesport. I don't know anyone of importance."

"C'mon! Why won't you help a fellow Sicilian? I witnessed the judge dismiss your case without a word. You obviously knew how to get to the judge."

"Hey, how many times do I have to tell you? I don't have the time for this." Paolo became angry at the insinuation he was lying.

"I am willing to give you fifty percent without any investment, as long as you can get the city to approve of our store. I am having a difficult time with them."

Tired of trying to explain to Antonio that he had no connections, Paolo began to excuse himself from the table. Antonio became irritated that Paolo would not assist a fellow Sicilian in his time of need.

Antonio may not have been a good businessman, but he had a persuasive way in manipulating people to do his bidding. However, convincing a Lomeo would take more than words, and Antonio soon realized that Paolo was not a typical recently arrived immigrant.

As his anxiety increased, his face became visibly red with anger, and then without notice, Antonio's head hit the table as he fell asleep.

Confused, Paolo looked at him sleeping and thought this guy must be joking or acting for effect. After about three minutes, Antonio woke up and explained to Paolo that he had a disease that caused him to fall fast asleep when he got excited with anger or anxiety.

His eyes beaming with anger and his jaws clenched, Paolo yelled, "Hey ciuccio, show more respect and don't take me as a fool to think a person could fall asleep at the first sign of stress."

Paolo never heard of narcolepsy and thought Antonio was either lying or just plan crazy. Either way, he wanted to leave the tavern and Antonio far behind. Antonio grabbed Paolo's hand as Paolo began to rise from the table, begging him to listen.

"Wait, Paolo, I am telling the truth. Ask around the neighborhood, our countrymen will tell you about my disease," Antonio begged.

Paolo, feeling the sincerity in his eyes, returned to his seat to hear Antonio's explanation, which was that his family had been cursed with this disease ever since his great-grandfather had refused to assist the local parish priest in Palermo.

"When my grandfather's father, Vincenzo, was a young man, the parish priest asked him to take responsibility for an unmarried village girl whom the priest had impregnated. My great-grandfather refused. The priest threatened to tell the village anyway that it was Vincenzo's child and the village would believe the priest over a poor village boy. When Vincenzo again refused, the priest said he would excommunicate Vincenzo's mother from the Church, knowing that this would deeply wound his mother.

"My great-grandfather always carried a knife, since he was a hired farm worker in the fields of Palermo. As the priest was talking, well, more like screaming, my great-grandfather pulled his knife from its sleeve tucked in the back of his pants.

"With a frightful look, the priest tried to retreat, but Vincenzo grabbed him from behind and slit his throat. Vincenzo was never tried for the murder, since the priest was a Frenchman, but the new priest told the parish that the Grazie family shall be cursed for three generations. So hopefully, my sons will not have to deal with this disease."

Paolo did not know what to make of this story and wished he could change the subject. Somewhat laughing but with concern that his new friend had mental health issues, Paolo said, "Antonio, I think I will call you Mangia Dorm from now on."

Mangia dorm is Sicilian for eat and sleep. Paolo made this little joke as a way to avoid the awkwardness of his peculiar situation. Another trick Paolo learned from his father: it is easy to avoid an uncomfortable situation with a quick-witted response.

"I don't think my wife, Maria, will like the nickname," Mangia Dorm laughed.

"OK, I will try to get the store permit. But remember, I am not making any promises, and I don't have any special friends."

Mangia Dorm and Paolo headed out of the tavern toward home, as Mangia Dorm detailed his idea to Paolo.

Chapter 7

The next Rockefeller?

Mangia Dorm had visions of a fruit and meat market that would sell specifically to the immigrant population. The Southern and Eastern European immigrants, no matter their country of origin, constantly complained about the inability to purchase authentic ethnic food in McKeesport. The city of Pittsburgh also had a diverse population of Southern and Eastern European immigrants, and had areas where authentic food and drink could be bought. However, McKeesport's blue-collar working population in the early 1920s consisted mainly of Northern Europeans, and with the Mon-Yough Valley industries recently recruiting labor from Southern and Eastern Europe because of their willingness to work for lower wages, Mangia Dorm figured that a truly ethnic store could succeed in McKeesport.

Paolo pondered the idea and discussed it with Rosalia once he arrived home. "Rosalia, I had the strangest conversation with Antonio Grazie this afternoon."

"Who is Antonio Grazie?"

"You have seen his wife and him at church. They are the people that dress like they are from Rome."

"I think I know who you mean. What did he want? You didn't lend him money, did you?" Rosalia sternly addressed Paolo.

"No, I didn't lend him money. What money would I give him? Anyway, he thinks he and I can start a store together. He wants to open a store that would serve people like us."

"What do you mean people like us? Sicilians?"

"He wants to serve new Americans from Southern Italy and the Slovaks. What do you think? I can sell my push cart and use the money to invest in a real store," Paolo expounded, looking excited.

Being an unusual woman for her day, Rosalia understood and enjoyed business discussions. "Mr. Grazie is on to something. I have noticed more and more new Americans who are from our part of the old country. We are the only people willing to do the dirty work in the mills, so our neighborhood should grow in future years."

Her only concern focused on the practical application of serving the needs of all the Southern and Eastern Europeans. The customs, foods, and drinks not only varied among Italians from various regions but also differed greatly between Southern and Eastern Europeans.

Using an example to prove the point, Rosalia told Paolo, "Compare the customs of our new neighbors, the Pastericks. They are from Poland, and Mrs. Pasterick prepares different meals from me. She prepares a dish called Haluski, where she mixes fried onions, salt, pepper, and butter with cabbage and wide egg noodles."

"I understand, but what should Mangia Dorm and I do? How do we solve this problem?"

"Who is Mangia Dorm?" Rosalia asked.

Laughing out loud, Paolo tried to explain Mangia Dorm's disease. "Well, Rosalia, what should we do?"

"Well, you could have a store that sells the staple items that all the ethnic groups use, such as cabbage, tomatoes, potatoes, and sausage."

Rosalia continued, "Or you could just sell the items that Italians use, and since we are Italian, hopefully the Italians will feel comfortable and loyal with fellow Italians. This way you only have to focus on specific items.

"Otherwise, if you try to service all the different consumers, you will have to have a store as large as a city block. You can't afford the inventory for a large store nor afford the rent of such a large store. I personally think you should just sell to Italians. I feel more at home with them."

Without knowing it, Rosalia was describing a modern-day Walmart when she referred to a store "as large as a city block." She may have been aware of The Great Atlantic and Pacific Tea Company, in future years known as A&P. A&P was the first true national grocery store in America. By the early 1920s it was starting to experiment with larger-spaced stores with a variety of inventory.

"Rosalia, I am not sure the other Italians will consider us family, since we are Sicilian and most of the immigrants I have met in McKeesport are from Naples. Plus, I am not sure that there are that many Italians in McKeesport to support the store," Paolo told her.

The two businessmen rejected Rosalia's idea to start a store that serviced only Italians. To have the broadest customer base with as little financial investment as possible, they settled on the idea of selling staple items to serve a larger population with a controlled inventory.

Knowing that Sean McDonough had previously told Mangia Dorm that he soon would lose his store to his creditors unless he found a buyer for it, Paolo decided to approach Mr. McDonough with an offer. Paolo woke early the next morning and walked from his Fairview home down the brick-laid Sinclair Street to McDonough's store. Paolo sat on the curb of Sixth Street waiting for McDonough to arrive.

Sean McDonough did not arrive until 9 a.m. It appeared that he had stayed up the entire night. His hair was a mess, his clothes were wrinkled, and he was missing buttons on the top half of his shirt. The tell-tale sign was the smell of alcohol seeping through the pores of Mc Donough's skin. However, McDonough did better than Mangia Dorm. Mangia Dorm did not arrive until after McDonough and Paolo had an agreement.

Paolo wondered why a proprietor whose business depended on the patronage of the steel workers during shift changes would not have arrived earlier than 9 a.m. The night shift and morning shift of National Tube ended and began at 7 a.m. This meant that a store owner who wanted to take advantage of the 7 a.m. shift would have to arrive for work no later than 6 a.m. to prepare the store for business by 7 a.m.

Paolo's fear of failure was somewhat lessened by McDonough's actions. McDonough was failing because he was not focused on success. Focusing and working toward success was not a problem for Paolo. Though he did not understand English well at the moment and had a lot to learn about American business ways and customs, he believed what he lacked in knowledge could be replaced with a positive attitude and the ability to keep pounding the proverbial door of success until it opened.

McDonough, recognizing Paolo from his encounter with Officer Rodkey, meekly approached Paolo with his hands held up at chest level. "Hey, I don't want any trouble. I didn't know Rodkey was going to give you a citation."

Confused and not understanding his English that well, Paolo could not understand why McDonough was mentioning Rodkey. "Mr. McDonough, I am here to talk to you about business. I am a friend of Antonio Grazie, and we would like to buy your store."

McDonough's relief was reflected by his large smile, and he extended his hand to Paolo and said, "Come in and sit down, and let's talk. Where is Antonio?"

"He will be here shortly, but I can discuss our arrangement."

Paolo and Mangia Dorm agreed to purchase McDonough's remaining inventory and assume the lease for the store space at the corner of Sixth and Sinclair streets.

Calling the space a store was a generous gesture. The space consisted of two floors, which included the cellar. The cellar made an excellent storage area for the produce and would double as an office space for Paolo. Paolo would park his truck on the Sinclair Street side of the store and unload his recently purchased produce to the cellar through a hatch door in the sidewalk. Opening the hatch would reveal a slide that could easily transport the produce from the sidewalk to the cellar. As long as there was a person in the cellar to handle the produce before it hit the floor, this system worked with just a little physical effort. Across the cellar were steps leading to the back of the retail part of the store on the first floor. It took great physical effort to retrieve the produce from the cellar to the wooden stands on the first floor. Fortunately, Paolo, at only five feet, seven inches tall, had the natural strength of a man twice his size.

The first floor space consisted of wooden floor planks not altogether flushed in place. The walls were white painted blocks where Paolo hung posters advertising the produce specials. It was Rosalia's job to construct the posters, as she was the only one of the two couples who could write in English. Neither Paolo nor Mangia Dorm had received enough education to write or read in Italian, let alone in English. With construction paper, paints, and a brush, Rosalia made the most simple forms look beautiful, at least to Paolo's eyes. The retail space had two entrances, one facing Sixth Street and the other on Sinclair Street. The space was basically a rectangle encompassing no more than 900 square feet, which mimicked the shape and dimensions of the cellar.

Though Paolo would have preferred to start a business in Pittsburgh, he calculated that this opportunity had a better chance of success than opening a new store in Pittsburgh. At least this store had some positive attributes. Foremost was its location on the corner of two busy streets and only three blocks from National Tube Works. This made finding customers with cash in their pockets easier. There was no better business model than locating a retail store close to a company with four thousand employees working around the clock. When the men finished work, a lot of them walked to the store with instructions from their wives to purchase the necessary items for the day's meal. In addition, the space was already configured as a retail market, so it took hardly any cash and relatively small effort to convert it to a space of Paolo's likening.

Paolo suggested changing the name of the store to Roma's Fruit Market. He did not want to be the same as every other small grocer with an eponymous store. He also worried that the non-Italians would have a difficult time pronouncing the name of the store if it was named Lomeo and Grazie. Showing their Southern Italian bias and envy of Northern Italy, they figured a store named after the most famous city in Italy and maybe the world would give the store immediate credibility with the upper middle-class people of McKeesport. Sure, their main customer base would be the mill workers from the Tube Works, but it was Paolo's dream and hope that in future years his store would also cater to the wealthier customer. Paolo figured that a wealthier customer may spend more than a mill worker thereby increasing Paolo's profit. In future years, Paolo would come to hate the name of the store. He would learn too late that it is the quality of the product and not the name that brings success to a business enterprise.

Beginning a business in America during the Roaring Twenties helped overcome the usual low cash flow of a new business. As long as the fire, smoke, and dirt spewed from the Mon-Yough mills darkened the day and brought artificial light to the night, customers had the money to spend on the specialty items sold at Roma's Fruit Market. Paolo and Mangia Dorm worked well together. Paolo had the ability to buy the best quality meats and fruits at the lowest possible prices, while Mangia Dorm's ability was to convince—in a friendly way—the customers to buy more than they initially wanted. This combination helped to make for a profitable enterprise.

Rosalia quietly saved the money Paolo brought home. Afraid of banks due to their unsavory behavior in Sicily and America, she literally saved the money in glass jars, hiding the jars in holes she dug in the dirt basement of their Fairview Avenue home, out of sight of Paolo and her two young children. By the end of the decade Paolo and Rosalia had two children, Joseph and John, with a third child on the way.

Mangia Dorm behaved more freely with his money. Being known as a rich married couple with many superficial friends made Mangia Dorm and his wife feel like true Americans. They never realized that to be a true American, one had to believe in a person's right to live without interference from government or mob rule. The by-product of such a system that protected a person's property and life from confiscation and harm was economic success.

Mangia Dorm and his wife were both born in Trapani, Sicily, in 1898, and married in Sicily before relocating to America in 1919.

His wife and he were less than physically attractive individuals. Other Sicilians in the McKeesport area referred to Maria Grazie as Facci de Porco, the English translation being "face of a pig." Crude for sure and probably also rude, but an uneducated population uses descriptive words to express their feelings, no matter how crude. Her preference for plaid dresses did nothing to hide her one hundred thirty pounds on a five-foot bone structure. Mangia Dorm stood about five feet four inches with a round body to carry his one hundred eighty-five pounds. With his slicked-back black hair he resembled a shady real estate investor more than a small business owner. A psychologist would say this unpleasant-looking couple overcompensated by spending lavishly on dinners or gifts for friends to relieve their feelings of inadequacy, both physically and financially. They both were gracious with their time for any charity or church work, as long as it could be seen by their friends. Mangia Dorm and Maria had no desire to perform charity without public recognition. The Grazies were also always the first to financially contribute to any church cause that they believed would be mentioned in the Sunday Mass bulletin. They never missed Mass with their three children. A socially seeking couple could never have anyone think they were less than perfect.

Rosalia easily became irritated when, inevitably, a parishioner or parish priest would ask, "Why don't you contribute your money and time like the Grazies?"

Paolo could easily ignore such slights, but Rosalia usually responded with anger and frustration. She would tell all who would ask, "My husband and I work while the Prince and Princess dance."

From the Ice to the Fire

By the end of the 1920s, the Grazies lived on the precipice of disaster unbeknownst to them but soon to become harshly known to them and many other Americans. The invisible dark clouds of economic ruin and despair were circling America, holding the hidden lightning bolt that would fundamentally change the relationship between the U.S. government and its citizens. The stock market crash of October 1929 wrecked the financial vehicle that Americans used to provide for their families and better their communities.

Not expecting the crash, President Herbert Hoover seemed to have received a head concussion from the violent shake and acted confused throughout his presidency. Contrary to current public perception, active government management of the economy began under the Hoover administration, not Franklin Roosevelt's administration. With the fear permeating throughout the country after the financial collapse, it was easy for the government to convince the populace that the life as they knew it was ending. Both presidents used this fear to institute publicly funded projects with large publicly traded stock companies and large industrial labor unions, as opposed to using small businesses and trade unions, to solve the perceived evilness and harshness of the business cycle. This change in the dynamics of the American market system would have dire consequences for Paolo and his family from this day until the day of his death.

With the money sent by Paolo to his mother over the years, his brother Eugico thought the path to quick riches went through America. Eugico did not understand that Paolo sent a large portion of his monthly revenue to his mother because he felt guilty about leaving his mother to manage the farm alone. Guilt has a way of eating a person's desire for independent success. His father and mother wanted him to go to America and start a Lomeo family dynasty. His guilt stemmed from his closeness to both parents and an obligation he felt as the oldest son to care for his parents. Somehow, sending money to his mother made him feel better, when in truth Agatina would have forgone the money just to see her son again. However, his small business on the corner of Sixth and Sinclair streets was not generating enough cash flow to support two families and pay for a trip to Sicily. As well, Paolo worked day and night to make the store a success, a schedule that was foreign to Mangia Dorm and not conducive to a boat trip across the Atlantic Ocean to Sicily.

Eugico raised enough funds to pay for his trip from Naples, Italy, to America. He never revealed how he raised the voyage money, but knowing his brother, Paolo figured that he earned the money in some unsavory way. Being seven years younger than Paolo, Eugico constantly tried to be the anti-Paolo while growing up. Whereas Paolo obediently listened to his parents and did his best to please them, Eugico rebelled from the strict structure that Giuseppe had placed on all his sons.

Eugico was enamored by the Mafiosos roaming the streets of Bagheria and Palermo, as if the two towns were their personal estates. Giuseppe's second son's perception of these criminals as "men of honor" and influence contradicted Giuseppe's opinion of these men. Giuseppe tried to explain and instruct Eugico that these men ruled by fear and were nothing more than a pack of wild dogs surrounding a helpless baby prior to pouncing on their prey. However, these men of honor's influence reached all aspects of Sicilian life. The Mafia was the organization to join if a person wanted to have influence and money in Sicily—the trade-off, however, was immoral and illegal conduct.

Unknowingly, Paolo and Giuseppe's relationship deeply affected Eugico. Most people would think their close relationship unintentionally hid Eugico from the view of his father. In reality, this probably was the family dynamic of the Lomeo family, but this conflict between the first and second sons to grab the attention of their father was not unique to the Lomeo family. Most cultures see conflicts between the oldest and next oldest son, especially in a society where the firstborn male receives all of the wealth of the father. For some reason, beyond the scope of this book, this conflict does not seem to happen to sons born after the second son. It may be that the later sons realize they do not have a high probability of inheriting any wealth through their father, so they do not concern themselves with such matters.

For Eugico, having no responsibility for the financial condition of the family was the true problem. No family member sought his thoughts or protection, as the family had Giuseppe or Paolo to reach out to. When a person has no obligations and feels separate from the family, he seeks an organization in which he is an integral part of the organization. Unfortunately, teenage males seek organizations that take physical risks or perform dangerous situations to prove that they are men of character like their boyhood heroes, such as Caesar and Lincoln. In Sicily, the most attractive organization to weak-minded and lost teenage males was the Mafia. Eugico decided his future prospects were better with the Mafia than the hardworking life course of his father.

Giuseppe relied on Paolo and expected Paolo to assume a greater portion of the responsibility of the operation of the farm, and Paolo gladly assumed this role as the leader-in-waiting of the family. When Eugico realized that his father and mother gave their blessing to Paolo to depart Sicily for America, he became angry and upset at what he considered unfair treatment by his parents. Even though Paolo had arranged for a farm manager to handle the day-to-day operation of the farm, so the burden of the farm would not fall solely on Eugico, Eugico again felt that his parents considered him intellectually, physically, and emotionally unable to succeed in America. Eugico thought his parents should have encouraged him to emigrate from Sicily to America, since he thought he had the courage and desire to be an American. What Eugico did not understand was that his father knew Eugico was not ready to be on his own in a land where the language and customs where different. Eugico was immature, irrational, and lazy.

Giuseppe loved Eugico with the same degree of love that he loved Paolo and all his children. Playing favorites among his children never occurred to Giuseppe, though he understood that each human being, even children from the same family, had different strengths and weaknesses. Eugico's strengths included his ability to take a risk without fear. The counter weakness was he never considered the consequences of his risk taking. Paolo may react emotionally if prompted by an event or by someone, but he did not have an innate gene to act on impulse like Eugico. Giuseppe knew the difference between Paolo and Eugico and tried to encourage their strengths, while pointing out their weaknesses. The big difference between the two sons was patience.

Paolo had more patience than Eugico, even though some would consider Paolo impatient at times. Eugico wanted his riches now and did not want to have to wait or work for it. He often said to his family and friends, "I will be dead before I can enjoy the rewards of hard labor.

Why not make the money quick and eat the fruit now while I can still enjoy it?"

Giuseppe would respond, in a loud clear voice, so that the point would be stressed to Eugico and overheard by Giuseppe's other younger children, "Yes, Eugico, it will take you years to obtain the riches of life, like a loving wife and wonderful children. But it is worth it, believe me. If you take to the life of a Mafioso, you will be dead, either physically or spiritually, before you realize the wrongness of your ways."

"Pa, I can't be killed. I am too strong and smart. And spiritually is just another word to manipulate my thoughts, like Mama's bible."

Agatina would always say, "I will pray for you, Eugico. You have a troubled soul, and you have so much to offer this world." A mother's love is forever, regardless of the actions of her child.

It also never occurred to Eugico to fire the farm manager and run the farm himself and try to emulate the course Paolo took. Eugico could have labored with meaning, saved enough money to depart for America, and thereby earned the respect of his family.

Never one to admit it, Eugico loved Paolo and, more importantly respected Paolo. Of course he was envious or maybe jealous of Paolo's relationship with their father, but deep inside Eugico knew that Paolo was a natural leader and moral person. Even though he did not follow Paolo's life examples, he knew he wanted his own sons to be more like Paolo than himself.

Before Paolo left for America, he and Eugico decided to go to a Bagheria tavern to have a good-bye meal and drink. Entering the small restaurant on Via Spataro in Bagheria, the two brothers took a table toward the center of the lounge. Neither brother having a lot of money, as they ordered a glass of wine and a plate of bread and cheese Paolo told Eugico, "It will soon be your turn to leave for America, so it is time for you to grow up and start taking responsibility for your actions. You are the head of the family now that father is dead and I am leaving for America. Mama needs you, and she needs to lean on someone. Like it or not, you are the one, and Patri would expect you to do it."

"That is great! A lecture from the prodigal son. You spend three years in the army without contributing to the farm. You arrive home to a hero's welcome, even during Patri's funeral. Now, you are running from the heavy lifting for the easy life in America. So quit telling me about obligations and responsibilities. You are taking care of yourself and that is what I plan to do."

Without thinking, Paolo quickly stood over Eugico, clenched his left hand into a fist, and slugged Eugico in the head, knocking him out of his chair. Eugico hit the floor like a stone to the ground. Screaming at a dazed Eugico, Paolo said, "You need to learn a little respect. No wonder I had to use my inheritance to hire a farm manager. You are irresponsible! Eugico, if you ever speak to me that way again, I will hurt you. I mean it!" The restaurant owner angrily told the two Lomeos to leave his establishment before he called the police. Paolo apologized for the disturbance and quickly grabbed Eugico by the collar, pulled him to his feet, and dragged him out of the restaurant.

Once on Via Spataro, Eugico realized that again his loud mouth brought him trouble. "I am sorry. You are right, Paolo, Patri deserves better. I will be a good son to our mother and brother to the rest of the family. Paolo, I will follow you to America, and you and I will be partners in some great American business."

Paolo, being a forgiving brother and knowing that his father would want him to change Eugico's life direction, told his brother, "Eugico, I would love to have you as a partner. Together, we can be an American success story, just as Patri hoped. I am your older brother, and I will always be there for you. Even when I am in America."

Eugico arrived in McKeesport in August 1926 at the age of twenty-three. The six years away from Paolo only exaggerated Eugico's warped sense of life. He had become a person with undying confidence regardless of any setback with a growing lack of intelligence to recognize the consequences of his actions. He came to McKeesport full of energy and ready to make his riches in America.

Upon seeing his brother's home on Fairview Avenue, the smoke and soot of the McKeesport mills, and witnessing the long hours Paolo worked, Eugico soon realized that America's freedom of speech and assembly did not bring riches. The combination of hard work and protection of property guaranteed by the U.S. Constitution brought success to the person willing to appreciate both. Working faithfully at any task was contrary to Eugico's idea of living. He no longer wanted to be a business partner of Paolo's. It only took him three years of living in America to know that he did not want Paolo's life. Paolo only had to live with Eugico for three years to comprehend and view him from the distance of time to see why their father was so worried about the final outcome of Eugico's life.

Eugico believed he could become rich with criminal conduct and the willingness to walk along the edge with the other criminals. Historically, Sicilians have been typecast in America and Italy as Mafia members regardless of the truthfulness of the allegation. Eugico satisfied this image and took some pride when people thought he was in the Mafia. He had a warped sense of success. By operating a betting house in the back room of a coffee house and working as a hired thug to collect money for the local Mafia chieftain, Eugico had more money than he ever imagined.

Paolo was disappointed in his brother and told him so when Eugico visited Paolo's Fairview Avenue home on March 27, 1929, for a late lunch or an early dinner, depending on your perspective. Eugico knew that business was usually slow after the on-rush of the second shift mill workers finished shopping and that Paolo would be at home for a quiet meal alone. The younger brother wanted to talk to his older brother about leaving the produce business and helping him with his criminal business.

Paolo told Eugico, "If you continue with this way of living, you will end up in jail or dead. I am not interested in either."

He tried to encourage his brother to respect his new country and not take advantage of its freedoms to commit crimes. "Eugico, this country has so much more to offer to an enterprising person than the life you are used to. It is different from Sicily. You don't have to ask permission from a corrupt government official or Mafioso to have an honest business. The criminals do not have the same respect and influence in America as they do in Sicily. You can have a business that Patri would be proud of."

"You don't know as much as you think, Paolo. America is the same as Sicily. Everyone is working the system. Look at Mangia Dorm and your other friends. They are all grabbing the money without much work. You are the only one living in a land that doesn't exist."

Eugico was seven years younger than Paolo and did not have the close relationship with their father that Paolo had. Paolo told him, "Patri wanted to be an American and wished his children would settle in America to better themselves and his grandchildren. He believed that in America our family could be successful. Here it doesn't matter about bloodlines or connections. It is all about the desire and willingness to take the risk to succeed. In any country there are bad things going on, and here is no different. I know that, but the American ideal is what makes this place different."

Shaking his head along with a smirk, Eugico thought this sentimentalism approached the unbelievable. Eugico pointed his finger in anger at Paolo. "You are amazing! You want me to feel guilty about my success. You don't know what our father would have thought about your little struggling business. He wanted to come to America to make more money and didn't buy the American propaganda. You left before the Fascists came to power. The Blackshirts used the same propaganda about their ideals to manipulate the people.

"Didn't the pardone just say these things about the great American life to entice us to come to America? Don't you see the soot from the mills? Don't you see most immigrants barely have enough to eat? Look at their clothes and faces! Neither has been cleaned in weeks, because they can't afford it. You are not fulfilling Patri's dream! I am!"

"Eugico, his dream wasn't to be a criminal. He could have done that in Sicily."

"Well, I am earning more than a beggar of a grocer," an angry Eugico screamed.

A comment describing his older brother as a failure lit the fuse hidden deep inside Paolo next to the dry gunpowder consisting of guilt and the anger of struggling to survive in America. Unloading a decade of rage and frustration on his ignorant brother, Paolo tackled him to the ground when the blanket of fear and regret covering his brother's face made him stop. Giuseppe would have been ashamed at the anger and rashness of Paolo's actions, especially with a family member.

Paolo helped Eugico from the ground. Eugico apologized to his older brother and hugged him like he used to do as a young boy in Sicily. He told Paolo, "I am sorry, Paolo. You have treated me well the last three years, especially considering all the bad things I have done to shame our family's name. You are right; Patri would be disappointed in me. I think he was always disappointed in me."

"That's not true, Eugico. He told me that he thought you were the smartest of all of us and that you could be someone if you would just believe in yourself." Sometimes an older brother has to couch the truth to ease a younger sibling's life train back onto the right track.

Under agreement with the local Mafia to do one more criminal act, Eugico promised his brother that he would lead a respectful life thereafter. For all of Eugico's faults, he always kept his promises, which is why Paolo believed him.

Departing after shaking hands and promising to see each other for Sunday dinner, Eugico stepped from the Fairview Avenue porch, walking quickly to a waiting car. Turning to Paolo, he said, "T'amu Frere." Love you, brother.

Driving the car was Mangia Dorm. Four in the afternoon seemed an odd time for the two young Sicilians to head off for a night of crime. Paolo watched the car drive down the brick-laid road, and raised his hand high while holding his father's lucky coin, waving good-bye to his brother. The sun sat in an odd position this afternoon, surely a bad omen for Eugico.

It was not until Wednesday afternoon, March 27, 1929, that Paolo realized that Mangia Dorm had introduced his brother to the criminal element in McKeesport. Only recently did he realize that Mangia Dorm himself held a low position in the McKeesport Mafia. Roma's Fruit Market's revenues equaled enough to barely support two families, and Paolo could not figure out how Mangia Dorm always had money to spend. Probably deep down he knew it but could not consciously admit it without asking his partner to leave the business. Paolo had worked so hard the last decade, and he did not have the courage to confront his partner, knowing it would be the end of the business. But now, he knew his failure to end his relationship with Mangia Dorm sooner had helped his brother become a player in the American criminal scene.

Rosalia noticed the concerned look on Paolo's face as he entered the front room after Eugico departed. "What's wrong?" she asked.

Photo courtesy of Pittsburgh Post-Gazette

Paolo and John loading some of their bushels on their small truck before the Teamsters stopped them. Photo courtesy of Pittsburgh Post-Gazette. (Pittsburgh Press October 1, 1945).

Photo courtesy of Pittsburgh Post-Gazette

Paolo surrounded by striking Teamsters trying to prevent him from retrieving his produce.
Photo courtesy of Pittsburgh Post-Gazette. (Pittsburgh Press October 5, 1945).

Paolo, with his head lowered and speaking barely above a whisper, told her. "Eugico and I had a small fight outside. He has finally agreed to stop the gambling house and working with the Mafia."

"Isn't that good? Why the worried look?"

"Well, I am responsible for his criminal ways. Just now Mangia Dorm picked him up outside to run an errand in Pittsburgh for the Mafia. I should have known! Mangia Dorm is an errand boy for them, and he convinced a naïve Eugico to join them these last three years."

Rosalia could not help but smile and laugh. "Paolo, I wouldn't call Eugico naïve. He is probably the one who recruited Mangia Dorm." Soberly looking at his beautiful wife, thinking he was so lucky to have met such a caring and loyal person, he said, "Maybe, but nonetheless Mangia Dorm's Mafia connections can only spell trouble for the fruit market. I should have seen this before today!"

"Let's just ask him to leave the store! You have been doing all the work anyway, so nothing much will change," Rosalia reminded her husband.

"I hope it is that easy. I hope my father is not upset with me," Paolo confessed to his wife.

"Why would your father care about throwing a "prince" like Mangia Dorm out of the store?" his confused wife responded.

Obviously, Rosalia did not realize Paolo's true concern. His father had always told Paolo, as the older brother, he was supposed to watch out for his younger brother. It was his job to make sure his younger siblings behaved properly. Giuseppe had told Paolo he was especially worried about Eugico. He thought Eugico had some of the same innate qualities of Agatina's father. Paolo knew his father was not giving a compliment. Now, he had let his father down. Eugico had become a criminal and a man that Eugico's future children would be ashamed of.

"Rosalia, my father would have expected me to control Eugico, just has he had done in Sicily before he died."

Rosalia never met Giuseppe, but from the profile described by her husband, she knew that a man of such integrity and intelligence would have understood that Paolo had no means to control the actions of his adult brother. "Paolo, there is no way you could have controlled the actions of a man. A father may be able to control his son as an adult, but no other person could. This is why a son needs to have a father. I assure you that your father understands."

"You are right," Paolo said, knowing she was right, but she hurt him without knowing it. A son does need to have his father, and he no longer had his to lean on for support or advice. He was by himself, a tightrope walker without a net. One wrong step could be a fatal step.

Although, he thought, he did have his father's coin, and in some way it brought him comfort and luck.

Our Lord above heard from Paolo for the first time in a long time this night. Rosalia believed in prayer and had always begged Paolo to take an active interest in his spiritual well-being. Paolo listened to her this evening. Their young son, born seven days before, stayed up with him throughout the night.

Mangia Dorm and Eugico drove to Benjamin's Butcher Shop, located in Pittsburgh at 5170 Butler Street. There they met with Benjamin Yamin, whose real name was Samuel Benjamin, but he now went by Benjamin Yamin to avoid the legal authorities from New York. With Yamin was another young Jewish man, Hyman Dodkin. Benjamin explained to Eugico and Mangia Dorm that he wanted to collect on the insurance policy for the four-story building at 5170 Butler Street. The building consisted of the butcher shop and a barber shop on the ground floor, along with apartments on the remaining three stories, all vacant except one apartment occupied by Yamin, his wife, and children, and another occupied by a young woman.

Dodkin asked the two Sicilians, "Help me unload these barrels of gasoline and rock powder."

Confused and shaking with fear, Mangia Dorm pleaded with Eugico to tell Yamin that this was not what they agreed to. "Eugico, I only agreed to help fake a burglary of the butcher and barber shops not burn down the whole building." They did not know how to handle gasoline and rock powder as incendiaries, especially to raze a four-story brick building. Also, the one hundred dollars they were promised was not worth the risk. Eugico approached Yamin with Mangia Dorm's concerns.

"Hey, Neofiti, my partner and I didn't come here to commit arson. You are not paying us enough. We only told our friends we would help you stage a burglary." Eugico was crude and treated people he did not respect with disregard. He shared the nineteenth-century European distrust of people practicing the Jewish religion. Neofiti is a derogatory Sicilian word for the Jewish people. Yamin either did not understand that Eugico was being offensive, or he did not care if there was a possibility that the two Sicilians would perform the arson.

Paolo did not have the same distrust of Jews as his younger brother. When Paolo was a young boy of thirteen in Bagheria, he, with a group of friends, decided to harass a group of Jewish men walking to the synagogue for services. Upon approaching the men on a wooden bridge, the boys threw stolen eggs from a local chicken coop at the men. Once the eggs were launched and landed on their intended targets, the boys ran in the opposite direction toward the safety of the urban streets of Bagheria. As Paolo was almost across the bridge, the decrepit bridge collapsed, sending Paolo hurtling into the stream below, shaken and confused. One of the Jewish men quickly rescued Paolo before he had a chance to drown. Wet and shivering from the cold water and fear, Paolo tried to express his sorrow for his participation in the egg throwing. Recognizing Paolo as the son of Giuseppe Lomeo, he said, "Paolo, do you think your father would be proud of you today?"

"Do you know my father?" Paolo nervously asked, knowing that if Giuseppe learned about his behavior today, Paolo would have more than eggs hitting his body this day.

"Yes, I know your father and you. Your father and you deliver your fruits to my uncle's store. Your father and I have been friends since our young adulthood."

"I recognize you now. I am sorry, Rabbi Roben. Please don't tell my father."

The rabbi agreed. "I will not tell your father, because I know he expects so much out of you. But only on two conditions. First, you personally apologize to my friends, and second, you tell your father what happened today."

Paolo looked shocked at the suggestion of confessing to his father. "Why would I tell my father? He will punish me and that is what I am trying to avoid."

"Well, maybe your consequences will be the same in the near future, but how often do you think your father will tell the story during your lifetime? How you confessed to him out of respect for him. Having the respect of your father is worth more than anything in this finite life." Paolo knew immediately that the rabbi was correct and kind enough to think of his father's feelings. "Rabbi, I will do as you say. My father said you were a man of God and intelligence, and I hope you will not let my bad behavior change your friendship with him."

"Giuseppe is the only non-Jew I respect. My friendship bond will remain strong regardless of his children's behavior. God be with you, son. Now, go home and spend time with better people," the rabbi said as he walked away from Paolo.

Roma's Fruit Market was positioned close to a number of Jewish-owned businesses in McKeesport. In particular, Paolo developed a friendship with Milton Sherman, a local dry cleaner. He learned throughout his young life that most people are the same, and it is only the elite of each culture that use hatred of minorities as a way to manipulate their fellow countrymen to believe that they need to have the elite class to protect them from these different people. Paolo also observed that some native Protestants of McKeesport discriminated against the Sicilians and Jews with impunity. The enemy of your enemy becomes your friend.

Being in his forties, Yamin thought he could bully these young Sicilian immigrants with threats that his connections with the Mafia would cause trouble for the two if they did not follow his instructions.

"I demand action or our friends will teach you about not listening to me."

Eugico, never one to be intimidated, quickly grabbed Yamin by the collar and shook him to the ground. Drawing his pistol to Yamin's head, he said, "Neofiti, the burning of your building is the least of your worries at the moment."

Dodkin and Mangia Dorm rushed over to calm Eugico and separate the two adversaries. Yamin, shaking with fear and realizing that he was dealing with a person who acted before he thought, quickly changed his attitude.

"Don Lomeo, I am sorry I offended you," Yamin apologized to Eugico. "I am under such pressure. I owe so many of our friends, and it makes me say crazy things. How about if I offer you more money to burn the building?"

"How much?" Eugico inquired.

Yamin offered to pay Eugico five hundred dollars if he would burn down the building. Eugico agreed by accepting a check made payable to cash. It never occurred to Eugico to ask for actual cash and not a check that could be dishonored by the bank when presented. Intelligence was not Eugico's strong suit. Eugico neatly folded the check and placed it into his pocket wallet.

As the Jewish men left the area, the two arsonists carefully carried the barrels of gasoline and rock powder to the basement, placing a barrel of each in the four different corners of the basement. Without planning, the men wore gloves because of the cold weather, which had an additional benefit of hiding their fingerprints at the crime scene.

Mangia Dorm's quick wit and ability to make people at ease with his personality did nothing to calm his fear of dangerous situations. He had purposefully emigrated from Sicily at the time of Italy's entrance in the Great War for fear of dying in battle. He avoided personal confrontation and tried to be friends with everyone. In better times, he would have made a good politician, never taking a stand and making people believe he actually was helping.

As Eugico soaked the burlap sacks in the barrels of gasoline, Mangia Dorm quietly climbed the basement staircase and yelled down to Eugico, "Paisan, I will wait outside and be the lookout."

Shaking his head in disbelief, Eugico screamed up at Mangia Dorm, "Fine, paisan. But since you lack the courage to help me, I am not sharing the five hundred dollars with you. I am doing all the work and taking all the risks."

Mangia Dorm was just glad Eugico did not force him to return to the basement. "Eugico, that is fine. I agree with you. You are the only one smart enough to do this safely. I am sure that is why they called you." Mangia Dorm, always the appeaser, was trying to use flattery to make sure his friend would stay his friend.

"Just get the car ready for a fast getaway," Eugico responded, frustrated and annoyed with his friend's weak ways. Eugico was hoping to be long gone from the scene when the building exploded.

Eugico slowly pulled eight burlap sacks from his winter overcoat. He then soaked the burlap sacks in one of the gasoline barrels. How he learned or who taught him how to commit arson would be a mystery through the remaining life of Paolo. Eugico proceeded to place each dripping wet burlap sack in each barrel of gasoline and rock powder, using the burlap sacks as fuses. He further tied bed sheets to the fuses to lengthen them. By extending the fuses, he was able to connect the fuses in the middle of the basement floor. Pouring oil and gasoline on the center knot, he hoped once the center knot was lit the fire would climb up the separate fuses and ignite the barrels of gasoline and rock powder. This way he would not have to light each fuse separately, giving him enough time to run up the staircase, through the building, and out to the waiting car for the getaway.

Lighting the center and taking a moment to admire his brilliance, Eugico headed for the steps. Taking every other step, he reached the basement door in seconds when he realized that he left his overcoat on the basement floor. It was not the coat that mattered, but the wallet in its pocket that contained the five-hundred-dollar check. Without thinking, a fatal trait of Eugico's, he turned and streamed down the steps with one hop to retrieve his coat. In one motion, he grabbed his coat and headed back up the steps—but too late. The incendiaries performed as planned, engulfing the building and Eugico in flames and smoke. As the McKeesport Daily News reported the next day, March 28, 1929, "Following the explosion, which rocked the Lawrenceville district, police and detectives rushed to the scene where their investigation revealed two powder cans, six oil cans, and old burlap sacks soaked in oil."

Eugico's scheme worked as planned except for his one fatal error. Eugico died a painful but quick death. The gutless Mangia Dorm, standing a block away next to his car, saw the explosion. Panicked and stricken with fear, he froze, watching the building burn without any evidence of his friend. As the occupants of the surrounding buildings came out to the street followed by the police, Mangia Dorm crept to his car, turned the engine slowly, and maneuvered the car in the opposite direction heading south back home to McKeesport.

As summarized in The Pittsburgh Press, March 28, 1929, "Eighteen pedestrians walking past the building were injured by flying glass and had to be taken to Dr. J. H. Zenseer's office for treatment." Yamin had told Eugico that the apartments were empty of people at the time, when in fact Elsie Weber, a beautiful eighteen-year-old woman with a slender but curving figure topped by natural blonde hair, was in her fourth-floor apartment. Yamin had told Eugico that Elsie had gone to visit her mother and saw no need for them to check her apartment before the explosion. However, Elsie was actually at home resting from a long day of work as a temporary secretary at H.J. Heinz and Company and preparing for her nighttime waitressing job at Frank's Tavern. Fortunately for Elsie, according to the same The Pittsburgh Press article, "Pittsburgh Fire Fighters were able to rescue her from the fire escape stairs. Only one victim, Amelia Redman, 47 had to be treated at a hospital, St. Margaret's Hospital, with a severe laceration in her right leg from the flying glass." With the number and types of injuries, the local Mafia would not be able to "fix" this case to help their friend Yamin. Yamin's pleas to Eugico to bring down the whole building, instead of just burning it, not only killed Eugico and injured innocent people, but also prevented the Mafia's police connections to quickly and quietly ditch the case.

Paolo woke early every morning to begin the hard work of running a fruit store. His business partner would never have entertained the idea of waking early for work. His idea of rising early for work was being at the store by 10 a.m. However, this morning was different.

Mangia Dorm, with his wife, arrived early in the morning at Paolo's home just as Paolo was departing to the wholesale fruit market area in Pittsburgh, known as the Strip District. Seeing his business partner standing in his front yard, he noticed that Mangia Dorm's clothes were disheveled, his hair unkempt, and he was holding a shaking cigarette in his mouth. This was contrary to Maria, who always dressed as if she were going to church, even in sad and difficult times such as this moment.

Paolo immediately thought his brother did something stupid and was sleeping in a jail waiting to be released on the bond Paolo surely would have to guarantee. "Hello, Maria. Mangia Dorm, what are you doing here? This is too early for you!"

Mangia Dorm held his head down looking at the ground, afraid to tell Paolo what had happened. He knew Paolo would not take this well. Mangia Dorm was not really worried about Paolo's loss, he worried about a possible violent reaction from Paolo toward him. Even in this most heartbreaking event for Paolo, Mangia Dorm could only think of himself and not offer any comfort, like a true friend would have.

"I have some bad news," Mangia Dorm said barely over a whisper while holding Maria's hand.

"OK, where is Eugico? I don't have time for this." Paolo reached for his wallet to give Mangia Dorm the bail money for his brother. Mangia Dorm quickly lifted his right arm with his right hand palm facing Paolo, motioning for Paolo to stop his thought.

"He is dead! Eugico is dead!" Mangia Dorm's stinging words drifted slowly toward Paolo, hovering over his head as they proceeded through the morning mist into the open kitchen window to the ears of Rosalia as she was preparing breakfast for her boys. Rosalia immediately headed for the front porch, not knowing how Paolo would react.

Would he react violently toward Mangia Dorm or begin crying like their newborn baby?

Paolo's worse fears had come true. His brother's stupidity killed him. He blamed Mangia Dorm, even though Eugico caused his own death by not listening to Paolo. This ended their business and personal relationship.

"Our friendship is over! You killed my brother!" Paolo screamed at Mangia Dorm, not caring whether he was being logical.

Meekly and untruthfully, Mangia Dorm said, "Paolo, I tried to talk him out of it. You know how he was. If he didn't listen to you, he surely wouldn't listen to me."

Paolo knew Eugico intimidated Mangia Dorm, and his brother would never have followed Mangia Dorm's advice. Paolo knew that Mangia Dorm was lying when he said he tried to convince Eugico not to burn the building. He had known both individuals for a long time as well as their separate personality traits and relationship. Eugico would have slapped Mangia Dorm silly if he even questioned Eugico's actions.

"You are such a liar. You are out of the business," Paolo informed Mangia Dorm.

"OK, Paolo, I understand. I will come by tomorrow to pick up my share of the store," Mangia Dorm said, wondering how his bluff of being paid for his share would grab Paolo. Mangia Dorm was a man of no courage, lacking in character and morals, and he knew it, but he thought he was smarter than both Lomeos.

"If you come by tomorrow, you will be seeing Eugico sooner than you had originally thought," Paolo spat.

Maria, unable to hold in her anger at the way her meek husband had refused to fight Paolo for his share of the store, screamed, "Paolo, you can't get away with this! We know people who will make you pay!"

Mangia Dorm grabbed his wife to prohibit her from approaching Paolo and Rosalia. He had known Paolo long enough to recognize that Paolo was about to lose control of his emotions. Rosalia stepped between Mangia Dorm and Maria and asked Maria to walk with her as she firmly held Maria's arm, directing her toward the front yard. The front yard was no more than a strip of land, which meant the women were essentially standing on the edge of Fairview Avenue.

With a soft and pleasant voice Rosalia told her, "Maria, it may be better for you to understand the situation you are in. No one at the church nor any of our paisans like you. Paolo can take his retribution without any worries of payback."

Maria carefully pondered Rosalia's words, and by the expression on Maria's face, Rosalia knew she had hit a nerve with her.

Never wanting to look weak and outmaneuvered, Maria responded, "Well, we have enough money without the store. With the look of your house, it seems you need the money more than us."

Rosalia held in her anger at this offensive remark because of her love for Paolo. She did not want Paolo to do something foolish and end up in jail for protecting the honor of a brother who would have never returned the favor to Paolo.

"You are right, Maria. I will tell Paolo that in order to show your love and friendship for us that you will pay for Eugico's tombstone. It would help heal his wounds especially after your hurtful words about his home."

Maria immediately knew if Rosalia told Paolo what she had just said about his home, this sunlit morning scene would turn dark quickly with possible harm coming to her husband and her.

Knowing when to quit—if anything, Maria knew how to survive—she said, "Rosalia, you are right. I have become emotional with the death of our dear friend, and my words today were said out of stress and grief. We will be happy to pay for your brother-in-law's tombstone." Rosalia quickly thanked Maria and started back toward her husband.

She reached Paolo and tenderly held his hand and nudged him forward into their little house.

Eugico was buried the following day at St. Mary's Cemetery on Grandview Avenue in McKeesport. The tombstone read "Jimmy G. Lomeo, Jan. 18, 1903–March 28, 1929." Everyone called him Jimmy even though his Sicilian name was Eugico. For some reason, Eugico liked the English nickname Jimmy and always introduced himself as Jimmy Lomeo.

The front page of The Pittsburgh Press, March 30, 1929, reported on the arson at 5170 Butler Street, stating that "James Lomeo, 26, of McKeesport died in the explosion." The headline read "Delay Yamin Hearing, Sleuths Press Probe of Fatal Meat Market Blast." Lieutenant David Corbett of the Pittsburgh Police Detective Division, Homicide Bureau, requested the postponement to continue the investigation into the death of Eugico.

The Pittsburgh police department told The Daily News, McKeesport, PA (March 29, 1929) that they "were convinced he [Eugico] was the 'touch off' man employed by the butcher and that through inexperience touched off the contraption rigged in the shop too soon, thus killing himself. In the pocket of the dead man detectives found a check signed by the butcher made payable to cash in the amount of five hundred dollars. Corbett said the deduction was that the 'touch off' man was paid the check on faith and that if he did not carry out the scheme the payment on the check would be stopped the next morning."

According to the police, "Benjamin [Yamin] is the owner of another Butler Street building razed by fire several weeks ago and also the owner of an automobile which burned last week, just a few days after the insurance policy was taken out.

"Benjamin refused to talk and pleaded ignorance to everything. While the 'touch off' man crept into the butcher shop where the combustibles were prepared, Benjamin took his family away. Several friends were visited and the Benjamin family was in the home of Mrs. Benjamin's mother when the explosion took place.

"How the explosion happened on the night his family was absent from their home, another shop and automobile owned by Benjamin recently burned, how the cans of powder were in his place Benjamin said was just fate. He said that although the check found in the 'touch off' man's possession was genuine, it must have been obtained while he was prowling through the place attempting robbery. Benjamin denied knowing Lomeo."

The district attorney of Allegheny County, Pennsylvania, Samuel H. Gardner, and police detectives conferred to charge Yamin with conspiracy to commit arson. However, the law enforcement officials believed the evidence against Yamin was so compelling that they considered a charge of felony-murder. Felony-murder is a charge based on the killing of a person in the commission of other statutory specified felonies. Arson was one of the specified felony crimes that would support a charge of felony-murder if a death occurred as a result of the arson action. Even though Eugico conspired to commit the arson, his death met the requirements of the law to support a charge of felony-murder against Yamin. According to The Pittsburgh Press, March 30, 1929, "The judge recommitted Yamin to the County Jail without bail, and Dodkin had been released by posting a bond as a material witness." Yamin was being charged with conspiracy to commit arson and murder. The actual trial of Benjamin Yamin would occur a year later—a year of great change for the Lomeo family and America.

Sending the telegram to Sicily to inform his mother of the death of her third child took an emotional toll on Paolo. The image of his mother reading the telegram was too much to bear. Surely, his mother would hold him responsible, as the older brother, for the death of Eugico. He wished he could see and talk to her and explain that family hierarchy had no influence in America. Eugico just would not listen, and when he finally did, it was too late. Paolo also had the telegrapher write that he was changing the name of his recently born son from Vincenzo, named after his departed friend Vincenzo Orlando, to James in honor of his dead brother. He had to explain that Eugico was called Jimmy in America and that the formal name for Jimmy is James.

At the same time, Paolo had to deal with managing the store alone. Mangia Dorm had never provided much physical support—he would rather talk than work—but his jokes and easy way had calmed Paolo's thoughts of doubt and anxiety. Paolo needed to learn how to adjust to his new life alone, without a connection to Sicily through his brother and without a connection to the social fiber of McKeesport through Mangia Dorm.

On Monday, April 1, 1929, being the first day as the sole owner of Roma's Fruit Market, Paolo woke up earlier than usual and headed to the store. As he unlocked the door and prepared the store for the day's business, Paolo reached into his pocket for his father's coin. Looking at it in his hand, he wondered if he had given the coin to Eugico, maybe Eugico's life would have been different. Why should he be the only one to be blessed with his father's greatest treasure? Remembering his mother handing the coin to him after his father's death and telling him that it was Giuseppe's wish that Paolo have the coin with him in America, he thought, who was he to disobey the wishes of his father?

Why did a man of thirty-three years with a caring wife and three sons have such doubts? His father always seemed so confident and had the correct answer for any situation. He wished he could talk to his father; he needed advice on how to move forward.

Just as the clock reached noon, Rosalia came to the store and brought Paolo a telegram that had been delivered to their home. It was from Bagharia, Sicily. He thought this could not be good. As he nervously tore open the envelope, he glanced at Rosalia in bewilderment and asked her to read the telegram. He had no formal education in Sicily or America, whereas Rosalia had attended school long enough in America to read most everyday items. She read it slowly, anticipating harsh or bad words, as the telegram was from Agatina. Rosalia, being a mother three times, should have known better.

It began with a sincere and warm-felt word of love and forgiveness, "Son." Agatina knew without hearing it how Paolo's feelings of guilt and failure as a big brother squeezed him into half of a man. The mother full of love in the few words limited by a telegram told her son that each individual has to be responsible for his own actions. Even though she had not seen Paolo in nine years, she had raised him and knew he cared for his brother. She also knew that her other American son's life moved fast and forward toward her Lord's home, hopefully.

Her Lord heard her pleas for Eugico on a daily basis, while her heart ached for Paolo. Without seeing Paolo, his wife, and his children, her motherly instincts told her he was doing well, and his family was proud of him.

After all, that is all a father really needs to know.

The end of the 1920s and the beginning of the 1930s brought a tough reality to America and Paolo. Paolo received a double dose of reality: the subsequent Yamin trial and the financial struggle to keep the store a viable business while the country was in the midst of the Great Depression. He could work toward solving the latter problem, but only the American court system could solve the former problem.

The Yamin trial began in June, but Judge Reid postponed the trial when one of the jurors became physically ill and had to be excused. Beginning a new trial on February 3, 1930, the case against Yamin weakened upon the death of Lieutenant Corbett. Corbett died on November 28, 1929, after complications from abdominal surgery at St. Francis Hospital in Pittsburgh. The death was unexpected, as Dave Corbett's physical presence and health held all indications that he would survive the surgery. His doctors could not explain the death, since all aspects of the surgery had gone well.

Assistant District Attorney Earl R. Jackson, the lead prosecutor in the case, started the case with the knowledge that the witness who knew the details of the arson and witnessed Yamin conspiring with Eugico could not be found. Corbett had previously interviewed this unknown witness and wanted to withhold his name from the official record. He knew that if the Mafia thought the witness would provide the testimony to convict Yamin of murder, the witness would be killed. Mr. Jackson had no choice but to drop the murder charge against Yamin, for without the unknown witness's testimony, it would be more than difficult to prove a conspiracy and therefore murder. The government kept the charge of arson because of the other incriminating evidence, such as Yamin's good fortune to have his family leave their residence on the night of the explosion. Additionally, he had insured the building for more than its worth. In direct examination of Fire Chief Callaghan and other witnesses, Jackson submitted evidence to the jury of the arson. However, Yamin testified in his own defense—a very unusual strategy in a criminal case.

Under our form of government, a criminal defendant is not required to testify at trial against his own interest. It is the burden of the government to prove guilt; the defendant does not have to prove he is innocent. Though on the surface this may seem to mean the same thing, in reality there is a huge difference between being found not guilty and being found innocent. To be found innocent, a jury would have to know with certainty that the defendant did not commit the crime. However, a finding of not guilty only means the evidence does not support the charge. America's Founding Fathers understood that to limit the overreaching power of government, it was important to have the government prove guilt. Otherwise, citizens could be charged and required to prove a negative. They would have to present evidence of the absence of their action. If proving innocence was the standard, the government could intimidate the population by threatening a charge, knowing that the chance of a conviction would be high. Unfortunately, Paolo did not understand the difference between not guilty and innocent. He could not understand why the judge permitted Yamin to testify to obvious untruths.

Yamin testified, as reported in the Pittsburgh Post-Gazette, February 4, 1930, edition, "I received a call from an unknown person warning me not to open a fruit department in my butcher shop."

The defendant continued, "I knew that Eugico Lomeo was actually in business with his brother, Paolo, and the Lomeos didn't want any more competition."

However, he had no explanation to the fact that Roma's Fruit Market, located twelve miles from his Butler Street shop, could not service the residents of the Lawrenceville section of Pittsburgh. Also, there were at least three other fruit stores located in McKeesport in direct competition with Roma's, so if the Lomeos were into extortion, it made more sense to harass their McKeesport competitors rather than Yamin.

Hoping to play on the Italian, especially Sicilian, stereotype that all Sicilians are in the Mafia and resort to violence to make a living, Yamin added to his testimony, "The fire to my other building and automobile happened after I told an Italian grocer I met in the Strip District that I wanted to expand into the fruit business."

Conveniently, Yamin could not recall the name of the Italian grocer, but he somehow remembered that this person was Italian.

The assistant district attorney had two rebuttal witnesses to impeach the credibility of the defendant. The first to testify was Teresa

Lord, the roommate of Elsie Weber. She had been rescued by the Pittsburgh Fire Department with Elsie, though the newspapers only reported Elsie as the sole occupant in the building at the time of the explosion.

She stated, under oath, that "Benjamin agreed to waive any rent payments in lieu of love." Speaking through tears and using a tissue provided by the judge to wipe her eyes and nose, she explained, "I was born in Johnstown. I don't have any brothers or sisters. My mother was too old to have another child. Papa and Mamma died in a car accident last Christmas when a drunk driver rear-ended their car. My mother's brother, Uncle Chaz, was unemployed, and I have five cousins, their children. Unc gave me the bus fare and I moved to Pittsburgh to find a job."

Attorney Jackson asked, "Miss Lord, how did you come to meet Mr. Yamin?"

"Mr. Jackson, as I walked off the bus Benjamin was in the depot and approached me. He said I looked lost and he wanted to help," Teresa explained.

"Why would you trust a complete stranger?" inquired Mr. Jackson.

Teresa, blushing at her own naiveté while trying to control her sobbing, explained, "Mr. Jackson, he said he was from the church and could help. He said he had an apartment I could have for free until I could find a job."

Having no real skills, she could only perform clerical services or work as a waitress at the local taverns. When she was unable to find a suitable job to pay her rent in a timely fashion, Yamin devised a scheme to lure Teresa into believing that he loved her and would soon leave his wife to be with her—a story as old as time, a devious man enticing a nice young lady on hard times with dreams of love, comfort, and security. As she regained her composure she continued testifying, "I gave Benjamin an ultimatum, either leave your wife or I would tell her about our affair. I felt horrible throughout the affair, especially every time I saw Mrs. Yamin and her children. Papa would be so disappointed in me."

The butcher promised his young love that by April 1 he would move his wife and children to his mother-in-law's home, then the two lovers would get married after the court granted his divorce. He made her promise to stay calm until April 1.

"I now know that he purposefully did not tell Mr. Lomeo that I was still in my fourth floor apartment, so that he could solve two problems with one crime."

Yamin had hoped his financial and love worries would be a thing of the past, like his building on Butler Street.

Paolo sat in the courtroom, stunned at Miss Lord's testimony. How did his brother ever meet such a hideous person like Yamin? His brother's personality bordered on the insane, but he had always showed the utmost respect to any lady. Their mother had made sure that all of her sons respected the role of women, an unusual concept in the early twentieth-century world of his childhood, and especially in the male- centric society of Sicily. Giuseppe respected and loved his wife and never would tolerate an ill word toward her in any conversation. Giuseppe stressed to Paolo, "Any man who cheats on his wife is no man."

Giuseppe never understood why Sicilian politicians and leaders were respected by the populace, when most of these men of society practiced infidelity as often as most people drank a different wine. "If a person is willing to violate a promise to a family member and bring public humiliation to the mother of his children, then in my opinion that person could not be trusted to act properly with the public's tax money," Giuseppe always complained.

Paolo observed the same attitude and behavior in his first decade in America. American politicians promised to take care of their constituents, even though they were unfaithful to their wives and families.

Trusting an elected official who made promises with no obvious intent of keeping them was dumb in Paolo's opinion. Shaking hands and showing respect to a person who not only made a lot of empty promises but also ran around on his wife contradicted every lesson Giuseppe taught Paolo. Paolo honored his father by always following Giuseppe's advice. He sorely missed his father. Sitting in the courtroom listening to the testimony about his brother, Paolo did not know if he should be angry at Eugico or Yamin, or the judge or the defense attorney. Were they all not responsible for the circus that Paolo saw in the courtroom? Why did the American justice system, known throughout the world as the leader of jurisprudence, permit and laud a defense attorney that fabricated a story to confuse the jury? Paolo had a sad and sick feeling seeing the judge lord over the courtroom like a Mafia don, and probably for the only time since his father's death, he wished there was no heaven. He did not want his father to view from heaven this play. Giuseppe deserved better.

The judge called a recess to the proceedings prior to Paolo's testimony. As Paolo was about to leave the courtroom for the hallway to smoke a cigarette, Joey "The Dime" Andoloni strolled into the courtroom. Andoloni was a reputed Mafia leader, and his nickname, The Dime, was given to him because he did not believe a human life was worth more than ten cents. Paolo quietly returned to his seat to watch the movements and motions of Andoloni. He first shook hands with the defense attorney, then the assistant district attorney, and headed toward the judge to say hello. Watching all of this, Paolo immediately thought that The Dime's presence ensured a favorable verdict for Yamin. Noticing Paolo in the courtroom, Andoloni walked over to Paolo with an extended hand and expressed his condolence for the death of Eugico. "Sorry for your loss, Paolo."

Paolo remaining seated in his chair, shaking his head in agreement and wondering how The Dime knew who he was. The Dime headed for the exit door after patting Paolo on the shoulder as Paolo thought Andoloni resembled a snake slithering out of the Garden of Eden.

The machinations of this case were all too much for Paolo. First, the only eyewitness could not be located, then the lead detective died without ever revealing the name of this witness, and now Andoloni arrived to ensure the result. Paolo knew the identity of the witness the D.A. wanted; it was Mangia Dorm. Previously, Mangia Dorm had begged Paolo not to reveal his identity, since the police would make him testify. Paolo and Mangia Dorm knew if he testified, the jury would have no other recourse but to say guilty regardless of Andoloni's influence. They also understood with all too much clarity that Mangia Dorm's life span would equal a week. Though still angry with Mangia Dorm, he did not want to be responsible for his death, as his death would not bring his brother back. However, now that he thought the fix was in, he approached Jackson and told him he knew the identity of the unknown witness. Looking shocked and perplexed, Jackson explained to Paolo he could not introduce the witness at this stage of the case. "I have already rested my case. We are at the rebuttal part, no new witness," he said, irritated at Paolo.

Paolo did not understand the procedures of a criminal court case. He did not know that the prosecutor presents the evidence, then the defense presents their case. The prosecution has the right of rebuttal only to counter any new argument that the defense argues to a judge or jury. It cannot present witnesses or evidence that relates to their case-in- chief. Paolo became upset at not understanding and at Jackson's attitude toward an uneducated immigrant.

With his strong Sicilian accent he told Jackson, "I may not understand the rules, but it seems you are afraid of The Dime."

Paolo used another of his father's tricks of manipulating an arrogant person. Giuseppe had explained to Paolo the reason a person speaks arrogantly and uses his superior knowledge or position to intimidate is because the person has a weak character and is afraid of life. Paolo learned from Giuseppe that a truly superior person with a strong moral character would always be respectful and take the time to make another person understand. If you strip away the mask of invincibility, the weak person will change his ways and try to appease you.

Jackson, taking the bait, softened his attitude and explained to Paolo that the case would have to be decided on the evidence already submitted. Jackson confidently told Paolo, "Yamin will be found guilty."

In fact, Jackson was confident enough that he had decided not to call Paolo as a rebuttal witness. He felt that the evidence was clear to any person that Yamin had conspired to set the fire. Wanting and desiring his father's advice, Paolo did not know if he should trust Jackson or plan his revenge against Andoloni for fixing the case. Reaching for his father's coin, clarity and reality set in. There was nothing Paolo could do at the moment, so he may as well stay for the verdict.

The jury slowly walked from the deliberation room, taking their seats in the jury box. Upon the request of the judge, the foreman of the jury read the verdict: "Guilty." The Pittsburgh Press reported it as "Samuel Benjamin, 42, butcher, 5170 Butler St. was found guilty of Arson by a jury verdict returned at 8:30 pm yesterday." It was a long day for Paolo, and after hearing the late evening verdict he just wanted to go home and forget about it. No verdict would bring his brother back to him.

Years later Paolo would learn that Andoloni wanted to see a guilty verdict, since it seemed that Yamin had reneged on some other criminal arrangement. This case had brought too much exposure to Yamin's activities, which could lead to Andoloni. Mushrooms, government, and Mafia grow better in the dark with very little exposure.

Chapter 8

The American Way?

Driving home after the arson trial, Paolo realized he had been in America for ten years, and his life was different from what he had imagined when he left Sicily all those years ago. America was "where gold lay on the streets just for the picking," though everyone had a different way to mine the gold. Some stole, some used political corruption, but most worked diligently to provide for their families. Though his life did not follow the course his father and he had talked about so many times in the orchard, he knew he had been more fortunate than most immigrants. He was his own boss, he began the store without any help, and he did not need to beg a union steward or political ward boss for a job.

A lot of his friends and neighbors worked hard in the mills, but they were working for the profit of others. They worked to provide comfort to people who were nothing like them and probably were the same people that thought dark-skinned Southern Europeans or round-headed Eastern Europeans diluted the quality of the American stock. These Anglo-Saxon or Northern Europeans, who traced their families' lines back to the American colonies, believed that only their kinfolk in Europe deserved to be Americans. The other immigrants were imitations who brought dishonor to the American way of life. Their hero, President Theodore Roosevelt, for all his progressive programs to entice the populace to vote for him and his elite friends, believed that the mixing of his type with the new immigrants would be the end of the supremacy of America. It seemed to escape these long-generation Americans that the difference between Northern Europeans and Southern Europeans had more to do with their system of governance and beliefs in individual rights than with the geography of their birth.

All human beings are creatures of God, and given the freedom to exercise their God-given rights of life, liberty, and the pursuit of happiness, they could accomplish amazing things. It had nothing to do with where a person was born, who his grandfather was, or the language he spoke. Americans who never lived under a despotic system could not appreciate the affects a free society could have on a person's ability to contribute to America.

Paolo worked hard every day to provide for his family. He survived the Great Depression without asking for government help, even though his business suffered during the early 1930s. Believing in himself and America, he knew that both would survive this economic crisis. The psychological depression that Americans of the 1930s felt had more to do with the feeling they lost something important rather than the actual loss they suffered. Of course, people suffered great financial harm, some losing their savings or their home, or both. However, the real devastation had to with the loss of hope. Most Americans believed that America's best days were behind it and the future only represented further suffering and sacrifice.

Although Paolo had experienced true financial hardship in Sicily and witnessed his father's and grandfather's struggle for financial survival with each whim of the political class of Northern Italy, a tonic made from the combination of knowledge and experience usually cures or solves most illnesses. This financial illness was no different. Paolo realized an investment into the self-reliant reputation of America would solve his financial problems. As long as his family was safe from physical harm, he knew he would ride out this low wave to surf the high wave of success once the economy recovered.

After years of listening to his grandfather and father, and then watching the political system in America, the election of Franklin Delano Roosevelt as president encompassed him with feelings of apprehension and fear. Though most of his neighbors and friends, in what today is called the working class, believed FDR would lead them out of the desert to the green valley of prosperity, Paolo felt differently.

He thought the New Deal programs were European socialist programs used to control the citizenry, just like the programs in Sicily. Not being a financially educated macroeconomist, Paolo did not understand how government deficit spending could create jobs if nothing of real value was being produced. Believing in neo-classical economics without knowing it, he thought if the elected officials and courts would protect the rights of small businesses against government intrusions and prevent businesses from growing too large as to rival the government, then everyone—small business owners, stockholders, bankers, union workers, and independent contractors—would have a better standard of living.

In Fascist Italy, the government chose the businesses that survived by regulating commerce activities to the benefit of their favorite companies and to the detriment of everyone else, including the workers of these favorite companies. FDR's speeches and programs sounded similar to Mussolini's without the vitriol. The rights of free speech and election protected under the American Constitution made it unlikely that FDR would become a dictator. How could Paolo know that FDR would break a tradition started by George Washington and seek re- election three times?

Feeling proud as a father watching his sons tease each other at the greatest of American holidays, Thanksgiving dinner, he wondered if his father would be proud. His youngest son, just barely over twelve years old, listened to every word his older brother John, who was twenty- one years old, said. He idolized his older brother and thought he could do no wrong. He did not have the same relationship with his oldest brother, Joseph. He felt Joseph liked being a Sicilian more than being an American, where John did not want to hear or think about the old country.

Paolo wondered if his two oldest sons would take over the store and possibly expand it. The store performed satisfactory to maintain a family in the lower middle class, but for some reason Paolo never could increase the business to lift his family to the middle or upper middle class. With some degree of envy, he watched the store down the street, Balsamo's Fruit Market, move to a larger store and offer a better selection of produce and meats. It helped that Balsamo's was closer to the entrance gate of National Tube and on the train tracks that ran through the middle of McKeesport.

November 1941 was a great time to be an American, especially compared with all the troubles in Europe. Hitler and Mussolini craved power and wanted to carve Europe into pieces to be traded among the Fascist powers. No matter how much Europeans were suffering, the American industry economy was booming due to the products needed to supply Britain with war materials, which stimulated McKeesport's local economy.

Knowing that America would eventually enter the war, regardless of the fancy words the American president and Congress used to convince America that no American blood would drench the European landscape, Paolo prepared Rosalia for the inevitable: her sons would be drafted into the European conflict. Being in America for twenty years, Paolo recognized the affinity most Americans had with their British cousins. America would defend their cousins. Paolo always followed world events with interest and believed that Hitler and Mussolini had to be stopped. To him, these Fascist dictators were just like the Mafia dons who controlled the flow of commerce throughout Sicily, except the dictators had more power. His only worry was that his two oldest sons would have to fight along with other young Americans at the risk of bodily harm or death. Deep down he had an unpatriotic selfish thought: Who would help him in the store if his two sons were drafted to war? He felt every one of his forty-six years in every bone of his body. He needed his sons to do the heavy lifting.

The war did come a few days later, on December 7, 1941. Eventually Joseph and a million other young men were drafted into the armed services to defend and fight for America across the globe. Since he was an Italian, the war department assigned Joseph to the Pacific theater. The draft board declared John 4-F, meaning his physical or mental abilities did not reach the level to be killed in a foreign land, even though John had no physical or mental weaknesses. Paolo never told anyone how he arranged the 4-F. How did John manage the store for four years during the war without a word from the War Department? It seems Paolo's lucky coin still worked. The home-front Lomeo family experienced the war effort like the rest of America's small business owners, doing their share to support their country and families.

The end of World War II brought peace throughout the world, except Paolo Lomeo was about to begin his own world war. A war that would terrorize his business, his life, and the well-being of his family.

As with most wars, Paolo's war started with a small event that would spread until it consumed all the participants. Germany surrendered to the Allied Expeditionary Forces on May 7, 1945, and everyone knew the war with Japan did not have much longer to last. Paolo, having experienced the inflation effects at the end of the First World War and remembering the stories that Giuseppe and Alberto told about the rising prices after the Italian aggression in Africa, knew America would experience a sharp rise in prices without wartime price restrictions. Anticipating that fresh fruit and produce staples, such as potatoes, would be in high demand during the fall and winter of 1945, he began stockpiling large amounts of produce in a refrigerated warehouse located in the Strip District area of Pittsburgh. The name of the business operating the refrigerated warehouse was Federal Cold Storage.

The Federal Cold Storage warehouse was a four-story cement building encompassing a whole city block. It was a rectangular building with few windows on each side of the lower level. The loading docks were located at the southern end of the warehouse. Trucks unloading and loading their produce would back up slowly over the brick-laid loading area for fear that the uneven pavement would cause their cargo to tip over inside their trucks.

The northern part of the building housed the manager's office. It was a small office that barely had enough room for the three staffers and manager who worked in the office. Most of the grocers knew the staffers on a first-name basis and would kindly offer them a couple of peaches or oranges as they picked up their bills of lading. A bill of lading is a document evidencing the amount of produce deposited in the warehouse and term of duration before the warehouse could legally dispose of the produce.

Penn Avenue, one of the main thoroughfares through the northwest section of the city of Pittsburgh, bordered the eastern face of Federal Cold Storage. There was a sidewalk between the avenue and eastern boundary of Federal Cold Storage's property. However, it was not busy with typical city pedestrians but rather with men involved in the produce business. This included the independent grocers, union dockworkers, and haulers for the major grocery retail chains.

The Allegheny River flowed in the distance about a quarter of a mile from the western side of the warehouse. This is the area where businessmen of all sorts conducted business transactions with a handshake. Some of the young men did not follow the time-honored tradition of honoring verbal commitments. The degeneration of this tradition started slowly so no one noticed any change, and then by the 1930s it was nonexistent.

As the summer turned into an Indian summer, Paolo's path to the American dream turned one hundred eighty degrees pointing toward Sicily. Labor unions throughout the United States were demanding higher wages from American industry after four years of wage controls established by a federal agency, the Office of Price Administration. Even though all Americans understood the need for emergency controls during the war years, it would be naïve to think that there were no complaints or whining from the people most directly affected. The executive officers of the different unions resented the suppression of wages while the factory owners were profiting from the war. In what seemed to be a coordinated effort between the different national unions, from the coal miners and steelworkers to bakers and bricklayers, the unions were striking to slow or shut down American business until their wages increased to match the outsized profits being made by American businesses. They also called for the work stoppage to compensate their members for four years of lost wages. It seemed a necessary fight, unless you were one of the marines on the coral reef of Peleliu who survived the brutal Japanese army's defense of that island; then you may have felt that the home-front political fight between business and labor was a selfish dance in an arena made safe by your personal sacrifice.

Is it not strange and unreal that men die in battle to protect our way of life, while home-front men of all economic classes, safely secured from war's harm, complain about their personal sacrifice? This pitiful refrain has been sung too often by politicians, business executives, and union leaders throughout our history.

As the labor strife began in Pittsburgh, Paolo had no hint that a business with no employees and operated by his family would become a target of one of the most powerful unions in America—the Teamsters, at the time a member of the American Federation of Labor.

In the middle of September 1945, Paolo had purchased plums and peaches from farms in Delaware and Maryland. His two sons, John and Joseph, drove the truck to pick up the produce to deliver the goods to the refrigerated warehouse. Following the proper and usual procedure, union workers unloaded the produce into the warehouse and gave the bills of lading to the two Lomeo sons. Then, on September 26, 1945, the Teamsters' local, Commission House and Produce Helpers Employes Local 944, called a general strike against eight-six of Pittsburgh's major fruit and vegetable wholesale houses. This basically stopped any produce from reaching the small fruit stores throughout the Pittsburgh region. The union insisted, as The Pittsburgh Press (October 1, 1945) reported, "it had a right to refuse to load or unload produce to and from non-members grocers and other customers of the wholesale houses." Local 944 wanted the independent business owners to join the union to increase their membership. Most of the fruit store owners initially resisted joining the union and purchased their produce from outside Pittsburgh to stock their stores. Eventually, these independent grocers would switch rather than fight, so as to avoid the stigma of challenging the union in the heart of the union movement in America.

However, Paolo had two different problems. First, he did not leave his mother in Sicily to be intimidated into joining a union. Second, he had an actual financial issue; he needed to retrieve his plums and peaches before the goods perished. Paolo could not afford to let his produce spoil and lose a great sum of money. The union argued that an initiation fee of ten dollars and three dollars a month was not unreasonable. In 2013 dollars, the thirteen dollars equals about six hundred dollars. It would seem that six hundred dollars meant a great deal to Roma's Fruit Market. However, the point that he had to retrieve the fruit now, regardless of the general strike, fell on deaf union ears. Paolo figured if he fought the union's right to prevent him from gathering his goods, the union would respect him, leave him alone, and fight with the politically loud-mouth grocers. His forty-nine years did nothing to increase his understanding of human nature and the dynamics of political power. No doubt Giuseppe would have explained it to Paolo.

He drove to the Strip District in the early morning of September 27 to retrieve his produce, only to have the strikers surround his truck and threaten him with violence if he did not leave the area. Barely able to drive back to McKeesport because of his blinding rage, Paolo had a hard time deciding how to get his fruit from the warehouse to his store. Waiting for Paolo as he parked his truck on Sinclair Street in front of Roma's was Alexander J. Bielski, a local McKeesport attorney. Mr. Bielski had heard about Paolo's confrontation at Federal Cold Storage and wanted to help. Slowly approaching Paolo with an extended hand, Attorney Bielski said, "Hi, Mr. Lomeo, I am Mr. Bielski. I am an attorney here in McKeesport."

"Yes, I know who you are. How I can help you?" Paolo quickly snapped while shaking his hand, thinking Bielski wanted to lecture him on the righteousness of the Teamsters' strike.

"I heard about your confrontation at the Strip this morning. I would like to help you."

Paolo thought how strange that his troubles reached home before he did. Paolo did not know Attorney Bielski well. "Sir, I can't afford an attorney. I can handle this on my own."

Alexander Bielski, a slender, well-dressed attorney, wanted to handle a case that would bring attention to his abilities as an attorney.

He knew fighting the powerful Teamsters in court would bring him the recognition he desired. His law practice had suffered during the war years, and he wanted to ride the boom of the post-war years.

Mr. Bielski asked, "Do you want to take a walk to Danny's Donuts for a cup of coffee to discuss the problem?" Danny's Donuts was an old-fashioned coffee shop on Sinclair Street a block away from Roma's.

Noticing Paolo was hot with anger, he draped his long slender arm over Paolo's shoulder and said, "Mr. Lomeo, please calm down and give me a chance to help. This is America, and no person or union can make a person join a union against his will."

Paolo began to feel the blood leave his eyes and slowly focused on the eyes of Mr. Bielski. Saying "we can fight" to protect his American right of free association were words to his liking, so Paolo followed Bielski to the coffee shop. Picking a window booth in the back of the small coffee shop, as the shop was always crowded in the morning with patrons, mostly night shift mill workers heading home in the early morning, Paolo sat with his back facing the wall, and Bielski sat across from him. Geneva, a young lady whose father befriended Paolo years ago, said, "Good morning, Mr. Bielski."

Bielski visited this place often when he needed to have a doughnut and coffee to think through a legal problem. Turning to Paolo,

Geneva held a wider smile, and said, "Good morning, Mr. Roma."

She liked Paolo, because Paolo always treated her father, Stan, with respect even though most of their neighbors and friends considered Stan the dumb one and poked fun at him.

The term "Mr. Roma" grated on Paolo. His name was Lomeo, but everyone thought his name was Roma since the store's name was Roma's Fruit Market. He had named the store Roma, Rome in Italian, because he believed at the time of forming the store that most Americans would find the term endearing and friendly, never realizing that the citizens of McKeesport would think his name was Roma. The confusion between the real name of the family and this fictitious name would continue throughout the school years of his grandchildren.

Attorney Bielski explained the legal situation and the political pressure Local 944 would use against Paolo. "Can I call you Paolo? Paolo, legally the warehouse has to release your goods to you. They have a legal obligation to protect your goods, since you are paying them for this service. However, what we have here today is that no one is willing to challenge the union. I believe if we went to court, a judge would enforce the law and protect our rights."

"I will call you Alex then?" Bielski nodded. "Alex, isn't a judge also subject to the political pressure of the union?" Paolo inquired, foreshadowing Paolo's future problem.

Being an honorable man, Mr. Bielski told Paolo, "The easiest course for you would be to take the path of least resistance and join the union." His answer, however, did not answer Paolo's question about the independence of the judiciary. As a man educated and trained in the law, he could not fathom the thought that a judge would be subdued to political pressure. The attorney had a lot to learn about the politics of elected judges in Allegheny County, Pennsylvania.

A union membership would not change Paolo's life or business, except the extra three dollars a month in union dues. Under the attorney's calculation, Paolo would lose at least four years of union dues if the ninety bushels of plums and peaches at Federal Cold Storage spoiled. Paolo disagreed with Bielski in part. "Sure, joining the union may solve my short-term problem; however, I am concerned with the long-term effects. My father wanted me to be a man of respect."

Giuseppe was a person a son could be proud of, and Paolo wanted his three sons to have the same respect for their father as Paolo had for his. To capitulate to this form of bullying would send the message to his children to live a life following the demands of the powerful and to fear their wrath. "If I cannot fight this battle when my life is not in jeopardy, what would I do when my life is truly in jeopardy?" Paolo rhetorically asked Bielski.

"Many Americans, including my eldest son, risked their lives in this war to stop tyranny. The least I could do is to stand up to a local bully," Paolo responded, answering his own rhetorical question.

The attorney understood the sentiment but disagreed with Paolo about the violence. After all, they were talking about challenging the Teamsters and their basic right to strike. He felt that both Paolo and he would be threatened with bodily harm or death. "You know they don't fool around? Also, they are connected and will use violence and intimidation to stop us."

Paolo knew by "connected" Bielski meant the Mafia.

Paolo slowly shook his head from side to side and then shrugged his shoulder, which meant to Bielski that Paolo knew the consequences of his actions. Both rising from the booth at the same time, standing face to face, they shook hands as honorable people do and agreed to fight this injustice.

Bielski took a quick liking to Paolo. Alexander was the son of an immigrant and saw the discrimination and recrimination his father endured to make sure his children became Americans. In a small way, he felt if he could help Paolo, he would be saying to his deceased father that he had not forgotten about his parents' hardships. Even now so many years later as a respected man of polite society, he still desired the respect of his immigrant father.

As the warriors for justice headed for the shop door, Geneva yelled, "Bye, Mr. Roma, and tell Johnny I said hi."

Paolo knew his son John had taken Geneva to the movies and other places over the last few months. Rosalia disapproved of her son dating this young American girl, even though Geneva's grandparents had emigrated from Poland only thirty years before. Geneva's parents also were neighbors of the Lomeos. The real issue was that Rosalia did not want her favorite son to marry a non-Sicilian, whereas Paolo wanted his son to marry a woman who would love and care for his son the way his mother had loved his father. A man needs to have a good partner in life, just like Paolo had Rosalia. Ethnicity may have brought Paolo and Rosalia together, but it was honesty and trust that kept them together to survive a not so easy life.

Paolo walked briskly up Sinclair Street to Roma's; he had a business to run and enough time was wasted today with this nonsense.

Chapter 9

Due process?

Attorney Bielski excitedly headed to his office to prepare his court petition asking for relief from the Teamster's strike at the produce yards. He filed this petition of injunction against Local 944 the next day, Friday, September 28, 1945. A petition of injunction is an action in which the moving party is asking the court to prevent the other party from acting a certain way. In this case, Bielski requested the court to stay the strike, so the union workers could load Paolo's produce onto a Roma's Fruit Market truck. The case was assigned to another McKeesport resident, Judge William A. Challener.

Bielski had his secretary call Paolo to let him know that their hearing was scheduled for next Monday. "Mr. Lomeo, this is Miss Kravitz, Mr. Bielski's secretary."

"Yes, I remember you. I think you come to the store sometimes." "My mother does. People say we look a lot alike. I just wanted to let you know that Mr. Bielski scheduled your hearing with Judge Challener for Monday. Do you know Judge Challener? He lives here in McKeesport. He is a really good judge."

The words "really good judge" hung in Paolo's ear long enough to slowly remove the fog of confusion and complexity of his predicament. The power elite of Allegheny County was about to teach him why any challenge was useless and maybe dangerous.

"Yes, I know him. Thank you, Miss Kravitz," Paolo said, resigned to his fate.

Challener had recently been appointed to the bench by the Republican governor of Pennsylvania, Edward Martin. He held himself out as a man of integrity, and his reputation among the legal community as a man of law confirmed his own self-inflated idea of himself. Random selection of judges in such politically charged cases happens only in idealistic books or movies. The political establishment needed to ensure Paolo's case never had a chance of success. Otherwise, the success of Paolo's petition challenging the union's method of causing collateral damage to nonparticipants in the employer-employee struggle, such as Paolo, would significantly reduce the bargaining power of the union movement.

Popular belief is that all business owners think and act alike—a monolithic group. However, the true reality paints a clouded picture in which the large businesses see the small businesses as intruders on their domain while promulgating the myth that all business types benefit America. By this time in America, the communities of business and politics had formed a working partnership in usurping the rights and liberties of the citizenry of America for their benefit for almost a century. The union establishment, a newly minted partner with business and politics, may have fought with its other partners on superficial issues, but when it came to maintaining power over the "rank and file" union members, or citizens, or consumers, each partner stopped his feud long enough to quash any hope of upsetting their delicate balance of power.

Challener's career had depended on politics. He had always been willing to please the powerfully connected people of society, to become a member of their elite club. From heading the judiciary committee of the Allegheny County Bar Association's investigation of political judges and attorneys to representing the business elite of Pittsburgh, Challener never hesitated to advocate the legal positions of the political and business apparatus. When Bielski telephoned Paolo to tell him that the case had been assigned to Judge Challener, Paolo immediately recognized that he would not have a fair hearing.

Oddly, a case that would be the topic of conversation throughout the courthouse and in the newspapers for the first eleven days of October 1945 consisted of three major characters—Challener, Bielski, and Paolo, all residents of McKeesport. Unfortunately, Paolo already knew Challener. Challener had visited Roma's some years prior to this case and had complained to Paolo that the bag of fruit he had purchased the day before had some spoiled fruit at the bottom of the bag.

"Mr. Roma, here is the spoiled fruit you hid at the bottom of the bag," Challener said in his lawyerly way.

Knowing William Challener from newspaper articles in The Daily News, McKeesport, PA and The Pittsburgh Press and through the grapevine of his customers, Paolo responded, "Mr. Challener, my name is Mr. Lomeo. Roma is just the name of the store. I didn't see you in the store yesterday. Are sure you didn't purchase your fruit at Balsamo's?"

His face turned red, as people of Irish descent tend to do when angered. "What are you saying? I can't understand your English, Mr. Roma. I know where I was yesterday, and I was here."

Paolo tried to control his temper, as he did not appreciate Challener repeating "Mr. Roma" when he just told him that his name was Lomeo. Paolo's voice quivered with anger as he said, "Mr. Challener, you are holding a Balsamo's bag and we don't sell their bags here."

Balsamo's Fruit Market, the largest fruit market in McKeesport, had a reusable burlap shopping bag. The bag had Balsamo's Fruit Market printed on both sides of the bag while the two handle straps at the top of the bag eased carrying a bag full of produce. Early on Balsamo's recognized the marketing success of handing out free shopping bags to the residents of McKeesport. Made of burlap material, the Balsamo's bag could be used for more than shopping. People used the bags to carry their picnic foods or as a small travel bag. However, most people in McKeesport had enough common sense and understood that other store proprietors would not appreciate them using a Balsamo's bag to shop in any other place but Balsamo's. Roma's financial condition prohibited Paolo from offering free burlap bags. He used the old familiar brown bag of different sizes.

"What? Speak slower. Just because I have their bag doesn't mean I shopped at their store yesterday. Can you understand that?"

Basically, he accused Paolo of cheating him. Never a good idea to call Paolo a cheater in any circumstance, but a really dumb idea to say it while in his store in front of his wife and son. Grabbing the taller man's right arm, squeezing his triceps from underneath with the palm of his right hand, Paolo angrily said, "Well, maybe you can understand this!" Paolo forcefully pushed him to the door exiting on Sinclair Street with the admonishment not to visit again. "You come here no more, Mr. Challener!"

Challener, taken by surprise, not expecting an uneducated immigrant with no social status to react to him so harshly, meekly exited the store without a word.

Observing her husband's action while waiting on another customer, Rosalia had politely excused herself but arrived too late to stop Challener's early departure. Looking perplexed at Paolo, Rosalia asked, "Paolo, what are you doing?"

In Sicilian, he said, "He was being offensive to me. He was critical of my weak English. I can't stand it."

She responded to her husband in English to show him that Americans spoke English. "Then you should have stayed in Sicily.

Americans are always critical of your accent, even though their parents had accents. You could have said no to him and asked him to leave in a more polite and businesslike way."

Paolo knew Rosalia was right. It was not actually the accusation of selling spoiled fruit that caused Paolo to lose his temper. Paolo believed that a business should try to make an unfriendly customer a loyal customer. If Judge Challener had said the same thing without the arrogant tones while repeatedly saying "what?" to highlight Paolo's accent and lack of education in the English language, Paolo would have given him a free bag of fruit to appease him. Paolo's actions manifested the psychological insecurity of America's immigrants. Most immigrants of the early twentieth century worried their accents made them something less than true Americans in the eyes of nonimmigrant Americans.

As he slowly hung up the telephone, he quietly sat in a chair next to it. Now Paolo thought his temper outburst with Challener years before could only spell trouble for him with a capital T. He could only think of what his father would have done in a similar circumstance. He already knew the answer, but he tried to rationalize to himself that Challener's actions that day in the store would have angered his father also. Giuseppe would not have tolerated any person showing such disrespect.

Sitting erect in the chair with his eyes noticing the different knots in the wooden-planked floor throughout his store, he reached in his right front pants pocket to find his father's coin. He twirled the coin in his hand without taking it out of his pocket. The smooth feeling of the coin with its little grooves seemed to calm his uneasy feeling. Paolo now knew that his father would have laughed at Challener's absurd excuse and offered him a free bag of fruit the next time Challener made a purchase in the store. Challener could have rejected the offer, but at least Paolo would have outsmarted a well-educated and respected attorney. If he accepted the offer, Paolo would have had a new customer. Any business owner would gladly give a free bag of fruit in exchange for a new customer who would hopefully spend a greater amount in future years.

At first Paolo lacked the understanding of the reality of his situation. He slowly recognized that the political establishment of Allegheny County could not permit a renegade to win a court challenge to their strike without losing the fear that the union establishment used to manipulate the "rank-file" workers and politicians. Paolo didn't know it at the moment, but the Teamsters needed to have this fight with Paolo to teach a lesson to anyone else thinking of challenging their supremacy in and out of the produce yards. Pettiness would not be Challener's primary motivation in this case, only a nice sweetener to his morning coffee.

Judge Challener did not deny the petition, but postponed the hearing until Monday, October 1. In open court he stated that he was granting the union's request for a postponement "in order not to inflame" the already tense situation in the Strip District. Regardless that a postponement was not supported in the law and only disadvantaged Paolo, Judge Challener supplanted his personal bias for a legal or logical rationale. Mr. Bielski told The Daily News, McKeesport, PA, "Lomeo's peaches and plums are rapidly nearing the spoilage stage."

"Why couldn't Judge Challener have ordered the fruit released and just instructed me not to violate the strike from now on?" Paolo wondered out loud to his attorney.

Paolo actually had analyzed the legal case in a commonsense way. Most legal issues, no matter how complex, can be solved with common sense. If Challener had issued such an order, Paolo's financial well-being would be unharmed, and Judge Challener would not have had to make a decision on the legitimacy of the strike. Meanwhile, Challener's decision did satisfy the union's demand for the court not to rule on the legitimacy of the strike while knowingly putting Paolo in harm's way. The union barely knew Challener and worried about how his Republican bias thinking would analyze the legal issues of a strike that effectively prohibited "mom and pop" stores from purchasing produce, thereby causing them to shutter their establishments. The union should have known their Republican friends would not have assigned the case to a judge friendly to a Sicilian shop owner.

Bielski argued to the court that he could understand a delay, if the items were bricks, stones, furniture, or even food with a slower rate of spoilage, such as potatoes. In this specific case, irreparable harm would occur to Paolo if the peaches and plums spoiled. Either Challener did not understand this simple logic problem or just ignored the obvious for the benefit of his political supporters. Bielski would be back in court early Monday morning.

Attorney Bielski arrived early Monday morning to the courtroom of Judge Challener. The Allegheny County Courthouse is a most unique building and looks more like a medieval castle than a courthouse. The entire five-story structure is built around an open-air courtyard with brown sandstone color granite blocks connected to the jail, which is made of the same material, across the street via a walking bridge copying the Bridge of Sighs in Venice, Italy.

As Mr. Bielski entered the almost empty courtroom, he met Ben P. Jubelirer, the attorney for Local 944. Shaking Mr. Bielski's hand, Jubelirer said, "This is a bomb waiting to explode. Each of our clients has the ability to lose control and act unreasonably."

Bielski did not know if Jubelirer intentionally meant to suggest his client would use violence if the Teamsters lost in court or if he truly believed Paolo had the same ability as the Teamsters to exact a physical penalty outside of these court proceedings. He quickly answered, "Well, I think your client of one hundred may have the edge on my fifty-year- old father of three."

With a chuckle, realizing that Bielski understood the dynamics of the union movement post–World War II, Attorney Jubelirer acknowledged the obvious. "I guess you are right. Do you want to sit down and see if we can settle this thing?"

"Yes, I think that would be a good idea."

Looking for the court clerk, they noticed Freddy, a long-time experienced court employee who usually was assigned to the newest members of the judiciary, sitting in his usual seat in front of the judge's bench reading the morning paper. Approaching Freddy, Mr. Jubelirer asked, "Freddy, can we use the judge's chamber for a private conference? We will need about thirty minutes."

"No, you can have fifteen minutes. I need to get the judge's desk ready for today's work," Freddy stated.

Mr. Bielski walked straight to the chair to the right of the judge's chamber desk, and the union's attorney took the seat on the left side of the desk. Mr. Jubelirer began the conversation, stating, "I don't want the court to decide any issues regarding the legitimacy of the work stoppage. I can agree to have your client retrieve his produce from the warehouse." "You will agree to let Mr. Lomeo retrieve his produce without any interference and without paying any dues to your union?" Bielski asked, unable to believe that the union would acquiesce so quickly and amenably.

"Yes, but only if you will withdraw your injunction petition."

Bielski emphasized to Jubelirer, "I only represent Paolo, and as long as Paolo can access his produce, I have no reason to fight the union's ability to strike."

Having an agreement, they approached Freddy again, informing him that they had an agreement, and there was no need to have a hearing. This was music to Freddy's ears. The unwritten job description of a judge's clerk was to strongly encourage the parties to settle their difference without a lengthy hearing or procedures. Though most lay people mistook this cajoling as a sign that judges and court employees did not want to work a full day, this unseen dance helped make the judicial system more efficient and most likely more equitable.

Upon the arrival of Judge Challener, Freddy called the court in session. The attorneys agreed on the record and Challener dismissed Bielski's petition. Bielski was happy he had a quick victory for Paolo, though somewhat sad that he could not showcase his trial skills to the public. Being a professional he hid his selfish feelings and called Paolo with the news. "Paolo, I have great news! The union agreed to let you get your fruit."

Paolo could not believe his good fortune. "Thank you, Mr. Bielski! I am glad you decided to visit me with this idea. I am happy."

As Bielski was speaking, Paolo began wondering why the union would cooperate with him and not the other grocers. As Paolo had anticipated, the prices for fresh produce had increased dramatically since he had purchased and stored the produce in the Federal Cold Storage warehouse. Paolo thought if he was born in America, and knew the language and customs better, he would have gained a nice profit in anticipating the increase in prices without all the hassle. Paolo could not shake the unsettling thought that this good news was not really good news. With all the stress and demands on owners, employees, consumers, and unions from the U.S. free market economy, why settle now, and with a one-person business owned by an immigrant from Sicily?

"Paolo, have you been listening to me?"

Bielski's words brought Paolo back to reality. He felt foolish for not listening to his attorney, an educated man. "Sorry, Alexander, I just can't believe it worked. Why did they settle?"

"We had to agree to dismiss our petition for the injunction. The petition is moot since the union has agreed to our demands."

Paolo had no understanding of the word moot, Bielski for a moment forgetting that his client had a limited understanding of American civil law procedure and words relating to the court system.

Bielski realized from Paolo's silence that he had violated the unwritten rule of attorneys representing the working class of America; he spoke in legal language as opposed to everyday English. Bielski, always the gentleman, quickly corrected his mistake.

"Paolo, we dropped the lawsuit because the judge agreed that you have the right to your peaches and plums," Bielski explained to his client. "Thank you, my friend. Do you think we should have stayed with the lawsuit until I had my fruit?" Paolo inquired of his legal representative. "No. This was not a secret agreement. We both spoke to Judge Challener in the presence of all in attendance and stated our agreement. I said I would drop the lawsuit if Jubelirer agreed no one would harass you at Federal Cold Storage. He agreed, and the judge said OK we are done today."

Not quite understanding his attorney, Paolo asked, "Who is Jubelirer?"

"Jubelirer is the Teamsters' attorney. He would be in a lot of trouble if he lied to the judge. Paolo, you don't have anything to worry about, OK? Your son John and you can pick up the fruit anytime today."

Paolo trusted his new friend. "OK, Mr. Bielski, I see. We can't go today. It is too late in the morning. The night shift mill workers will be here soon, and John and I have to wait on the workers before they head home to sleep. Thank you for your help. I will stop by your office tomorrow after I pick up my fruit. I want to give you a few of the peaches and plums you helped rescue for me. Good-bye, my friend. "

Paolo hung up the telephone and saw his two oldest sons, John and Joseph, waiting for him to find out what happened in court. They watched as their father slowly hung up the telephone and seemed to turn to them in slow motion. Slowly they saw his face turn as bright as the rising morning sun with joy and relief at the same time. The sons knew he had good news for them. Paolo, for the first time in his adult life, felt the equal of Giuseppe. As he slowly turned to face his sons, their faces reflected the look of sons who idolized a father after a hard-won battle. Paolo had waited his whole life for that look. His sons were in awe of him, he thought or at least hoped, the same way he was in awe of his own father.

Hugging John as Joseph watched, Paolo said, "Boys, we won!

We can pick up our fruit tomorrow."

Joseph's feeling of elation quickly dissipated as he witnessed the strong father-son bond between John and Paolo. Joseph had recently returned from the war, serving in the army as a truck driver in the Pacific theater. He lost four years of bonding with his father, and

John filled the traditional role of the oldest son because of Joseph's war absence from Paolo's life—an inner psychological wound that Joseph would never fully recover from during his lifetime.

"Tonight, after Jimmy comes home from school, we all are going out to have dinner," Paolo said in a voice only slightly less than a scream. Immigrant families did not usually have dinner out for the simple reason they could not afford it. But this day was special. Paolo's victory saved the family enough money to eat out every day for the next year. Only if Paolo's life truly rolled this smoothly, he would have more than a small fruit market in McKeesport.

Jubelirer received an angry and threatening call from Joey "The Dime" Andoloni on Monday evening. "Why did you settle with Roma's attorney?" The Dime demanded.

Jubelirer stammered and spoke quietly like a child being scolded by his father. "I was worried that Challener would say the strike was illegal against the independent grocers, since they didn't have employees." Jubelirer's legal judgment would have been correct assuming an independent judiciary existed in Allegheny County, Pennsylvania, in 1945.

Screaming through the telephone at Jubelirer, Andoloni lectured, "What made you think the judge would have decided against us? Do you think we don't have enough influence to convince, by hook or crook, an insignificant state court judge? Allowing one grocer to cross the picket line will embolden the other grocers to break the other picket lines in the city."

"He is not crossing the picket lines. We are letting him in," Jubelirer asserted, trying to appease The Dime.

"Are we supposed to pay you? Most of the grocers are immigrants and uneducated. They will not know why Roma is getting his fruit. They will just see and know that he got his fruit and they didn't. I will take care of it. Don't do anything more until you hear from me," The Dime said, putting down the telephone without waiting for the Teamsters attorney's response.

Labor unions across the country were on strike or threatening a strike. All the large labor unions were demanding higher compensation because of the lack of pay raises during the war years. October 1945 was a tense month for business and labor. Pittsburgh was no different. The Teamsters drew an embargo circle around the Pittsburgh area preventing the supplying of the small fruit markets throughout the region. The dawn patrol, as the independent grocers were called, arose early every morning except Sundays to drive their own trucks to the Strip District to purchase produce from the different wholesalers. These independent grocers were the only retail produce sellers affected by the embargo. The large retail shops, such as the A&P, barely noticed the strike. These large grocers already had union workers, and therefore the warehouse workers gladly loaded their trucks and rail cars.

In fact, these large sellers encouraged and supported the Teamsters in their effort to unionize the small grocers. Secretly providing funds to the union to compensate the strikers for missed workdays, the big retailers wanted their small but numerous competitors out of the way. Believing a double standard existed in the food business, they had to use union labor, whereas the small independent grocers did not have this burden. They were all too happy to assist their normal business enemy even if it ruined the businesses and lives of the small grocers.

The Dime would speak to the Teamsters in the morning to make sure they prevented Paolo from entering the warehouse. Figuring that Bielski would be back in court seeking relief from the breach of the court settlement agreement, Jubelirer had strict instructions from The Dime not to negotiate a new settlement. Jubelirer's job consisted of convincing the court to support the strike against Paolo and, therefore, the other grocers, or at least to have the hearing postponed for as long as possible to apply financial hardship on Roma's. The longer the strike continued without any relief for the grocers, the sooner their businesses would be under great financial strain, causing the grocers to either join the union ranks or close their stores.

Paolo and John arose early Tuesday morning to drive their two trucks to Federal Cold Storage's warehouse to get their gold. As both trucks crept slowly through the strikers lined on Smallman Street, a street on the western side of the warehouse and parallel to the Allegheny River, both separately thought that the air was more hostile than they had expected. Paolo pulled his truck next to the police car stationed a block away from the warehouse. John parked behind him. Paolo approached John, instructing him to stay in the cab. "I will find out if there is a problem. I was afraid of this. Bielski was too naïve."

John, slightly above a whisper, said, "OK, Pop. Watch yourself." Paolo looked at John with a mixture of thanks for the kindness and perplexity at the obvious. As Paolo reached the strike line, the jeers started.

The strikers screamed, "Go home, scab," "Hey, dago, go back to the Boot," "Wop," and "sons of bitches and Mussolini." They knew Paolo. He had been friends with most of the warehouse workers for years. Now these friends had blood in their eyes and evil in their hearts, not realizing that Paolo was one of them. He was only crossing the picket line to protect his family. Paolo had empathy for the strikers, as they were doing what they thought was right to protect their families. He did not participate with the other independent grocers who were forming an association to confront the union to loudly pronounce their disgust of the union. The angry strikers did not realize that they had a true friend in Paolo.

Paolo had learned well enough from Alberto that a common man cannot do the right thing without hurting himself with no appreciation from society. Suddenly, feeling a sense of peace and finally understanding the lessons he had learned throughout his life helped illuminate the path to his family's salvation. Before his epiphany, Paolo would have not let the strikers' offensive and derogatory words go unanswered, which was exactly what the leaders of the strikers wanted. They wanted the police to arrest Paolo for starting the violence that would surely have occurred this day if Paolo had let his emotions control his actions. Seeing trouble, one of the strikers approached Paolo and told him, as a friend, to stay away. "Paolo, go home. They are out to get you," the friend explained.

"What happened? My attorney had an agreement with your attorney," Paolo responded.

The fiery rhetoric spoke by the union leaders at the early morning union meeting excited the strikers to ignore their attorney's agreement and prevent Paolo from entering the warehouse. "They told us that you lied in court. That you were secretly working for Federal Cold Storage to break the strike. Everyone then started to scream that they wouldn't let any scab into the warehouse."

Shaking his head, his face reflecting the rage his soul felt, he slowly walked back to his trucks. Paolo and John were badly outnumbered, and the four police officers did nothing to discourage or reduce the excitement of the warehouse workers. John asked Paolo, "Now what?"

Losing confidence as the illuminated path fell dark with his anger, Paolo felt incompetent as a father when he said, "I am not sure."

John looked at his father with a puzzled glance. "Didn't the judge agree we could get our produce?"

"This is bigger than the judge. We have a real problem. Let's go home." Paolo walked to his truck and wondered how he ended up in this situation. More importantly, how would he resolve this situation? Giuseppe would know what to do, but he wasn't here. Paolo regretted his son could not have a father like his father. Of course, a son always believes his father is "all knowing," and a father is always worried that he is not providing the proper guidance to his son. Paolo didn't realize it, but John respected his father and stared in wonderment at how cool and calm Paolo handled the situation while instructing John to drive back home.

Again, the news of Paolo's rejection reached McKeesport before he did. Alexander Bielski was waiting for Paolo when he arrived at Roma's. Rarely did Bielski become angry when a case did not work his way. However, this was different. He had a promise from an attorney and judge, two officers of the court. Bielski took the breach of this promise as a sign of personal disrespect. More importantly to him, it humiliated him as a professional. Bielski, facing Paolo, placed his hand on his heart. "I promise you I will be in court as soon as it opens tomorrow with a new petition."

Paolo, working under a new set of personal parameters, held his friend's hand and reassured Alexander. "I know this is not your fault. This was a breach of honor by the union's attorney, not you. You can't control another person. The problem is I don't think anyone can control these thugs."

Appreciating the sentiment, Bielski ran toward his office to prepare for tomorrow's battle, not realizing Paolo's thinking about a quiet resolution had changed.

As Bielski sat in Challener's courtroom reading the morning newspaper, Pittsburgh Post-Gazette, he perused the article about General Patton's dismissal as the military governor of Bavaria, Germany, by Allied Supreme Commander Dwight Eisenhower. A year before, on October 3, 1944, Patton was an American hero and now he was being dismissed with less respect than a private who never saw battle. Paolo's attorney thought how easily public perceptions change with the changing sentiment of the political class. Patton had been a source of trouble for Eisenhower for many years, and Patton's successor as military governor, Lieutenant General Lucian K. Truscott, probably should have replaced Patton three years before in the battle for northern Africa. However, Bielski correctly thought, the political class used Patton's popularity for their election purposes and then once he was no longer useful they dispensed with him.

As Bielski finished the article, Jubelirer walked into the courtroom with the confidence of a boy asked to play point guard on his fifth grade basketball team for the first time. Jubelirer knew he had sandbagged Bielski and expected a rough treatment from his opponent. Standing at the far end of the jury box waiting for Judge Challener's appearance, Jubelirer did not make eye contact with Bielski.

Bielski walked toward the Teamsters' attorney and asked, "Hey, buster, what happened? You made me look like a fool. I am asking Challener to sanction not only your client but you. You are a jerk."

Shrugging his shoulders, trying to hustle and harass Bielski the way The Dime hustled and harassed him, Jubelirer said with a tone of superiority, "It is something out of my control. You can act high and mighty, but you are unrealistic. You are living in a dreamland. There is no way the Teamsters are letting your client into the warehouse."

"I bet the judge won't agree. Remember you are not only facing me, but you broke your word to the judge," Bielski responded.

"You are proving my point. You are living in a dream land," Jubelirer quipped. "I am warning you that harm to your client will occur if Paolo tries to gain access to the warehouse regardless of the court's decision this morning."

Unbelievably, Jubelirer first told him that the breaking of his promise was out of his control and in the next sentence threatened Bielski's client with bodily harm. Laughing with derision, Bielski told Jubelirer, "Obviously, you have never met Paolo. Otherwise you would know that this threat would not be made without impunity."

However, Jubelirer's threat was not a meaningless threat. At about the same time of their hearing, some Teamsters decided to follow Andoloni's advice and physically enforce the strike. As the Pittsburgh Post-Gazette reported the following morning, "Morris Mazer, the owner of Curtisville Fruit and Produce Company headquartered in the Strip District, and his nephew David Lowenthal had stopped their truck at a red light at the intersection of Wylie Avenue and Tunnel Street when four men parked their truck to block Mazur's truck. Then two of them exited the truck and launched an attack with metal pipes on Mazur and Lowenthal. Lowenthal finally started the truck, swerved on to the sidewalk to avoid the striker's truck and then sped away. Mazur and Lowenthal reported the assault to the police and the police refused to investigate due to a lack of evidence."

News of Mazur's attack spread quickly throughout the grocer network, and Paolo learned about the attack while waiting on a customer with the little remaining produce he had in the store. John overheard the conversation between the customer and his father and thought that no matter what the court decided the Teamsters would not let them enter the warehouse without a fight.

After the customer left, John told Paolo, "Pop, maybe it would better to avoid the trouble. No amount of fruit is worth your life. Plus, we could purchase our fruit from the warehouses in Altoona and Johnstown. That is what the other stores are doing."

"Son, I appreciate you thinking of me. If they would let me just get the fruit I already purchased, then I won't go back there. We have too much money out. I have no choice."

Freddy called the court in session, and Judge Challener took the bench and called Paolo's case. The courtroom resembled most courtrooms in the United States. The senses of any visitors entering the courtroom, through a large, light brown wooden door with a window encased in the middle third of the door with bold black letters reading "Judge William Challener" below words reading "Courtroom No. 4," would be overwhelmed by the full atmosphere of the room. A center aisle bordered on each side by four rows of brown wooden chairs with eight chairs in each row would invite the visitors to partake in the activities of the day. Each row of chairs was bound together, having the look of one long bench with the purpose of keeping the rows straight and preventing the moving or separating of any one chair from the others. After passing the rows of chairs, wooden banisters separated the rows from the rest of the courtroom. Five feet further in the front of each banister sat two long attorney tables. The left table was designated for the defendant in the different cases, and the right table was for the plaintiffs.

The jury box sat against the right wall ahead of the attorneys' tables. It is called a box, but it is actually a rectangular space elevated slightly above the courtroom floor. The white painted right wall of the courtroom acted as the back length side of the rectangle box. The other three sides of the rectangle were outlined by mahogany wood rising about three feet from the elevated floor of the box. Jurors could enter the box through a small cut-out entrance on the width side closest to the row of chairs. Inside of the jury box were two rows of brown wooden chairs. Each row had seven chairs for a total of fourteen chairs. In most cases, the judge would ask the attorneys to choose twelve jurors and two alternate jurors to act as substitutes for any of the twelve who could not continue their public service throughout the duration of the trial.

The wall furthest from the large wooden door consisted mainly of glass that would bring sunlight into the courtroom on the few days of sunshine in Pittsburgh. In front of this large glass window sat the judge, about fifteen feet from the attorneys' tables. This area of the courtroom is called the bench. The bench, a large mahogany wood "bench" desk with a throne like chair where the judge sat, was centered in the middle of the glass window and positioned almost the entire width of the courtroom above all the participants and spectators in the courtroom. Another mahogany banister separated the bench from the rest of the courtroom. This part of the courtroom is commonly referred to as the "bar." Attorneys were not permitted to go beyond the bar during any proceeding.

All the walls reflected years of use, as the white paint had faded with time to look a dingy yellow, highlighting the sober and depressing decisions emanating from this courtroom.

Bielski made two motions this morning while standing on the right side of the bar facing His Honor. He renewed his petition for an injunction against the strikers and added two new actions. One cause of action requested Challener to reprimand Local 944 and Jubelirer for intentionally violating their previous settlement agreement. The second action asked for the release of Paolo's fruit through a replevin action.

Replevin is a legal term meaning that Federal Cold Storage was illegally withholding Paolo's property and should return it regardless of the difficulty or costs. Attorneys usually file alternative motions to give the judge options, in case the judge does not view the case in the same way as the attorney. Bielski stated for the record, "Your Honor, yesterday my client, Mr. Lomeo, was prevented by Local 944 warehouse employees from removing his goods per your order approving our settlement."

"Is this true, Mr. Jubelirer?" asked Judge Challener.

"Yes, Your Honor," said the Teamsters' attorney as he stood to the left of Mr. Bielski at the bar.

"How and why did this happen when we had an agreement in place?"

Jubelirer stated for the court record, "Judge, if one man can remove his goods, then a thousand others would be permitted to do the same."

Challener further inquired, "And what is wrong with that?" "Your Honor, if you decided that anyone or everyone could violate our strike then effectively you have canceled the union's right to strike. It would be a strike in name only. Our fathers fought for years for the right to strike, and we can't lose it over a dispute with a small-time grocer," Jubelirer implored.

As Bielski listened attentively to his opponent's arguments, he wondered how Paolo would react to the description of Paolo as a small- time grocer in open court. It showed that the Teamsters had no respect for Paolo.

Ensuring union support in any future personal political endeavor, Judge Challener said, "Mr. Jubelirer, that is a point I hadn't considered." Bielski interjected to change and challenge Challener's thinking. "Please, Your Honor, Mr. Jubelirer's argument is baseless. We are not talking about a business that employs Teamsters or even has employees. Mr. Lomeo has no employees and has no ability to affect the strike. This case is no different from a person who had his wallet stolen and the thief hid the wallet in a safe deposit box at the local bank. We are only asking you to instruct the bank to return the stolen wallet. We are not asking you to make a judgment on the actions of the thief."

Hearing Bielski's rebuttal, the judge became silent. The only people in the courtroom were the judge, attorneys, and two court employees, and all remained still and silent as Challener pondered his dilemma. Finally, Freddy rose from his chair and walked toward Bielski with an extended hand. Grabbing Bielski's hand, he bent slightly toward Bielski's left ear whispering, "That was the best argument I have heard in thirty years of working in this courtroom. Too bad it will not do any good."

Challener and Jubelirer stared in disbelief at Freddy's bold action and watched him as he casually returned to his station. Rumor had it that Freddy was somehow related to Davey Lawrence, the political boss of Pittsburgh and future governor of Pennsylvania. Freddy could take chances with a judge or powerfully connected attorneys other court employees would never dare.

Using the most of his experience, legal skills, and education, Challener resolved his dilemma of choosing between the strikers and Paolo. Challener approved Bielski's replevin action, so Paolo could legally retrieve his produce while postponing the injunction petition hearing until October 8, 1945. This way history would say that the court upheld Paolo's property rights, and at the same time the current politicians and union members would know that their right to strike went unchallenged. Challener thought once Paolo loaded his fruit on his truck the injunction would become moot, and he would never have to decide the legitimacy of the strike. Did Challener truly believe that the Teamsters would obey his order?

The judge's order instructed the Sheriff's Office of Allegheny County, Pennsylvania, to serve the writ of replevin on J.C. Hetherington, General Manager of Federal Cold Storage, by 9:30 a.m. the following morning.

Bielski experienced this charade in a dream-like state of mind. He knew the union would never honor the writ, and Challener had decided to bury the injunction petition in the graveyard of the judicial calendar of the Allegheny County Court of Common Pleas.

Jubelirer felt relief. Andoloni should be satisfied now. Jubelirer's intelligence and experience told him the same thing as Challener's and Bielski's. The injunction petition's postponement meant it would never receive a fair hearing, and the Teamsters would not let a small insignificant Sicilian immigrant win regardless of the demands of the court order.

Prior to traversing the exit threshold of the courtroom, Alexander Bielski turned back to look at the judge sitting on the bench, catching him signing the court order, and noticed the sun's rays that beamed through the glass window behind the judge had suddenly dissipated, leaving only a gray hue throughout the courtroom.

Chapter 10

Pickets and plums?

As Judge Challener was denying Bielski's injunction petition with Jubelirer feeling the thrill of victory, Paolo was entering the real fight. The Teamsters arrived at Roma's Fruit Market and set up a picket line around both entrances of the store. The store sat at the corner of Sixth and Sinclair streets, with an entrance on each street. McKeesport, being very close to Homestead, Pennsylvania, the place where the true union movement started in the United States, had a strong union presence and following. Most citizens of McKeesport were connected to the different labor unions in some fashion. The Teamsters knew most customers of Roma's, who were mostly from the working class of McKeesport, would not cross a picket line no matter how well they knew Paolo or his family. The vise was being set and about to press the squeeze on the Lomeo family.

Paolo and John drove past the store prior to leaving for the Strip District and were shocked when they saw the picket line. "Pop, what is going on? Look, they are picketing the store," John exclaimed to his father. Paolo sat in the driver's seat as John sat to his right on the front bench seat of the truck.

Trying to stay calm so as not to worry John, Paolo said, "I guess things didn't work out for Bielski this morning."

Rosalia usually operated the store if John or Paolo was not available to manage the morning shift. Most mornings either Paolo or John would head to the Strip District to purchase their daily supply of produce while the other stayed in the store to wait on their morning customers. Before leaving home, the family's discussion resolved that both Paolo and John would go together this day, since at the time they were not sure what the court would decide.

Paolo turned his truck around and drove back home to see

Rosalia. Quickly leaving the cab of the truck, asking John to stay in the cab, Paolo started yelling prior to entering the home, "Rose, Rose you can't go to work!"

Rosalia felt the urgency of the message as Paolo ran from the truck calling for her loudly enough to wake up their neighbors earlier than expected. Cleaning the kitchen after her son James had just finished breakfast, she covered the six feet from the kitchen to the front porch in two steps. Meeting Paolo on the porch she nervously asked, "What?"

Entering the home, Paolo hugged Rosalia, and shaking with concern, stated, "The Teamsters have surrounded the store."

"What do you mean surrounded the store? Why?"

Paolo's heart rate slowly started to recover and he more calmly tried to explain the situation to her. "The Teamsters have started a strike of our store. Their men have blocked each entrance. They want trouble."

"Can they do this?"

Becoming frustrated with fear, Paolo released his insecurities on the person he loved the most. "Rose, don't say silly things. Can they do this? They are doing it!"

Her face changed from that of a caring mother and wife to a person in agony. Paolo, as the protector of the family, had violated the protector's code of conduct; he shifted the burden of the problem on another family member. Immediately feeling guilty and thinking Giuseppe would have never acted so selfishly, he apologized to his wife. "Rose, I am sorry. I am scared."

Rosalia grabbed his hand and asked him to sit down. "Paolo, I am scared too. But I know you will take care of it. Just stay calm and think before you do anything, please. We can lose a couple of bushels of plums, but we can't lose you."

God had graced Paolo with a marriage to a caring and smart woman. Thinking of Giuseppe, he took his coin out of his pocket as Rosalia talked to him. His father had been right—a good marriage can solve most problems. He begged his wife, "Rosalia, stay home and keep the store closed until John and I come back from Pittsburgh."

Rosalia knew that Paolo only used her Sicilian name Rosalia rather than the American version Rose when he was seriously concerned. She did not like the name Rose as Paolo did not appreciate his American Paul, but she and Paolo thought using their American names helped them assimilate into American society.

James prepared to head out the door for school when he witnessed this interaction between his parents. Being a teenager, and not really focused on the family's immediate problems, he knew something important had just happened. He quickly went to his father and asked, "Should I stay home with Mama?"

Paolo, looking at his son with the focus of a person on a mission from his own father, told his youngest son, "Your schooling is the most important goal of this family. No matter what happens to me, you have to finish your education." James would be the first Lomeo to graduate from high school, as the older sons left school after eighth grade to help their father in the store.

"Pop, what do you mean if something happens to you? Do you think they will kill you?"

Paolo, trying to hide his fear and regretting his slip of the tongue, said, "Jimmy it will take more than a few hunky thugs to kill me. You go to school and let me worry about this. OK?"

"OK, Pop. I will see you when I come home tonight," James said, relieved that he had to worry only about teenage life's problems.

Obeying his father, James headed for school worrying about his family.

As Paolo kissed Rosalia, ready to head out the door, the telephone rang. Rosalia seemed shocked by an early morning call and quickly answered the phone. "Hello. Hello, Mr. Bielski. Yes, Paolo is here. Yes, he also wants to talk to you."

Paolo, hearing only one side of the conversation, stood behind Rosalia ready to talk to his attorney friend. Rosalia turned to Paolo and handed him the telephone receiver. "Hello, Mr. Bielski. We have a problem."

Bielski interrupted and did not understand that Paolo had made a declarative sentence and was not asking a question. "Paolo, the judge gave us our order. The union is not allowed to interfere with you." Bielski purposefully hid his real thoughts about the union's intentions, since he had no hard evidence of their plan.

"Well, maybe the word did not reach the strikers. They have surrounded my store," Paolo angrily told his attorney with a tint of fear.

Taken aback by the turn of events, Bielski responded, "I am still in Pittsburgh. I will go see the judge. This is a clear violation of our order."

Tired of the courtroom antics, Paolo said, "Mr. Bielski you have done all you can. I am going to Federal Cold Storage and getting my fruit. I am tired, and my family is breaking from the stress. I will resolve this today. Thank you." Paolo, not wanting Bielski to speak reasonably to him and convince him to stay home until the court acted properly, hung up the telephone without waiting to hear a good-bye from his attorney.

Rosalia agreed to stay home until 10 a.m., when the streets would be busy with witnesses, preventing the picketers from trying anything foolish to harm Rosalia or the store. In the meantime she would ask Joseph, her eldest son, to walk to the store to make sure the Teamsters did not vandalize the place. Feeling sure that his family would be safe, Paolo and John left for Pittsburgh in two separate vehicles. John drove the truck, and Paolo took the family Ford sedan, following close behind his son. As he was leaving, he lowered the left front window of his sedan to say good-bye to Rosalia. "I will back soon. Call the police if there are any problems."

"Paolo, please be careful. If there is any trouble, come back home.

Remember, you have John with you, and he is only a young boy," Rosalia begged her husband. A mother always sees her child as young and innocent regardless of the child's age, even when the child is in the second decade of his life.

Paolo entered the Strip District crawling behind John's truck as it stopped at the loading dock at the southern side of the Federal Cold Storage Company's warehouse. Due to the delay caused by his concern with the picket line at his store, Paolo arrived at the produce yards later than normal at 10 a.m. Noticing the sun rising to his right with the morning temperature reaching fifty-three degrees Fahrenheit, Paolo dreamt of the October mornings of the Sicily of his youth. An unusually warm October morning with the heat of hatred simultaneously rising with the air temperature forecast a rough day ahead for the Lomeos.

It seemed to John that there were a thousand strikers screaming scab, dago, and whop and threatening father and son with harm. Most of the strikers carried pipes, held the pipes in one hand, and banged the pipes on their free hands. Thomas Taylor, steward of the warehouse workers, told The Pittsburgh Press, "They [the Lomeos] are scabbing us out of our jobs."

Mr. Taylor did not seem to realize that the Lomeos did not want his job at the warehouse and, in fact, needed to have the warehouse employees to load their trucks. Taylor's intelligence level should have been questioned by the reporter with such an illogical statement.

Paolo stepped out of his car and walked through the crowd of strikers. John, fearing for his life, stayed in the truck. Every door to the warehouse was locked, except one small door to the left of the larger garage doors usually used to transport the goods from the warehouse to the waiting trucks. It would be almost impossible for Paolo to load his produce through this door, but he would try. He located a flatbed dolly just to the right of the door; it seeming to have been placed in full view expecting Paolo to use it. He pushed it to the center of the warehouse. Mr. Hetherington, the manager, stepped with meaning toward Paolo and asked, "Mr. Lomeo, please leave now before this place erupts."

"I have every right to be here. You know that the judge agreed with me. You are afraid, but I have more to lose than you," Paolo responded.

Mr. Hetherington, recognizing Paolo was right, shook his head side to side as he spoke. "Mr. Lomeo, for us both, I hope you know what you are doing."

Paolo ignored him and asked, "Can you point out to me where my plums and peaches are?" Hetherington pointed to his left. Pushing his dolly toward the area, Paolo found his bushels and began loading them on the flatbed dolly. As he loaded the produce, he wished the warehouse workers would help, since he felt all of his fifty years. He pushed the dolly across the floor, out the small door, and onto the dock.

He motioned to John by waving his right hand and saying in a loud voice over the Teamsters' derogatory shouts, "John, open the back of the truck and help me load the truck."

Hesitantly, John exited the truck, opened the back of it, and jumped up to the dock to start loading. Scanning the crowd and seeing the anger in their faces, John began fearing for his own safety.

Noticing his son's apprehension, he said in Sicilian so the Teamsters would not understand, "John, pay attention to the fruit. The sooner we load this truck and get out of here, the better. It will take them awhile to realize that they should stop us now and not after we load the truck."

Confused, John replied, "They will just block the truck and not let us leave."

"I would rather be in a four-ton truck facing this crowd than in the open like now," Paolo hurriedly explained to his son.

John realized his father was right and started taking the bushels off the dolly into the truck as fast as he could. Being a twenty-four-year-old man standing about five feet nine and one-half inches tall with a slender but a muscular build enclosed in an olive tan skin topped with jet black eyes and hair, he looked the part of a stereotypical Sicilian immigrant. Paolo could not keep pace with John, though he did his share of unloading and loading of the bushels to the truck.

Paolo and John repeated the same action until all ninety bushels were loaded into his truck. All the while, the strikers were screaming at Paolo and John and made death threats to them. "Kill the WOPS! Find a rope and let's drag the Lomeos through the streets!" yelled the crowd.

The longer the strikers screamed, the more threatening they became. Whispering among them began. Paolo became frightened and worried about the striking Teamsters' next move. He knew the whispering could mean only one thing—they were planning physical harm to John and him.

Standing some distance away but in full view of the strikers stood nine Pittsburgh police officers and two sheriff's deputies that Judge Challener had ordered to the warehouse. These law enforcement officers stood by and did nothing to control the situation. It is a sad day when men who have taken an oath to protect all refuse, out of fear or politics, to help ordinary citizens avoid physical harm. Watching the police officers and deputies, the Teamsters' leaders in the crowd recognized the law officers would do nothing to help the Lomeos.

Paolo instructed John in Sicilian, "Drive the truck home and don't stop for traffic lights, stalled cars, people, or any other obstacles that the Teamsters place in your way. Get to McKeesport without stopping! I will follow behind you. Don't worry about it, even if I stop. You keep going no matter what! Understand?"

"Pop, I am scared. I can't do it! Someone will stop me and kill me. Let's just leave the truck and drive home in the car!"

"John, listen to me! You get in that truck now and start the engine. You are going to get us killed if you act like a frightened child!

I am afraid too, but we have to get home. You are wasting time. Get going!"

Paolo headed through the crowd to his car parked about seventy-five feet from the truck. He pushed a few young men standing by his car and entered the driver's seat of the Ford. John climbed into the cab of the truck as his father was entering the Ford. Just as John started the engine to the truck, someone yelled, "Circle the truck!"

The strikers circled the truck and Paolo heard someone scream, "Let's tip it over and show these dagos."

Paolo jumped out of his car and ran into the crowd to protect his son. Filled with anger, Paolo stood in front of the truck, slowly opened his sweater, and revealed his holster holding a Smith & Wesson .32 caliber revolver. Without saying a word, he unbuttoned the flap on his holster and placed his right hand on the butt of the revolver. Seeing this action in slow motion, every striker stopped where they were standing. The leader of the Teamsters this day, Steward Thomas Taylor, having known Paolo for many years as Paolo had a good working relationship with all the warehouse workers until today, approached Paolo with his hands held at chest level. "Paolo, easy does it. How do you plan shooting us all with that small revolver? You don't have enough bullets."

Paolo stared at Taylor as though Taylor did not deserve to live and see his family again. Paolo stressed to Taylor, as clear as he could with his Sicilian accent, "My friend, I may not have enough bullets to kill all of you, but I have enough bullets to kill you!"

Knowing Taylor was the union steward and the leader inciting the crowd the day before, he determined that killing Taylor would frighten and give pause to the mostly young men with little life experience in the crowd. Taylor, concerned that he would lose the respect of his men, decided it was his time to become bellicose with Paolo. "Lomeo, you are a little dago. You pull that gun, I will kick the crap out of you!"

Taylor was a large man. He stood six feet three inches and weighed one hundred ninety-five pounds. A person does not become a union steward in the fiercest union in the country without having proven himself in physical altercations. The young Teamsters knew Taylor's reputation as a tough guy and figured Paolo had bitten off more than he could chew.

Paolo's body quivered with anger, and he could feel the blood in his fingertips as his eyes became blind with rage. Taylor felt the heat of Paolo's rage even though he stood three feet away. "Taylor, you open your mouth with one more word, I am going to kill you right there where you are standing. I hope you told your wife and kids you loved them today before you came here. I did! Say dago again!" Paolo spoke forcefully but almost quietly as he pulled his gun with his right hand from his belt holster attached to his right hip. He did not raise his Smith & Wesson, but held the gun in his hand with his arm extended parallel to his right leg. Still blind with rage and acting on instinct, Paolo said, "Well, Taylor, what do you want to do?"

Taylor could only keep his eyes on Paolo's gun and the twitching of Paolo's right hand. He followed every little involuntary movement of the muscles in his belligerent's right hand.

Taylor, standing more than eight inches taller than Paolo's five feet seven inches, shook with fear and the crowd became silent. Screaming to John, Paolo said, "Head home, son, and don't stop for any reason."

With the strikers still standing in front of his truck, John's courage visited his soul after seeing his father's actions, and he stepped on the accelerator, pushing the truck through the parting sea of strikers down Smallman Street toward McKeesport, some twelve miles away.

Paolo walked slowly back to his car without a man looking at him, placed his gun on the right front seat, and left the Strip District, following John to McKeesport.

Before leaving the courtroom, Bielski learned what happened to Paolo at the warehouse and began to worry about his safety. He asked Freddy if he could use the telephone in the judge's chamber to call the Pittsburgh police to escort Paolo and his son to the city line. According to The Pittsburgh Press, the Pittsburgh police told Bielski that they "had three scout cars, an ambulance, and nine policemen at the cold storage company to protect him but they wouldn't escort him anywhere."

Paolo followed closely behind John, and they drove through the city without any incidents.

Bielski placed a call to the police officer for Dravosburg. Dravosburg, Pennsylvania, a very small hamlet between Pittsburgh and McKeesport, with only one police officer on duty, agreed to escort Bielski's clients to the McKeesport line. The officer's squad car with lights flashing waited for Roma's fruit truck at Bettis Airfield and signaled John to follow him. Paolo was relieved to see the Dravosburg police car. As John looked backward out the left window, Paolo waved to John to follow the police car. After what John had just been through with the Pittsburgh police and county sheriff just standing by as the strikers surrounded them, John worried that the Dravosburg police officer was laying a trap for his father and him. Trusting his father's instincts, John stayed with the police car as it proceeded down the Dravosburg hill to the McKeesport border. The officer pulled over to the shoulder of the road to let the McKeesport grocers pass. Paolo saluted the officer as he crossed the borderline.

After calling Dravosburg, Bielski telephoned the McKeesport police department. This police department, unlike the Pittsburgh police department, was funded by the tax dollars Bielski and Paolo paid as small business owners, and as residents of the city. Initially, the McKeesport police department had agreed with Attorney Bielski to escort his clients through McKeesport to their store. However, the police never met the Lomeos. Bielski later learned that the McKeesport police chief, Guy Rodkey had countermanded the order. This was the same Guy Rodkey who had issued the citation to Paolo years before. The Pittsburgh Press reported that Rodkey "issued orders to the policemen that they were not to meet Lomeo, this is 100% union town." When an officer questioned the order and asked the chief hadn't they taken an oath to protect everyone, Rodkey replied, "You're not going to take the scout car; let that blankety blank protect himself."

Remember, this was 1945, and the newspapers had more class than today and used the term "blankety blank" instead of the actual language. Everyone reading the paper knew exactly what he said. He probably said something like "let that dago, whop, scab protect himself."

Rodkey had political ambitions and wanted to use the power of the Office of Chief of Police not for the good of the community but to advance his political career. He wanted to be a city councilman, and knowing most people were connected with the unions in some fashion, tried to be seen as the protector of the union cause. In fact, he was a candidate for city council, with the November election only a few weeks away. What he failed to calculate into his equation was that most people, especially Americans, do not approve of a government official using his political power to hurt another person.

When Rodkey realized that Paolo's gun permit had been issued by his department eight years ago, he quickly calculated that if he revoked the permit, Paolo would have to surrender his gun. He basically was sending a message to any thug that Paolo now did not have the means to protect his family and himself. Rodkey, dressed in his dress police uniform with a medal or two on his chest, met Paolo and John at the store just as they pulled to the curb to park their vehicles. Rodkey approached with a menacing look and said, "I need your revolver."

"Why? I have a permit for it," Paolo hesitantly responded. "Look, Mr. Dago. Your Mafia style may work downtown, but not in my town."

Paolo, his muscles still pumped with blood and adrenaline from his Pittsburgh encounter, thought about reacting quickly and violently against this usurper. For the first time in his life, he used rational thought while under the influence of high emotions. "Chief, I am Mafia? Who paid you to act like Mussolini?"

"If you keep talking back to me I will arrest you. Let's see how long you last in jail!"

Paolo looked around and felt uneasy when he realized that Rodkey arrived at the store without a partner or other police cars. Why would a chief of police do this alone? Did the other officers refuse to cooperate in this unlawful action, or did the chief want no witnesses to his abuse of power? "Do you plan on arresting me by yourself?" Paolo inquired.

Operating the store with her son Joseph in Paolo and John's absence, Rosalia watched in disbelief as her husband and son encountered the police chief on the Sixth Street sidewalk. Not realizing what had occurred earlier at the Federal Cold Storage warehouse, Rosalia thought Paolo had done something stupid when she prayed and pleaded with him to remain calm before he left for Pittsburgh. Paolo and Rosalia never had a chance to speak together prior to the arrival of Guy Rodkey, since Rodkey's appearance almost seemed planned to occur at the moment of Paolo's arrival to catch Paolo off guard.

As the exchange of words between the combatants flew through the air like fast balls pitched by Pittsburgh Pirate pitcher Mace Brown, Paolo constantly kept glancing over to Rosalia, who watched this sidewalk drama from inside the store. Paolo could read Rosalia's face and eyes to know that she wanted him to cooperate with Rodkey before Rodkey actually did arrest him. Paolo thought to himself during this verbal altercation that it was better to retreat when the odds were against you, so you could challenge your adversary when the advantage was on your side. Also, Chief Rodkey would like nothing more than to arrest him and have the newspapers say that Chief of Police Rodkey arrested Paolo Lomeo, the scab. Publicity is the ego infusion that all politicians thrive on.

Knowing Paolo was not an easy individual to bully, Rodkey headed back to his car to dispatch a backup police officer. As Rodkey asked for additional police help over the car radio, Paolo approached him while holding the gun with the barrel facing Paolo, so Rodkey could grab the handle. "Here, now please leave my store unless you plan to shut us down."

The chief said, "Now you are starting to wise up. Maybe you will learn that this is a union town."

Paolo inquired where Rodkey had purchased the new shutters recently installed at Rodkey's residence. Stunned, Rodkey glanced at the officer who had just arrived to assist him, then at John standing next to his father, and then to Paolo. Abruptly, Rodkey said, "It doesn't matter, you will be out of business within a week," and directed his officer to follow him to their respective cars.

After the police left, John confusedly looked at his father and asked, "Why did you asked about his shutters?"

Paolo explained, "He is experienced enough to understand the implication of my question. The message is that if any harm comes to my family, I know where he lives and would return the favor."

Was there any doubt, after today's events, in Rodkey's mind that retribution would come quickly and hard? Chief Rodkey lost the election that year. Based on his future actions as a councilman in later years, he obviously did not understand that the true meaning of America meant that all people should be treated the same.

The headline of the October 8, 1945, edition of The Pittsburgh Press read "PRODUCE STRIKE HITS JOHNSTOWN, Principal Supplier Closed by Teamsters." The article detailed how the produce strike that embargoed Pittsburgh spread to Johnstown, Pennsylvania, when the wholesaler that supplied ninety percent of perishable goods to two hundred fifty independent grocers was closed by Teamsters Local 110. Joseph Walling, manager of Walling & Company, said his "thirteen employees were called off the platform by Local 110. One of our customers, a McKeesport dealer who had been buying from us for a year, arrived this morning with two of his own trucks and a third he hired from an associate produce man. The union had told us we could deliver to the McKeesport man so we went ahead and loaded the three trucks. After we did that, the union called our employees out on strike because we loaded the third truck. We're closed up tight."

The Teamsters tightened the grip on Pittsburgh's independent grocers by demanding that wholesalers in Youngstown, Altoona, and Johnstown not load produce to any trucks belonging to Pittsburgh-area grocers. J.A. Nelson & Company's Don Nelson, a wholesaler from Altoona, told The Pittsburgh Press that "the union told him he could only sell to firms from Johnstown, Altoona, and Greensburg that were current customers." The strike at Walling & Company ended at 9 p.m. when the company agreed not to sell to any grocers from the Pittsburgh region. The newspaper asked if this included the McKeesport dealer, and Mr. Walling replied that "the union didn't tell me who I couldn't sell to but I am not taking any chances. I'm lucky I'm in business. The union can make or break me."

Paolo had the same feeling. The union prevented him from purchasing produce from any of his normal vendors. This was the same plight of the other independent grocers, except the union had not formed a picket line around the other stores. This special treatment was reserved for the only grocer to challenge the union's demand that independent store owners join their ranks. So, even if he could buy produce from a wholesaler willing to disobey the union, Roma's union member customers may not be willing to cross the picket line. Paolo worried that his store would have to close; he only had a small amount of produce left. Though his loyal customers were willing to cross the picket lines because of his lower prices, his wooden fruit stands would soon be empty. He did not blame the store picketers for his problems.

He knew they were only following orders and were not of independent minds. In fact, Paolo invited the picketers into the store for coffee on the cold mornings. Learning from Giuseppe that it is easier and more effective to fight one general than one thousand soldiers, Paolo decided to befriend the picketers.

The next day Paolo's old business partner and the person he blamed for Eugico's death, Mangia Dorm, willingly crossed the picket line to see Paolo. Seeing a friendly face and a person of no courage walk through the picketers boosted Paolo's confidence that life would be back to normal very soon. Greeting his old friend with a hug, he said, "Antonio, I am glad you came. It has been a rough couple of days."

"No worries Paolo, I am glad I came too," Mangia Dorm said even though Mangia Dorm looked pale and had the expression of a man visiting a friend on his deathbed. Mangia Dorm sheepishly asked, "Can we talk in private? I have some news from the union."

Motioning toward the storage area at the back of the store, Paolo went forward with Mangia Dorm following him. "I could use some good news at the moment, my friend," Paolo said as they entered the storage area. This storage area did double duty as an office with a small desk and telephone and a place where the smaller boxes of fruit, such as strawberries and blueberries, could be stored. The larger items were always stored in the basement storage area and then brought up the integral steps to shop level. Standing in a storage area with dimensions of three feet by three feet, Mangia Dorm felt uncomfortable. He had thought Paolo would just have had them speak in the corner next to the exit door to Sinclair Street. He thought he might need a quick access to the street once Paolo heard his news.

Hanging his head low, and unwilling to look into Paolo's eyes, Mangia Dorm said, "Paolo, I have bad news for you."

Paolo, seeing his friend's shaking knees, asked him to sit down as he placed his arm around the shoulders of Mangia Dorm. "Antonio, don't let this thing get to you. Your news can't be as bad as what I have already been through. What did you hear? They plan on running me out of business? I already know this."

Mangia Dorm accepted Paolo's offer to sit down, since to do otherwise might trigger the violent response Mangia Dorm feared. "Paolo, the Mafia is putting pressure on me and my family. I am in their debt, you know this, right? I gambled too much and now they want payment."

Paolo started feeling uneasy and anxious; for all of Mangia Dorm's faults, he had never gambled. Mangia Dorm was too greedy to spend his money on anyone but himself. "Antonio, you never gambled before. What is going on?"

"OK, Paolo, but listen to me first before you get mad. Andoloni came to see me yesterday. He wants me to ask you to drop your court case and join the union. He says you are making the union look bad, and it is causing them problems with the other grocers."

"Good, I hope the other grocers join me. This way we can stop this nonsense," Paolo shouted to Mangia Dorm with a fake confidence in his ability to defeat the most powerful union in the country.

Finally looking directly at Paolo up from his seated position, Mangia Dorm explained. "Paolo, you are not understanding me. I am not just a messenger. They want me to help them. I will have to testify against you! Just join and let's get out of this mess."

"Testify? What can you testify to? You haven't worked at the store for sixteen years," Paolo insisted.

"Paolo, The Dime threatened to kill me if I don't testify. I have to go to the Pittsburgh police tomorrow," Mangia Dorm cried. Lowering his head again, Mangia Dorm explained. "Andoloni wants me to say that I was the witness that Corbett referred to in his file. I have to say that you and your brother and I were working for Yamin to burn down his building."

Angry but confused, Paolo threw up his hands. "You are unbelievable! You kill Eugico and now you want to kill me! Get out of here!"

Mangia Dorm slowly stood up, never making eye contact, and hurriedly walked out the Sinclair Street exit. He was afraid Paolo would change his mind and take out his anger and revenge on him.

Paolo had immediately understood; he would be charged with murdering his own brother. Murder is not a charge that has a statute of limitations. A case from sixteen years ago in which all the evidence had been destroyed and witnesses too far removed to be found still could be tried.

Rosalia watched as Mangia Dorm walked out of the store, and her husband just standing and staring into the blank wall in the storage area. Recognizing something was terribly wrong, she excused herself from the only customer in the store. She knew her husband needed her. "Paolo, what is wrong? What did Mangia Dorm say to you?"

"Nothing, Rose, I don't feel well. I am going to walk home. Tell John to close the store, and I will see you at home." Paolo kissed his wife on the cheek, turned to the Sixth Street door, and headed home.

Sitting at the kitchen table in his home alone, Paolo begged for guidance from his father. But all he heard was silence. He felt truly alone for the first time in his life. He laid his coin on the table and stared at it, thinking his good luck charm would bring an idea to him. It did not. He knew he had no choice but to capitulate to the union's demand.

This organization was able to convince a judge to postpone his suit for a permanent injunction, revoke his gun permit, stop customers from visiting his store, and prevent him from purchasing fruit and vegetables for his business. There was no doubt in Paolo's mind that they could convince a jury that a Sicilian immigrant would conspire with his brother and other criminals to commit arson and murder. Paolo could fight physically and economically for his American right to operate his business, but he could not fight if the government stole his liberty. He could not risk going to jail. His family needed him. Joseph, just discharged from four years of army war duty, needed time to adjust to civilian life. John, though a smart and dedicated worker, did not have the experience or necessary skills to challenge the Teamsters. Paolo felt inadequate in this fight. He did not want to put his favorite son through it. James was too young; he was still in high school. This being 1945, a woman, even one as intelligent as Rosalia, would never receive the respect or understanding of the court or its attorneys. His only choice was to instruct his attorney to end this fight. Paolo Lomeo would soon be a Teamster. The thought repulsed him.

Paolo arose from the table resolved in his course of action and ready to move on with his life. He picked up the coin from the table and before placing it in his pocket, he held it in his open right hand to stare at Lady Liberty impressed into the coin. Lady Liberty had previously held Paolo spellbound. She seemed to look at him, and her look always reassured Paolo. However, this day, Lady Liberty provided him no comfort. She looked sad and sorry that a good American would incur such treatment from the American court system. Paolo thought if the judge had done his job, Andoloni would not have had the opportunity to pressure Paolo to join the union. He placed the coin in his pocket and started from his home to Bielski's office. The twelve-minute walk seemed like a long walk to the gallows. He dreaded telling Bielski and having to admit defeat to a bully.

Anxiously, Attorney Benjamin Jubelirer waited in his office for the telephone call he feared the most. Every day since the strike began, Jubelirer would provide an update to a Washington, D.C., attorney, James Tomasello. Jubelirer really did not know who Tomasello represented or advised or his connection to the Teamsters, though Andoloni paid close attention to any order given by Mr. Tomasello.

His secretary knocked and opened his office door without waiting for Jubelirer's customary "yeah" and quizzically said that Mr. Tomasello was waiting for him. As he reached for the bulky telephone on the credenza behind his desk, the secretary, realizing her boss misunderstood, excitedly said, "Mr. Tomasello is not on the phone; he is in the waiting room."

Never having met Tomasello, and knowing him only from reputation, he understood that Tomasello did not accept excuses and only wanted results. Didn't he have the judge deny Bielski's temporary injunction? Didn't the judge postpone the hearing for the permanent injunction? Wasn't Lomeo's business basically closed, no produce to sell, nor customers to sell to? Why did Tomasello bother to travel from D.C. to Pittsburgh to see him in person instead of calling?

Rising from his chair and skipping with girly steps, Jubelirer opened the door and entered his waiting room in one skip. Trying to alleviate the tension that he felt upon seeing Tomasello, Jubelirer said, "Mr. Tomasello, I presume."

James Tomasello presented himself well. He was dressed in a gray three-piece suit, white handkerchief in his left coat pocket, a blue and yellow striped tie knotted with a dimple in the middle, all accented with black shoes polished with a shine. This was a man that commanded respect. "Yes."

Jubelirer, standing slightly stooped and head lowered, greeted Tomasello with a wimpy handshake while introducing himself. "I am Ben Jubelirer. Well, I guess you know that."

Mr. Tomasello, looking perturbed, asked, "Mr. Jubelirer, could we have a private conversation in your office instead of your waiting room?"

"Yes, of course, please follow me." Tomasello walked ahead of Jubelirer through the waiting room and opened door into Mr. Jubelirer's officer where the secretary had stood as a statue, afraid to move until ordered by her boss. "Ruth, don't just stand there. Get Mr. Tomasello a cup of coffee."

"Excuse me, Mr. Tomasello. I am sorry. Do you take your coffee black?" asked the secretary.

"No, thank you. I never drink coffee. But a glass of Coke or water would be fine."

"No problem, Mr. Tomasello. I can go downstairs to the restaurant in the lobby and get you a Coca-Cola." The secretary, Ruth Mikuska, had thought how polite and gentlemanly Tomasello acted, especially compared to her boss. She could never dream of working with an attorney of Tomasello's caliber due to her limited education and experience.

"Excuse me, young lady, where are you from?" Tomasello asked Ruth before she exited the room.

Ruth responded, "I live in Bloomfield with my parents."

"No, no, Ruth, Mr. Tomasello doesn't know where Bloomfield is. She lives in the city. She lives in the Italian part of the city. That part is called Bloomfield." Jubelirer tried to act as professional as Tomasello while he embarrassed Ruth for her lack of sophistication. She blushed in embarrassment, and Tomasello felt her uneasiness, and now knew why his Teamsters friends lacked a thoughtful game plan to unionize the independent grocers. Ruth did not look Italian. She was too tall and her face too round to be of Italian descent.

"Are you Italian then?" Tomasello inquired.

With a chuckle Jubelirer interjected, "No, she is not Italian. Her pa works at the Iron City Beer plant, and it is in Bloomfield."

Turning away from Ruth's glance and glancing at Jubelirer in a menacing and intimidating way, Tomasello said, "Quit interrupting our conversation. She is perfectly able to speak for herself." Feeling that Ruth must tolerate and endure these little slights each day, Tomasello thought of his own mother's struggles when she first came to America. "You weren't born in the U.S. I can tell. You said Coca-Cola. I wasn't born here either, but I try to avoid the little slips that will give it away. Say Coke next time. OK?"

Feeling happy that a professional man respected her, she said, "Yes sir, I will remember." With a smile she said, "I will get your Coke now." She left for the lobby restaurant a more confident woman than this morning.

"Please, sit down, Mr. Tomasello. You must be tired from your travels."

Tomasello remain standing, so Jubelirer did not dare sit down even though he desperately wanted to sit to stop his knees from shaking. Jubelirer inquired, "How can I help you? Everything is in order."

Tomasello was upset. "No, everything is not in order. You are letting a small-time grocer named Roma give our friends such a difficult time."

Jubelirer, wanting to protect his job and defend his representation, said, "The court postponed the case. The judge liked my argument. He will agree with me. I am sure of it."

"I am not sure of it. Didn't Roma get his fruit regardless of the strike?" Tomasello retorted.

"Yes, but that is it. No one will sell him any produce. He will be out of business within a week."

"If he is not and appeals any court decision, it could set a precedent. This case could affect our other strikers across the country. You should have had the men at night take Roma's produce out of the warehouse and deliver it to his store. There wouldn't have been all this publicity, and the other grocers wouldn't have realized it. You have to think!"

Jubelirer explained, "Mr. Tomasello, I received a called from Don Andoloni right before you came here. He said Lomeo is dropping his suit tomorrow. Andoloni had something on Lomeo and told him to drop the suit or else. I guess a little blackmail goes a long way." For the first time in their brief meeting, Jubelirer felt the equal of Tomasello.

He thought to himself—since he did not have the courage to say it out loud—we Pittsburghers can handle things. We don't need to have some D.C. attorney talk to us like children.

Puzzled and looking awkward, Tomasello said, "Who is Lomeo? Now it was Jubelirer's turn to act confident and all knowing.

"Lomeo is the grocer. His name is not Roma, that is just the name of his store. People do call him Paul Roma, but his actual name is Paolo Lomeo."

"Paolo Lomeo from Bagheria?"

"I never heard of Bagheria, but Andoloni told me Lomeo had emigrated from Sicily in the twenties, though I am unsure of the town."

Shaking his head, smiling with approval, Tomasello remembered his conversations with a young Paolo Lomeo years ago in Northern Italy. "Are you able to arrange an appointment with Mr. Lomeo?" asked Tomasello.

Jubelirer said, "I will contact Lomeo's attorney to see if they are willing to meet with you and me."

Excusing his lack of clarity, Tomasello said he was not asking to meet with Paolo's attorney and Jubelirer. "Excuse me, Mr. Jubelirer. I want to meet with Paolo alone."

"This is highly unusual. Andoloni will not like it," a surprised Jubelirer said.

"Mr. Jubelirer, just arrange it. I don't work for Andoloni. Andoloni is a small-time thug. You listen to me," Tomasello angrily responded.

Jubelirer had mistakenly and inadvertently questioned Tomasello's authority. Never a good idea in dealing with people in Tomasello's line of work. Immediately realizing his mistake, Jubelirer said, "I will see what I can arrange. I am sure I can do it."

Bielski and Paolo met that afternoon to discuss their course of action. Currently, the court's agenda for tomorrow was the hearing on the permanent injunction, and Bielski's new motion asking the court to order Chief Rodkey to return Paolo's gun and reinstate the gun permit.

"Mr. Bielski, I have to quit the fight." Paolo explained his visit by Mangia Dorm. "I can't risk a lengthy murder trial, even though it's untrue. Look at what they have done so far. It isn't hard to imagine that they could buy a jury to find me guilty."

Paolo and Bielski knew Jubelirer and Andoloni had outmaneuvered them, and it was best not to delay the final outcome a day longer. Local 944 still would prevent him from purchasing goods at Walling & Company, prevent him from storing his produce at Federal Cold Storage Company, and not remove the picket line. Paolo had to settle the case.

Bielski agreed. "Once you settle the case and join Local 944, your business operations would not be interfered with any longer."

"I hope. But I am not sure of anything," Paolo said. Paolo left Bielski's office after agreeing to meet Bielski in court tomorrow, Wednesday, October 10, 1945.

Chapter 11

Prophet in the Wilderness?

Below the fold on page one of the October 10, 1945, edition of The Pittsburgh Press the bold headline that brought cheer to some and sadness to others read, "PRODUCE MAN GIVES UP FIGHT, DECIDES TO JOIN UNION, Lomeo, Blasting Courts and Police, Says T h e r e ' s Nothing Else He can Do." The reporter wrote, "Paul Lomeo threw in the sponge today and decided to join the union. The stocky McKeesport fruit and produce dealer, who was the first independent merchant to resist current efforts of the produce workers to unionize them, agreed to sign up as a member of Local 944, Commission House Drivers and Produce Workers. The union got a $10 initiation fee and dues of $3 for one month from Mr. Lomeo. Mr. Lomeo through his attorney, Alexander J. Bielski, made it plain that he was not joining because he wants to. He is joining, he said, because:

> "I have appealed to the Courts; I have appealed to all law agencies for the protection of my business, my property and myself, I have received nothing. Court proceedings are ignored, legal actions are hindered and delayed, and my last means of defense—a permit to carry a gun—today was taken away from me. In order to protect my business and the well-being of my family and myself, I have resigned to the inevitable and have joined Local 944. I refused to be a Prophet in the Wilderness."

Before signing the statement prepared by his attorney, Mr. Lomeo listened attentively as his son Joseph, a veteran of four years in service and discharged only a few days ago, read it to him in Italian.

Mr. Lomeo nodded resignedly, picked up a pen and signed. "What else can I do?" he asked as he laid down the pen. "I can't get police to protect me or the court either."

After paying his thirteen dollars to Harvey Bierman, business agent of the union, and signing his application for membership, Mr. Lomeo found he was suddenly back in business.

Mr. Bierman telephoned Walling & Co at Johnstown and instructed that firm that they could sell produce to Mr. Lomeo without getting into any future difficulty. Walling & Co employes had been called out on strike for doing it once.

Mr. Bierman also telephoned the Federal Cold Storage & Co and said it would be all right for Mr. Lomeo to move his merchandise from the warehouse."

Even though Bielski had filed a motion for the return of Paolo's gun, Bielski and Paolo learned through Freddy, Judge Challener's clerk, that Chief Rodkey would return Paolo's permit and gun as soon as Paolo joined the union. There was never a hearing regarding the gun issue, and Paolo's gun and permit were waiting for him when he returned to Roma's.

Jubelirer offered to shake Paolo's hand as Paolo was exiting the courtroom. "Mr. Lomeo, no hard feelings. You are one of us now. Call me if you need anything."

Paolo stared in disbelief at Jubelirer and just walked passed him to the door and into the courthouse hallway. Walking down the hallway, Paolo heard in Sicilian, "Don Lomeo, please wait, I need to talk to you." Turning around, Paolo faced the well-dressed James Tomasello, and he thought that the last twenty-seven years had treated Don Tomasello well.

Recognizing his old attorney, though confused as to why he was here today, Paolo greeted his old friend by saying, "It is nice to see a friendly face."

Tomasello asked Paolo in Sicilian, "Do you have a moment to talk confidentially?"

Entering a coffee shop a few blocks from the courthouse, both men sat down, joining the late-morning customers for their coffee break. Tomasello insisted on calling Paolo "Don Lomeo" as a sign of respect and refusing Paolo's offer to call him Paolo. "Don Lomeo, you deserve the honor. You are a man of principle."

James Tomasello worked with large business corporations and knew presidents, senators, and Congress members, whereas Paolo had one small store with no employees with few dollars saved for his retirement. "I should be addressing you as Don. You helped me so many years ago when you didn't have to."

Tomasello believed otherwise. Tomasello explained, "I have to confess to you. I have been following your case. I represent the Teamsters' headquarters. I called Jubelirer every day for updates and to give him advice. I didn't know it was you. Jubelirer kept referring to Roma or Roma's Fruit Market. I never heard the name Lomeo until yesterday in Jubelirer's office."

"I understand. You were just doing your job. It's OK," Paolo reassured Tomasello.

"No, it is not OK. This was unfair to you. I should have known it was you. You would be the only person with the courage and stubbornness to fight with the Teamsters and Pittsburgh's political establishment," Tomasello said with a slight smile and small touch of pride.

Feeling uncomfortable and wanting to just go home, Paolo said, "It's OK." Continuing his explanation, almost ignoring Paolo's presence, Tomasello tried to explain the political situation. "Truman is not happy with all unions at the moment. These post-war strikes by all the unions are putting a vise grip on the economy. But the Teamsters' president told Truman if he did not agree with us, we would not support him in the upcoming elections. We couldn't have a regular guy win a fight with the union. It would have given fuel to Truman's fire." Tomasello wanted Paolo to have the full picture so he could understand Tomasello's actions. "Don Lomeo, forgive me! I should have handled this better."

Paolo accepted his friend's apology. "Don Tomasello, I have thought of you often. It's funny, during this fight I kept thinking if

Don Tomasello was my attorney, this case would have been over in minutes." "Your attorney is a good attorney. He made the right arguments. He just didn't understand the politics of it."

"That is my point," Paolo said, shaking his head in agreement.

"I accept your apology. You didn't need to do so though." Giuseppe had always taught his children to accept a sincere apology.

Today was surreal. Paolo had gone into court as a defeated man, and now he again felt that he controlled his destiny. He asked Tomasello, "Why do you feel it necessary to make sure I respect and forgive you?"

Don Tomasello said, "You remind me of my father. My father believed in the American ideal that all men are equal and that the good Americans should assist each other to ensure that the evil Americans do not turn America into another corrupt European country.

"No one had defended your rights and I had as much to do with it as anyone. I called my wife last night and told her about what had happened. How I met a man I knew years ago when I was a good man. I lost my way. The money and power intoxicated me. My father had warned me not to be tempted by the gold.

"I am glad my father is not alive to see what I have become over the last twenty years."

Paolo disagreed and said, "I am sure that your father would be proud of your financial success and social status. I hope the same for my boys."

The ambassador, as some people still referred to Tomasello, knew Paolo was being kind. "Thank you for the kind words." Self-confessing out loud, not really talking to Paolo but to his own father, Tomasello continued, "My father wanted me to become an honorable person. A person willing to give up material wants to protect the rights of those less fortunate. I should have done this for you, a fellow Sicilian."

"You didn't know it was me. You did help me. Remember, you helped me when I was a young soldier. You got me out of that murder charge."

Paolo subconsciously must have imitated his long-time friend, as he also started self-confessing out loud, but not to Tomasello. He seemed to want to get twenty-seven years of guilt off his soul. Paolo continued, "I still carry the guilt of killing the Frenchman for the last twenty-seven years. I never had the chance to tell my father, as my father died soon after I returned from the war. I never had the courage to tell my wife. I feel guilty that I didn't tell her after all these years. I don't want her to think of me as a bad person."

Reaching his hand across the table and patting his younger friend on the arm, Tomasello said, "You did not kill the French doctor! The doctor was seriously wounded, and the hospital doctors thought he might die, but he recovered and returned to France. In fact, the doctor's brother joined the doctor in helping the Nazis when the Germans invaded France in 1940. I guess in hindsight, it may have been better if you had killed that damn Frenchman."

Paolo could not believe what he was hearing. He had carried this burden all these years, and he had not even killed the doctor.

October 10, 1945, may have seemed a difficult day for Paolo Lomeo, if one was to read the newspapers, but if one had spoken with Paolo, he would have said this was one of the best days of his life.

Parting company, Paolo and Don Tomasello walked toward Paolo's car. Tomasello assured Paolo, "I will talk to Andoloni to make sure you have no further trouble with my clients or Andoloni. He will follow my instructions."

Paolo again thanked his friend and said, "I would be proud if my youngest boy could be an attorney like you."

Smiling and shaking his head in disagreement, James Tomasello told Paolo, "Tell your son to choose another line of work. He will meet a better class of people."

This would be the last time the two friends would see each other; both would be dead within a year and a half.

Chapter 12

What price faith?

The below paragraph is an exact reprint from the Editorial Page of The Pittsburgh Press, October 11, 1945.

"PAUL LOMEO is now a member of Local 944, Commission House Drivers and Produce Workers, A.F. of L.

"It cost him $13 in cash and the pride he had in his American citizenship. It cost him his belief in the justice of the courts. It cost him his belief that policemen live up to their oaths to uphold the law without fear or favor.

"Mr. Lomeo didn't want to join the union. Why should he? He wasn't an employ of anyone. He owned a business. He doesn't have any employes. His fruit and produce business in McKeesport was built up by himself in 20 years of hard work. Helping him to run it now are three sons and Mrs. Lomeo.

"One of those sons was discharged from the Army a few days ago after serving 35 months and taking part in 10 battles. He was out fighting for the preservation of the things his father believed in.

"But whether or not Mr. Lomeo wanted to join the union made no difference to the union. It had decided to organize the small independent dealers and grocers who drove their own trucks to the Pittsburgh produce yards.

"This decision was in violation of the union's signed agreement with the wholesalers. When the wholesalers insisted upon observing that agreement, the union called their employes out on strike. The union members gain nothing individually from this strike but the opportunity to watch their leaders take in new members at $13 a crack.

"Mr. Lomeo wasn't going to be coerced into joining. He went to court when he couldn't get his produce out of a warehouse because of union interference. His petition for an injunction against this interference was refused. But Mr. Lomeo wasn't licked yet.

"His attorney got a writ of replevin, which permitted him to get some of his produce from the warehouse. His next problem was to transport it to his store in McKeesport without interference.

"He appealed to the police for an escort. Pittsburgh police turned him down. The lone policeman on duty in Dravosburg did not. He escorted him through that borough.

"But McKeesport, his home city, where he raised his family, where he pays his taxes, where he built up a business and a reputation as a good citizen, let him down.

"The police chief not only refused him an escort, but also took away the permit he had held to carry a gun to protect his life and property. According to Mr. Lomeo's attorney, Alexander J. Bielski, Police Chief Guy Rodkey called Mr. Lomeo, a 'strike breaker.'

"Is it any wonder that Mr. Lomeo finally gave up the fight and join the union?

"Is it any wonder that he doesn't understand now what his son was fighting for almost four years?

"Mr. Lomeo saw what the union could do for him after it had his money. He saw the business agent pick up a telephone and call the cold storage warehouse to tell them it was all right to deliver Mr. Lomeo's property to him. He saw him telephone a Johnstown dealer and tell him he could sell to Mr. Lomeo without having a strike close his plant.

"Mr. Lomeo was back in business.

"The courts didn't put him there. The police had no part in it. "ALL MR. LOMEO HAD TO DO WAS PAY $13- AND LOSE HIS FAITH."

Chapter 13

Is it over?

    Life returned to normal for the Lomeo family. Business revenues resumed to pre-strike levels, the old routine returned, and their family was whole again after four years of Joseph's army tour fighting the Japanese in the Pacific theater. Joseph slowly regained his posture as a civilian, while John's leadership in Roma's increased as Paolo slowly decreased his involvement in the store. Paolo believed his two sons could manage the store together. He had a similar feeling after he had left Sicily knowing his mother had a good manager for the farm. He secretly wished John and Joseph would eventually move the location of the store to a larger space, so Roma's could offer a greater variety of produce and hopefully expand into selling different types of cheeses.

    Paolo now turned his attention to his youngest son. It was his dream to have James go to college and become an attorney like Mr. Bielski or Don Tomasello. Even after all the injustice he had experienced, he hoped his son would go to law school and protect the rights of those less fortunate. Paolo felt rich, not with money, but with knowing his little American family had taken root in America and hopefully would grow into a large, strong American family. As John directed Joseph on the proper way to stack the boxes in the rear storage room, Paolo pulled his half dime from his pocket and flipped it in the air with pleasure.

    He suddenly heard John scream with pain, as Joseph accidentally placed a heavy box on John's hand. Taking his eyes from the coin to John, Paolo lost sight of the coin in midair and watched it hit the worn wooden floor and roll on its side under the front door on Sinclair Street. Knowing John was fine, Paolo rushed to the door and grabbed the coin before it ended in the storm drain below the curb. As the cold

December wind blew down Sinclair Street bringing a chill to Paolo, he was sure glad he did not lose his lucky charm on such a gray, miserable day.

Roma's Fruit Market was preparing for the busiest day of the holiday season, December 24. They had so much to do prior to tomorrow. Paolo told his sons, "John and Joe, I want you two to clean the store windows and stack the Christmas trees on Sinclair Street." In 1945, most people purchased their trees on the morning of Christmas Eve and decorated the tree that evening.

"OK, Pa. But we should leave some in the storage room so it looks like we are selling trees too quickly. Maybe we can charge a little more for the last few ones, if the customers feel desperate," John told his father.

"No, John. This is Christmas, and we only need to make our normal profit. Plus, some of these customers stayed with us through the strike," Paolo said.

Joseph and John began stacking the Christmas trees as instructed but were acting like two school kids giggling about girls instead of men of twenty-eight and twenty-six years old, respectively. They had plans together this evening. John asked, "Pa, can Joe and I go home early tonight? I have arranged a double date with Geneva and her girlfriend." Always one to negotiate, and happy to see his sons bonding together after so many years apart, Paolo said, "Yes, but you two have to open the store on time tomorrow. Also, you have to work all day. I am staying home this Christmas Eve." Paolo trusted John. If John said he would open the store on time and stay late until the store closed, Paolo did not have to worry.

John agreed, "OK. But I was going to take Jimmy to purchase a new suit for his graduation tomorrow. Can you take him to the Famous for the suit?" James would be the first Lomeo to graduate from high school. Buying a suit six months before graduation only manifested their pride in this accomplishment.

The art of negotiating seemed to run in their family, and with a chuckle and slap on the back, Paolo agreed. "Go ahead, boys. Have fun but be careful. Remember you have to get up early." John and Joseph left for home.

Being home from the war and ready to return to a normal life, Joseph was excited to have a date. Rosalia, however, was not as excited. After the boys departed the store, Rosalia angrily told Paolo, "Paolo, don't encourage John to date Geneva. This can only lead to trouble for us."

Paolo laughed and addressed her by her American name. "Rose, what are you worried about?" Most of Roma's customers were middle-class folks, either immigrants or first-generation Americans from all parts of Europe. Going by the name Rose was the same as using the name Mary; it was pleasing and non-offensive to all ethnicities.

Rosalia became even more irritated. "Paolo, you know encouraging this makes me mad. But you still do it!"

"Rose, please stop. We are in America now, and your temper is making me laugh too hard," Paolo said, still chuckling.

"John is a man and not a kid, and soon he will be married. How loud will you laugh if our grandchildren are not Italian?"

Paolo could think of worse problems than having grandchildren of mixed blood. Paolo's liberated mind showed his keen intelligence even while breaking a social taboo. Paolo told Rosalia, "Rose, you will just have to appreciate Sunday meals with pigs in a blanket."

This was the first good laugh Paolo had had in some time. Paolo closed up the store thinking about his upcoming day with James and having a day off from the store. He thought, for the first time, that he deserved the day off, especially after all that he had been through this year.

At 3:10 a.m. on December 24, 1945, the telephone rang like a bad tune throughout the home at 618 Fairview Avenue, McKeesport, Pennsylvania. Half asleep, James stumbled out of bed to answer the telephone. It was Joseph talking, or more like crying, but not making any sense. "Jimmy, get Pop. Get Pop! John is dead!"

Hearing the words but not comprehending, James screamed into the receiver, "Joe, stop it! Come home, get out of the bar. It is late." Finally, James understood Joseph's words and yelled for his father in Sicilian. "Pa, come quickly! There is real trouble!"

Paolo slowly rose out of bed, thinking why they could not just let him sleep. James, with tears streaming down his face, handed the telephone receiver to his father. Joseph did not have the courage to tell his father that John was dead. Now crying uncontrollably he said, "Pa, come to the hospital quickly. John is hurt badly."

McKeesport Hospital was located only a mile from their home. Paolo and James left without telling Rosalia. She remained in a peaceful sleep, the last night she rested peacefully until her death on December 13, 1978.

Father and son arrived at the emergency room and encountered Joseph covered in blood. His head, hands, suit jacket, pants, and shoes had John's blood painted in large blotted splashes. James fainted and hit his head on a waiting room chair, bouncing on and off the floor before resting face down. The attending nurse ran to treat James, who required six stitches in his head.

Joseph hugged his father, crying and explaining what had happened. The front page, column three of The Daily News, McKeesport, PA of December 24, 1945, covered the story succinctly without the gruesome details. The headline read "McKeesporter Fatally injured When Hit By Automobile," and the article continued, "Lomeo was killed instantly about 2:45 am today when he was struck by a car while fixing a flat tire on his own automobile. The accident occurred on Fifth Avenue near Forest Avenue in East McKeesport, according to Police Chief Miller and Patrolman Henry Lenhart. The officers said Lomeo, his brother Joseph, and another passenger, had pulled to the curb along the street to change the tire which had gone flat while they were enroute home. John was kneeling beside the left rear wheel when he was struck by Arthur J. Fry, a soldier, residing at 7120 McClure Avenue, Swissvale, Pennsylvania. The victim was brought to

McKeesport Hospital where he was pronounced dead of a fractured skull and other injuries."

Telling Rosalia that her favorite son was dead would not be easy. Paolo helped a still dizzy James and carefully watched Joseph as they walked toward the car. Joseph was still in shock from this Christmas Eve tragedy. All the living male Lomeos came home together in a state of disrepair to face the only female of the household. Sensing something was wrong, Rosalia nervously asked, "Where is John?"

Seeing Joseph covered in blood, Paolo reached Rosalia just as she fainted and fell to the floor of their small kitchen. Lying on the floor together, both knew that their lives would never be the same. James and Joseph watched forlornly as the ball of human flesh comprised of their parents shook in grief.

During this time, Paolo continued working at the store and doing the things he did every day but without the same energy and desire.

He had to conduct business with people in a state of disbelief. Here he was working at the store, while his son lay in his home for the funeral viewing. The only day he did not go to the store was on the day of the funeral. John was laid to rest a few days after Christmas at St. Joseph Catholic Cemetery in North Versailles, Pennsylvania, a township located adjacent to McKeesport.

Knowing that he had to continue his life and provide for his family, he struggled each day to head to work. The confusing part was that the police never came to interview Joseph or inform Paolo when charges would be filed against Arthur Fry. After about two months, Paolo contacted the East McKeesport Police and asked for the status of the case. Chief Miller told Paolo, "We are unable to find Fry. We can't interview him if we can't find him."

"The paper said he was in the army. Did you check with them? Did you go to his home in Swissvale?" Paolo asked.

The chief responded, "District Attorney Artemas Leslie told us to let the case sit, as his office will not prosecute Mr. Fry."

Without any explanation, his son's murder could not raise the interest of any law enforcement officers, but his small insignificant fruit market grabbed the interest of the whole Pittsburgh region. Even his friend James Tomasello, a D.C. attorney, had been involved in his fight with the Teamsters. Now, for some reason, a death of a human being could not interest any person in authority.

Thinking of his friend Don Tomasello, he remembered that his friend had told him at their last meeting to call if Paolo had any problems. However, Paolo did not know how to find him. He called and asked Attorney Bielski if he could track down James Tomasello. After a few days, Bielski gave Paolo the telephone number to Scott & Johnson, a Washington, D.C., law firm, where Tomasello worked. Scott & Johnson had deep political connections, especially with the Democratic Party.

Later that day, Bielski called his grocer friend. "Paolo, I decided to call Mr. Tomasello for you."

"Great! Did you tell him what happen to John? Can he help?"

"Paolo, I have bad news. Tomasello is dead. He died a few days ago."

"How? Was he sick?" Paolo inquired, knowing Bielski did not have the answers.

"I don't know, the receptionist at the law firm wouldn't tell me. She just told me he died and nothing more," Bielski said, actually not believing he could not get the information.

"Will there be a viewing? What paper would have it?"

Wanting to help his grieving friend, Bielski said, "I will find out. Probably the Washington Post. I will let you know as soon as I find out."

Paolo's instincts told him that Tomasello's employer not revealing the details of his friend's death was in some way related to John's death. Contacting the Washington Post, Bielski learned a little information about Tomasello's death and the funeral arrangements. Placing a call to his client, Bielski explained, "Paolo, Tomasello was killed while crossing a street."

Hearing the words brought chills to Paolo; too coincidental to his son's death. "Did the paper say what happened?"

"Yes, Mr. Tomasello was crossing Wisconsin Avenue at M Street in Georgetown at around one p.m. I guess he was walking back to his office from lunch when a car hit him."

"Georgetown, I thought he worked in Washington. Where is Georgetown?"

Bielski explained, "Georgetown is a section of Washington, D.C. It is an affluent and influential part of the city."

Paolo, already knowing the answer, asked, "Did the person stop? Do they know who was driving the car?"

"No, it was a hit and run. I called the Washington, D.C., police department. They have no idea who was driving. No witnesses could be found."

His fears being confirmed by his attorney, Paolo shook his head and said, "Of course not. They made sure of that. Guess America is more like Sicily than I knew."

Bielski did not have to ask who "they" were. He knew Paolo meant the Mafia. "The viewing is in a couple of days, if you wanted to go. Drop by the office, and my secretary will give you the address to the funeral home."

Paolo decided to pay his respects and attend the viewing of his friend. After hanging up the telephone, he slowly walked with his head down across his small store to the customer counter to update Rosalia about Tomasello's death. Rosalia's face had a perpetual frown ever since John's death, one that would not leave her face until her own death some thirty-two years later.

"Rose, I want to go to Washington to pay my respect to Don Tomasello. Would you come with me? I don't feel well, and I don't want to drive by myself."

"Why should we go? We don't even know him. Isn't he the one that helped the union?"

"Rose, he was a good man. He lost his way for some time but he was a good man. He was the older brother I never had but always wanted. I never told you this and it may change your feelings for me."

"Paolo, I love you. Nothing would change my feelings for you. You know this already," Rosalia said as she hugged Paolo. Paolo could feel her grief for John in every muscle twitch in her body.

"When I was in the army I shot someone and was charged with murder."

"Don't people in the army shoot other people all the time?" Rosalia asked, confused.

"No, I shot a French doctor on our side. He was a butcher and killed my friend. Anyway, that isn't important. Don Tomasello was a young American attorney who defended me at the court martial. The French wanted me executed that day, but Tomasello used his influence and had the case dismissed. I am not sure exactly what he did, but I was free to go home."

Paolo began to cry as a customer entered the store who then quickly turned around to leave. Paolo continued, "I never told anyone. I was so embarrassed and ashamed. I carried it with me during the trip home. The thought of me telling my father was unbearable. But I never had the chance. He would have comforted me. I carried this guilt for all these years. I never enjoyed my life because of the guilt."

"Paolo, you probably did nothing wrong. No one can fix a murder charge. Not even the great Don Tomasello," Rosalia said sarcastically.

"That isn't fair. You don't know what he did or didn't do. He was a true friend. Well, forget it, I will go by myself," Paolo angrily responded but knowing his wife's grief made her say a hurtful thing to him.

"I am sorry, Paolo. I will go with you."

"Can I finish my story?" Without waiting for Rosalia to respond, Paolo began, "Remember when I went to court and settled the case? Don Tomasello was in court. We had coffee together. He said he didn't know it was me. He would have stopped the case immediately if he did. Tomasello also said I didn't kill the French doctor. Don Tomasello said the doctor lived and became a French Nazi. I was so relieved when he told me."

"OK, that is why you came home happy that day. You left that morning looking sad and defeated. I was afraid you would do something dumb. Then you came home. You didn't mention the case and went on with business like you didn't have a care in the world. Jimmy even saw it. He asked me why Pop was so happy after losing the fight. I didn't have an answer for him. I will go with you for sure. Who will watch the store?"

"Joseph can. He knows enough to run it for a few days," Paolo said as he squeezed the only woman he ever loved really hard. The only other person that could ever squeeze a person they loved tighter would be Paolo's great-granddaughter, Juliet.

"Also, I think it will be good for us to get away for a few days together. We never really did that like true Americans," Paolo said with a smile. Rosalia nodded her head in agreement, smiling back at her husband.

Paolo was not feeling well. He did not want to travel alone for such a long distance. He felt lethargic, and his stamina seemed to be decreasing every day. Rosalia, always the loyal wife, agreed to go even though she wanted to stay home and never leave it. Today, she would have been diagnosed with mental depression.

The long trip did wonders for the grieving parents. Traveling over the Appalachian Mountains in Pennsylvania and Maryland to D.C. was one of the most scenic journeys the two had taken. Taking some time to find the funeral home in the busy area of Georgetown, Paolo and Rosalia were hesitant to enter the funeral home after they noticed the style of dress of the people going into and leaving the funeral home. Clearly, the people visiting Don Tomasello were men of respect and ladies of society. The suits and dresses were of the finest quality, and they strolled instead of walking through Georgetown. Paolo, knowing Rosalia was always somewhat self-conscious of her dress, told her, "We are here to visit our friend and the other people's concerns don't matter."

They entered the large lobby of the funeral home and immediately went to the viewing room with the most people. As they stood in line waiting their turn to give their sympathy, an elegant and refined woman at the head of the casket noticed Paolo and Rosalia. Their style gave them away. Mrs. Tomasello knew that Paolo and Rosalia were there out of true concern and not for public appearance or politics. She politely greeted them, "Thank you for coming to see my husband. How did you know him?"

Paolo said, "Your husband and I were old friends during my time in the Italian army. I was fortunate to see and talk to him recently when he visited Pittsburgh."

Mrs. Tomasello asked, "Sir, what is your name?"

"This is my wife, Rosalia, and my name is Paolo Lomeo."

As the last vowel of "Paolo Lomeo" left Paolo's lips, Mrs. Tomasello started to shake with fear.

"Please, can you follow me? I need to talk to you both," Mrs. Tomasello begged.

Finding a quiet place in the funeral home to talk, Mrs. Tomasello explained, looking straight into Paolo's eyes just like Paolo's mother used to do when he was a child. "You are not safe here. Don Lomeo and Mrs. Lomeo, I truly appreciate your concern to drive such a long way to pay your respects to my husband. But it wasn't a good idea. My husband told me what happened to you. He was afraid for your safety. I am afraid someone will recognize you here. You should leave as soon as you can."

Reaching to touch the grieving Mrs. Tomasello, Rosalia said, "We will leave if our presence is causing you problems. Paolo only wanted to show his respect for your husband."

Looking at Paolo, almost ignoring Rosalia's comments, Mrs. Tomasello said with sincere concern, "Your presence is not a problem for me. I am worried about you. You are easy prey in this city."

Paolo sensed her fear and wondered if she had knowledge of another assassination plan against the Lomeo family, namely himself. He thought she surely knew that the Mafia did not usually kill the wives of their targets. They killed only the men. Maybe she did not know, and her fear for Paolo's safety was actually her fear for her safety. Mrs. Tomasello did not act or look like her heritage was Italian. She seemed well educated and had the mannerisms and manners of high society. Paolo figured she had no idea how to care for herself without her husband.

"Mrs. Tomasello, please don't worry about me. I will be OK." Trying to ease her fear, he explained somewhat clumsily, "They don't usually attack the wife. I am not sure if you are familiar with their ways, but we are. But we will stay with you until you feel safe."

Just as she started to speak, a young lady walked into the private room. "Excuse me, Grandma, people are asking for you. What should I say?"

"Mr. Lomeo and Mrs. Lomeo, I would like to introduce you to my granddaughter, Lucia. Lucia, this is Mr. Lomeo and Mrs. Lomeo, good friends of your grandfather."

Nodding their heads, Paolo and Rosalia just smiled, not knowing what to say and feeling uneasy. Paolo finally said, "We are sorry for your loss. Your grandfather was a good man."

"Run along and I will come in a minute." With that Paolo and Rosalia were alone again with Mrs. Tomasello. "I appreciate the offer. I now see why my husband trusted and respected you so much. Even though I was born in the United States, my parents came from Catania. As you will probably find out someday, I may as well tell you now, my uncle was Giuseppe Esposito."

All Sicilian-Americans were familiar with the name Giuseppe Esposito. According to the Federal Bureau of Investigation, Giuseppe Esposito was the first Sicilian Mafia member to immigrate to America after allegedly murdering the chancellor, vice chancellor, and eleven wealthy landowners in Sicily. He was eventually extradited to Rome in 1881 to stand trial for the murders.

"I am not worried about my safety. My family has already made arrangements to solve my problems," said Mrs. Tomasello.

Rosalia seemed confused about her statement, but not Paolo. Paolo knew by "arrangements" she meant that her safety was guaranteed and retribution would visit the people who ordered and committed the murder of her husband.

Feeling a little stupid thinking he knew more than a well-educated lady of society and the niece of a Mafia boss, Paolo said, "Well, we have a long trip home. We will leave you with your family. Again, we are sorry for your loss."

"Don Lomeo, please be careful. You don't have any protection. My family can't help since you are not part of their society. They will try to hurt you or your sons."

Rosalia began to cry as Mrs. Tomasello finished her warning. Unable to control herself, Rosalia blurted out, "They have already killed our son! The day before Christmas!"

Paolo hurriedly hugged his wife and apologized to Mrs. Tomasello. "It has been hard for us this last month. I was trying to get a hold of Don Tomasello to see if he could help me. The police will not investigate our son's killing."

Mrs. Tomasello's heart began racing as she became light-headed. She had to take a seat before she fainted and collapsed on the floor. Paolo sighted a pitcher of water on the little table in the corner of the room. He ran to it, filled a glass with the water, and handed it to Mrs. Tomasello.

Regaining her composure she said, "Please, wait here." She left the room and headed directly toward the telephone in the hallway of the funeral home. Her conversation with the unknown person seemed to Paolo and Rosalia to last for hours, when in reality it was a short conversation of a few minutes.

Returning to Paolo and Rosalia, she hugged Rosalia as one mother does to comfort another mother. "I am so sorry for your loss.

You didn't have to drive all this way. I am sorry I didn't know this had happened. You will not have any more problems. Don Lomeo, no one will cause you harm from now on. I can't say how I know, but please believe me."

Paolo understood without being told. Her telephone call was to her family, and the message would be sent to the Pittsburgh Mafia to stand down against the Lomeo family. "Thank you, Mrs. Tomasello."

Though they were at different stations in society, Don Tomasello and Paolo Lomeo were men of the same fabric. Paolo wondered what type of person he would have become if he had the opportunities and temptations that Tomasello experienced. Would he have remained a person his father could be proud of? Or would he have been seduced by the glitter of money and power?

Saying good-bye, Rosalia and Mrs. Tomasello held each other for a long time and in Sicilian blessed each other. Mrs. Tomasello then turned to address Paolo. "Thank you for helping my husband."

"Pardon me. I didn't help your husband. He helped me."

She continued, not acknowledging Paolo's comment. "As a young man my husband was a person to be proud of, but as he became more well-known and richer, he lost his way. He became everything his father hated. That all changed a few months ago when he met with you, Don Lomeo, last October.

"He told me that you were a man his father would have been proud of. You defended yourself, and believed in yourself, regardless of your material success. James Tomasello had an epiphany. His father talked about success and respect, but he did not mean financial success or the fake respect it brought. He meant success in raising a morally based family and having dignity and honor as a person. His epiphany led to his death, though his Lord will forgive him since he repented prior to his death."

The years of 1946 and 1947 were eventful for America with the post-war boom on. But for Paolo the days seemed to drag on longer as the years churned on. The only bright spot was the birth of Joseph's first son on March 15, 1947. Rosalia asked Joseph to violate the old Sicilian rule of naming the first son after the paternal grandfather by naming this new life after her dead son. Joseph, not wanting to disappoint his mother, named his first son John in honor of his dead brother.

With Paolo feeling worse every day over the last year, his sons convinced him that he should see a doctor. Being a true Lomeo, visiting a doctor meant he was really sick, and he was. Paolo trusted his doctor, Dr. Hebner. Dr. Hebner had settled in McKeesport after graduating from The Ohio State University. He had met his wife, Natalie, at a charity dance held at a church in Upper Arlington, Ohio. Natalie Hebner was raised in McKeesport and wanted to raise her family there.

Dr. Hebner had known Paolo for a long time but hadn't seen him since the death of his son. Seeing Paolo for the first time in the waiting room of his medical office full of patients, Dr. Hebner could not hide his reaction. "Paolo are you OK? What is wrong? Come with me now!" Dr. Hebner's concern frightened Paolo.

"Doctor, I can wait. You have these other patients," Paolo nervously said, not wanting to face the medical issue he knew he had.

Paolo followed the doctor through the waiting room door into a hallway with two rooms on each side. Pointing to the first door on the right, Dr. Hebner instructed, "Paolo, go in. I will be in in a second. Strip down to your tightie-whities."

When Dr. Hebner entered the exam room Paolo was sitting on the exam table with his head down. "Paolo, tell me what is going on. How are you feeling?"

"Well, I have been exhausted for some time. I get dizzy every once in a while, and I have these rashes all over," Paolo said, revealing the rash spots under his arms and on his legs.

"What about your ankles and feet?"

"They have been swelling up along with my hands."

Dr. Hebner performed the usual exam by checking Paolo's heart and lungs while taking notice of Paolo's difficulty with breathing. After some thought and a small time of silence, Dr. Hebner said, "Paolo, I don't have good news. Your kidneys are failing."

"What does that mean? Is there medicine I can take?"

"Paolo, there is no cure for this. You probably have a few weeks at most."

Stunned by the news, Paolo fainted and fell to the ground head first; fortunately, he did not seriously injure himself. Dr. Hebner rushed to turn Paolo on his back and put a warm compress on his head. Paolo finally regained consciousness and apologized to Dr. Hebner. "I am sorry. Now what do I do? Will it be painful?"

With the doctor's assistance, Paolo stood on his feet and then sat down on the exam table to hear Dr. Hebner's prognosis.

"Do you want me to take you home? I can explain it to Rose."

"No, I will be fine. I just don't want to be a burden on my family. They have had enough pain the last two years," Paolo said, gaining his composure.

Dr. Hebner hesitated but knew being blunt and concise was the best medicine to dealing with such shocking news. "Paolo, you will not be in any pain. Your body will shut down, and your breathing will become laborious."

Dr. Hebner noticed the confusion on Paolo's face after he spoke the word laborious. Trying to clarify he continued, "You will have a hard time breathing as your kidneys fail. As the kidneys fail the other organs, such as the lungs, will stop working. This will only happen in the last few hours of your life. You should prepare for it. You should prepare your family for it."

"I don't want my family to see me dying such a harsh death. This would be torture for Rosalia," Paolo spoke as he began to cry, thinking of the emotional pain his death would cause his family.

"Is there a way a avoid this?" Paolo asked, thinking he would drive away and die in the woods so his family would not be able to view his slow, cruel dance with life on this earth.

"Well, I can admit you to the hospital, and when you slip into an unconscious state, I will tell your family it is time to say good-bye. Until this time, you will be able to see and hear them and possibly speak to them. But once you are unconscious, you will still be alive medically, but your brain will not register their presence. Your laborious breathing will not start until you are unconscious. I will tell them that have you gone, and they will leave you, never witnessing your gasping for oxygen as your body involuntarily tries to breathe."

Paolo began feeling better and began to rise from his seated position when Dr. Hebner offered his arm for assistance. Paolo appreciated his friend's offer to do his best to ease his family's sadness and expressed it with a hug—an uncommon reaction among men in 1948. "Thank you, my friend. God be with you," Paolo said as he exited the exam room and headed for the exit door of the medical office.

After leaving Dr. Hebner's office, Paolo thought it would be best to take a drive to calm his nerves before telling his family. Paolo decided to leave McKeesport and head toward the woods he used for hunting in today's Monroeville, Pennsylvania. Parking his car on the dirt path into the woods, Paolo, without his shotgun, glided effortlessly into the woods. He felt like the young Paolo in Sicily who used to run instead of walk on his hunting trips with his father. Finally resting against a tree, sitting down with his back leaning on the tree trunk, he thought he heard his father calling him. "Paolo, Paolo, stay there. I want to talk to you."

Rising up, he stood to see a man resembling his father walking toward him. As the figure got closer, Paolo's heart rate rose. "Who are you? What do you want?" Paolo screamed.

"Paolo, it's me! Don't worry, it's me. It's your father."

Rubbing with his right hand the bump above his left eyebrow caused by the fall in Dr. Hebner's office, Paolo thought the bump caused him to hallucinate. Not believing his eyes, he ignored the man standing in front of him. Then Paolo had a sickening feeling that this man was not a hallucination, but a hired assassin working for the Mafia to finish their nasty business. Having left his shotgun in the car, Paolo began wondering how he would defend himself, especially now when his physical state would be no match for a Mafia hit man.

Holding his hands above his head to ease Paolo's visible state of agitation, Giuseppe said, "Paolo! Paolo, relax, son. It's me! I know it is hard to believe. Frankly, I am not sure how I got here either."

Paolo reached inside his sweater where his pistol would normally rest to indicate to this man that Paolo could defend himself. "Stay there. What do you want?"

The man stepped forward without concern that Paolo had a gun. "Paolo, it's your father. Believe me!"

Keeping his hands high above his head he continued to speak. "Let me tell you a story I am sure you never told anyone, not even me. Then you tell me if I have it right. Once when you were young you had a little trouble with Rabbi Roben. He recognized you. You begged him not to tell me. Am I right?"

As his vision became blurry, his ears began hearing a buzzing noise like a Spitfire plane was approaching, and his head felt like Joe Louis had hit with him with a quick left jab. Paolo fell silent and slowly sat down again against the tree. This man knew the story, but how? He was right. Paolo never told anyone that story. Paolo actually had forgotten about the incident, it was so many years ago. Looking up at the man and learning how to keep his senses the way his father had taught him, he said, "If I never told anyone, then how do you know about it?"

"You are always thinking. Rabbi and I had been friends for many years. He told me. He wanted to make sure I knew, so that you were not falling into a bad group like your brother Eugico did after I had gone. We agreed that I would not say anything to you, since we both thought keeping you guessing would keep you out of trouble. I guess Rabbi was right."

"You know about Eugico? I am sorry. I tried, but he just wouldn't listen to me."

"Paolo, it wasn't your fault. It was my fault for leaving too early. If I hadn't gone, Eugico may have been something important. He had the energy and attitude. His compass was pointed in the wrong direction. I am not sure who to blame, but it surely isn't you."

Recovering from his dizzy spell, Paolo slowly stood up to get a closer look at this man. Was this actually his father? Giuseppe stepped close enough to Paolo to touch him. He reached out and placed his hand on Paolo's shoulder. Paolo started to cry.

"Pa, things are so bad for me now. The doctor just told me I will die soon. My young boy is not even twenty years old, and my oldest boy is almost thirty. They both need me. They are lost and confused men."

"Paolo, I am sure they will be fine. You are a good man, and you have taught them well."

"Pa, that isn't true. I am afraid the last two years I haven't been much of a father. I didn't feel like doing anything but lying in bed. I am not sure if it was my disease or the death of John." Paolo assumed this spirit would know about John and his death. Giuseppe seemed confused and paused before hugging his son.

Paolo recognized his father's confusion. Even though he had not seen his father in years, he still knew his father better than anyone.

Trying to explain, Paolo said, "John was my middle son. We worked together at my store. He didn't go to the war. You know about the war?" Giuseppe shrugged his shoulders, signaling he did not know, but

Paolo just continued without further explanation. "He was a good boy, actually a man. I had a dispute with the Teamsters."

Giuseppe interjected without being rude, "Teamsters?"

"The Teamsters are a union controlled by the Mafia. Pa, America has the same Mafia we had in Bagheria. They are just as evil. They killed John."

Paolo started to cry again. "I killed John. I shouldn't have challenged them. I knew they would take revenge, and they did. I should have been like everyone else and ignored it, and let someone else deal with it. If I had, John would be alive, and my other two boys wouldn't be in such bad shape.

"John was the leader of the other two. Without John, I am afraid they will not know what to do or how to be a father in America."

Giuseppe consoled his son. He understood the heartache, and the feeling of desperation of words unsaid and advice not given. Giuseppe had the same feeling when he died. "I had so much to tell you before you left for America, but God never gave me the chance. I died suddenly. You have an opportunity to tell them what you need to tell them. Paolo, you may not realize it, but that is a wonderful gift. Most people regret they didn't say I love you to the people they loved before it was too late."

"You are right. I didn't have that opportunity with John, but I do with Joseph and James. I am just not sure what I should say to them. How do I give them fifty-two years of experience in a few days?"

"Just give them advice that can last forever. Tell them to be honest and understand that their behavior and actions will affect their children way after they are gone."

"OK, that is what I will say. What about John's death? The police won't investigate. No one will help me."

"I know you are a true American now. You said 'OK,'" Giuseppe proudly said. "If the police won't protect you, then you have to protect yourself. God is a just God. If the police won't prosecute and punish John's murderer, then you have the right to."

"John was hit by a car while changing a tire. Do I go after the driver?" Paolo asked, unable to articulate the word kill. He knew killing any human being was against the teaching of his church, so saying "go after" eased his mind for violating the Church's teachings.

"No, the driver was just the puppet. You can kill him, but you don't have time to take revenge on every bad actor in this play. You will die soon yourself. You need to kill the person who gave the order," Giuseppe explained, not afraid to use the word kill to pay back the person who killed his grandson.

"I am sure the Mafia gave the order. But I am not sure who in the Mafia."

His father asked, "After the death of John, did some person connected with the union seem especially thoughtful and forgiving?" "Yes, I thought it was strange but kind. My wife even questioned it, but thought old warriors became friends after a tragedy. Joey "The Dime" is the killer! I should have known," Paolo said, looking down at his muddy boots, not able to look at the disappointment in his father's eyes for being so naïve.

Joey "The Dime" Andoloni had spent an extraordinary amount time at John's funeral viewing. He also had the warehouse workers deliver Roma's produce directly to the store during the few weeks after John's death, saving Paolo the trip to Pittsburgh. Paolo, at the time, thought Don Tomasello's instructions to The Dime was Andoloni's motivation. A son continually learns from his father, even long after the father's death. "Paolo, it isn't your fault. Remember, I had many more years of experience dealing with the Mafia. My father explained it to me during the workers' strike before you were born. It is my fault. I should have known that the Mafia would be in America and try to force you to do bad things," Giuseppe reassured his son.

Paolo knew his father was only saying this to make him feel better, but hearing his father condone his inaction relieved his guilt about John's death.

Watching his father walking away, Paolo ran to him from behind with the 1870 Liberty Seated Half Dime in his hand. He handed it to his father, saying, "Patri, thanks for the coin. But I don't need it anymore."

Giuseppe, surprised by the offer, asked, "Why?"

Paolo told his father, "I have learned to handle life's problems on my own. I don't need to have a good luck charm. Anyway, it hasn't brought me any luck lately."

"You thought it was a good luck charm? Did you think I believed in luck?"

"Sorry, Pa, I didn't mean any disrespect. I know you relied on the coin for your salvation."

Giuseppe smiled and said, "If that's true, the coin didn't work. I never left Sicily. I died too early to see you grow into a man. I never saw any of my grandchildren. The coin wasn't for me. It was for you."

"I don't understand."

"Yes, finding an American coin was exciting to me. I kept the coin because the value to me was that it was from America. It made feel like an American. But once you were born, I knew I would never leave Sicily. I began thinking of the coin differently. I wanted you to have the coin as a reminder of me and realize that no matter how bad life seems it eventually becomes better after time."

Even though Paolo felt weak and dazed from seeing his father, he became fully cognizant that the 1870 Liberty Seated Half Dime was a symbol of hope and not a good luck piece. "I understand now, Pa. You wanted me to keep hope alive, so I wouldn't give up."

Giuseppe, full of pride, pulled his son's head close to his. "Paolo, I love you. I only wanted the best for you! You keep the coin and give it to your children."

"Which one?"

Giuseppe thought for a moment, realizing Paolo could not give one coin to two sons, knowing giving the coin to one would hurt the other son. "Well, I see your problem. Why don't we give the coin to John? Joseph and James are already in America, the land of hope. John is starting a new adventure. He may need to have hope to get through it."

Paolo smiled at his father. He had not felt this happy and completely satisfied since all those years back when his father and he would sit in the orchards discussing Paolo's future. "That is perfect. Will you give it to him?"

"Yes, I will make sure he has it," Giuseppe reassured his son. Paolo hated to depart with the only thing that reminded him of

Sicily, but he knew his father was right. He slowly reached into his pocket and handed the coin to Giuseppe. Giuseppe took the coin, gripping it with a smile. His long-last friend had come back for a visit.

Repeating the scene on the day of his death in Sicily thirty years before, Giuseppe casually walked away from Paolo. He continued walking down the valley and up the hill where he had come from. Paolo stood watching his father. Barely visible over the crest, Giuseppe glanced over his right shoulder, winked at Paolo, and said, "You handled the fire better than I could have. I am so proud of you! You were the best son a father could have. I love you!"

Then he disappeared.

Dr. Hebner called Rosalia after Paolo had left his office. He knew Paolo would never tell his wife that he was dying. Hebner wanted to make his friend's last days as easy as possible. When Paolo arrived home dragging himself through his front door, Rosalia was waiting for him. He could tell from her face that she knew. Paolo was relieved that his friend had called and explained it to Rosalia. He did not have the will or want to discuss it with his beloved wife. She rushed to him, held him tight, and said, "I love you. I am here for you."

"Rosalia, I love you. I am glad I met you. I was surprised that you agreed to marry me. I hope I was a good husband."

With tears streaming down her cheek and her body shaking with grief, she said, "Paolo, marrying you was the best decision I ever made. I never regretted it. Now let's get you to bed. You had a long day. You need to rest!"

Paolo agreed, and as he rested in bed he tried to tell Rosalia about seeing his father in the woods. She told Paolo, "Please sleep. You are worn out. You need to save your strength. We can talk about it tomorrow."

Paolo died that evening, February 3, 1948, at home in his sleep without the coin in his pocket. His sons thought he had lost the coin in the woods and were disappointed that it could not be passed down the generations of the Lomeo family tree. They never learned that Paolo's actions were more valuable than any coin. He had taught them to be honorable, to respect their families, and to defend oneself against the people of greed and power. Paolo never was able to return the favor for John's death, never had the time to explain himself to his two living sons, and never held his wife again. He died too soon.

Notes

The articles, books, and websites cited below were in most incidents used in more than one chapter, but are only cited once in these Notes under the chapter where the information initially appeared.

The newspaper articles refer to Paolo as Paul Lomeo.

Some of the information in this book was based on oral statements or stories given to me by various people. I did my best to verify the oral information. If there was a conflict between the oral information and information verified with my primary sources, I used the primary source information.

CHAPTER ONE

Jacques Petit's name and involvement could not be verified. He is a fictional character.

James Tomasello's name, position in the U.S. Armed Services, and involvement could not be verified. He is a fictional character.

Luigi Boselli's name and involvement could not be verified. He is a fictional character.

Antonio Di Rudini and Carlo Di Rudini were actual people but their involvement in Paolo's martial hearing could not be verified, en.wikipedia.org/wiki/Antonio_di_Rudini.

Gabriele D' Annuzio was an actual person but his involvement in Paolo's martial hearing could not be verified. Biographical Information for Gabriele D'Annuzio, en. *Wikipedia.org/wiki/Gabriele_D"Annuzio*, Italy From Revolution to Republic, 1700 to Present, (1995), Spencer M. Di Scala, and La Storia, Jerre Mangione and Ben Morreale, (1992).

CHAPTER TWO

Mother Superior Tarsila's interaction with Paolo could not be verified. She is a fictional character.

Antonio Maggiore's name and relationship could not be verified. He is a fictional character.

Treaty of London of 1915, www.history.com/this-day-in-history/allies-sign-treaty-of-london.

Triple Alliance, *Italy From Revolution to Republic, 1700 to Present*, (1995), Spencer M. Di Scala.

Giuseppe Garibaldi, *Italy From Revolution to Republic, 1700 to Present,* (1995), Spencer M. Di Scala and La Storia, Jerre Mangione and Ben Morreale, (1992).

John Patterson was an actual person. His interaction with Alberto could not be confirmed. Alberto did meet an American during his youth during Garibaldi's expedition to Sicily. He believed his American friend was from Pittsburgh and had died early in life. John Patterson's plight was explained in a museum exhibit at the Fredericksburg and Spotsylvania National Military Park.

CHAPTER THREE

Benito Mussolini, *Italy From Revolution to Republic, 1700 to Present*, (1995), Spencer M. Di Scala and La Storia, Jerre Mangione and Ben Morreale, (1992).

Fasci Siciliani, *Italy From Revolution to Republic, 1700 to Present,* (1995), Spencer M. Di Scala and *La Storia,* Jerre Mangione and Ben Morreale, (1992).

CHAPTER FOUR

Birds of Passage, *La Storia*, Jerre Mangione and Ben Morreale, (1992).

Pardone, *La Storia,* Jerre Mangione and Ben Morreale, (1992).

Americanos, La Storia, Jerre Mangione and Ben Morreale, (1992).

Paolo's ship manifest, *New York Passenger Arrival Lists (Ellis Island) 1982-1924 for Paolo Lomeo at ellisisland.org.*

RMS Olympic, *en.wikipedia.org/wiki/RMS_Olympic.*

Carnegie, McCandless and Company, *en.wikipedia.org/wiki/Edgar_Thomson_Steel_Works*.

The people Paolo met on Olympic are fictional characters.

CHAPTER FIVE

History and Culture of Northern Italians, *Italy From Revolution to Republic, 1700 to Present*, (1995), Spencer M. Di Scala and *La Storia*, Jerre Mangione and Ben Morreale, (1992).

Ellis Island Experience, Italy From Revolution to Republic, 1700 to Present, (1995), Spencer M. Di Scala and *La Storia*, Jerre Mangione and Ben Morreale, (1992).

Dr. Alex Hilton is a fictional character. This part of the story is a composite of the Author's grandparents' Ellis Island experience.

Angelo Di Carlo's name and involvement could not be verified. He is a fictional character.

Broadway Limited, *en.wikipedia.org/wiki/Broadway_Limited*. The actual train Paolo took from New York, NY, to Harrisburg could not be verified.

The grocery store owned and managed by Mr. Cali could not be verified. He is a fictional character. The actual lives of the Calis could not be verified.

Mrs. Laughlin's name could not be verified. She is a fictional character. David McGillis's name could not be verified. He is a fictional character.

CHAPTER SIX

Josephine Mangini's name could not be verified. This Author recollects meeting a person he called "Mama JoJo" as a five-year-old boy, but cannot recall her actual family name. Rosalia did tell this Author that she lived with Mama JoJo when she first moved to McKeesport, PA. She is a fictional character.

Grocer McDonough's name could not be verified. This Author could not verify the former owner of the produce store. Oral stories by Rosalia and other relatives said the store was purchased from an insolvent owner.

Citation issued by Officer Rodkey to Paolo could not be verified. Telli's name and involvement could not be verified.

Antonio Grazie, Mangia Dorm, could not be confirmed. Paolo, according to oral stories, did have a partner in the store for the first few years.

Mangia Dorm is a composite of people known to this Author. This is a fictional character.

McKeesport History of 1920s, en.wikipedia.org/wiki/McKeesport_Pennsylvania.

Mayor'sstatement, *www.library.pitt.edu/labor_legacy McKeesport3Strikesframe2.htm* and The Pittsburgh Press, page 1, July 26, 1901, and The Independent, Volume LIII, page 1768, July-September, 1901, Regents of The University of Minnesota.

CHAPTER SEVEN

Pastericks are fictional characters.

This Author can recall the physical look of Roma's Fruit Market. It seemed to the Author that the store probably did not change a lot from 1930s to the early 1970s.

"Probers Find Dead Man in Ruined Store", subtitle, "Victim has $500 check signed by Proprietor. Powder Tin Found," The Pittsburgh Press, page 1, March 28, 1929.

"Local Man Dies in Fire", subtitle, "Pittsburgh Police Think He Touched Off Butcher Shop Blast," The Daily News, McKeesport, PA, page 1 and page 27, March 29, 1929.

"Delay Yamin Hearing", subtitle, "Sleuths Pres Probe of Fatal Meat Market Blast", The Pittsburgh Press, page 1, March 30, 1929.

"Butcher Held in Shop Blast", subtitle, "Charged with Plotting to Secure $17,000 Insurance," Pittsburgh Post-Gazette, page 1, April 3, 1929.

"Police Attend Corbett Burial", subtitle, "Funeral Services Held Yesterday for Head of City of Homicide Squad, Pittsburgh Post-Gazette, page 3, December 3, 1929.

"Seek Missing Arson Witness", subtitle, "Attorney's Office Reveals Name Unknown Since Officer Died, The Pittsburgh Press, page 12, February 2, 1930.

"Arson Trail Opens Today", subtitle, "Butler Street Man Faces Charge in Blast, Pittsburgh Post-Gazette, page 1, February 3, 1930.

"Seeks to Refute Arson Charge", subtitle, "Butcher Testifies Blast in Shop Due to Feud with Racketeers, The Pittsburgh Press, page 1, February 4, 1930.

"Jury Finds Butcher Is Guilty of Arson", subtitle, "Defense Counsel to Ask New Trial Today", The Pittsburgh Press, page 1, February 6, 1930.

Tombstone of Jimmy Lomeo, www.usgarchives.net/pa/allegheny/tsphoto/ stmarygerman-mckeepsort/lomeo-jimmy.jpg.

Joey "The Dime" Andoloni's name could not be verified. This is a fictional character.

CHAPTER EIGHT

Dollar Conversion to 2013 Dollars, www.dollartimes.com/calculators/inflation.htm

"Produce Dealers Buy Out of City", The Pittsburgh Press, page 4, October 1, 1945.

"Produce Men To By-Pass Terminal Here", Pittsburgh Post-Gazette, page 1 and page 4, October 1, 1945.

"Producer Dealer Again Sues Union", The Pittsburgh Press, page 6, October 3, 1945.

"Court Besieged by Produce Men", Pittsburgh Post-Gazette, page 4, October 4, 1945.

"Produce Peace Chances Remote", The Pittsburgh Press, page 1 and page 4,

From the Ice to the Fire

October 4, 1945.

"Produce Strike Deadlock Still Tight as Ever", Pittsburgh Post-Gazette, page 1 and page 4, October 5, 1945.

"Warehousemen in Produce Strike", The Pittsburgh Press, page 1, page 2 and page 8, October 5, 1945.

"Produce Strike Likely to Spread", The Pittsburgh Press, page 1 and page 3, October 6, 1945.

"Produce Strike Hit Dealers for $800,000", The Pittsburgh Press, page 1 and page 6, October 7, 1945.

"Produce Strike Hits Johnstown", The Pittsburgh Press, page 1 and page 4, October 8, 1945.

"Produce Union Put Embargo Around City", subtitle, "Strikes Threatened in Nearby Cities", The Pittsburgh Press, page 1 and page 5, October 9, 1945.

The word "employee" was spelled "employe" by the unions and newspapers of 1945.

CHAPTER NINE

Judge William Challener Biographical Information, The Pittsburgh Press, page 6, February 27, 1945.

Judge William Challener's courtroom number could not be verified.

CHAPTER TEN

Ruth Mikuska is a fictional character.

CHAPTER ELEVEN

"Produce Man Gives Up Fight, Decides to Join the Union", subtitle, "Lomeo Blasting Courts and Police, says there's Nothing Else He Can Do". Prophet in the Wilderness speech to the Court, The Pittsburgh Press, page 1 and page 2, October 10, 1945.

"Lomeo Regains His Gun Permit". The article states that Chief Rodkey did not know whether he had the legal right to revoke the permit, but "took the action as a precautionary measure to prevent trouble." Though Judge Kennedy sustained Paolo's appeal, he commended Rodkey for using such caution and said he would have done the same himself. The Pittsburgh Press, page 6, October 23, 1945. Author's comment: Seems odd that a judge would agree that Rodkey violated Paolo's constitutional right to protect himself against violence and then state from the bench that he agrees with Rodkey's action. Would Judge Kennedy have ruled in favor of Paolo if Paolo had not joined the Teamsters two weeks prior?

CHAPTER TWELVE

"What Price Faith?", The Pittsburgh Press, Editorial Page, page 14, October 11, 1945.

CHAPTER THIRTEEN

"2 Men Killed in Accidents on Highways", subtitle, "McKeesporter Fatally injured when hit by Automobile", article on the death of John Lomeo, The Daily News, McKeesport, PA, Front Page, December 24, 1945.

Arthur Fry was listed in newspaper articles as residing in Swissvale, Pennsylvania. Swissvale is a small borough close to the city of McKeesport.

Obituary of John Lomeo, The Daily News, McKeesport, PA, page 15, December 24, 1945.

The actual cause of death of James Tomasello could not be verified. Paolo and Rosalia did attend a funeral in Washington, D.C., but the actual date and location could not be verified. It had to occur prior to February 3, 1948.

Obituary of Paul Lomeo (Roma), The Daily News, McKeesport, PA, page 15, February 3, 1948. The Daily News used the alias Roma, since most residents of McKeesport believed Paolo's last name was Roma.

Scott & Johnson law firm is a fictional law firm.

The character of Mrs. Tomasello could not be verified. Accordingly, the family relationship between Mrs. Tomasello and Giuseppe Esposito could not be verified. She is a fictional character.

Giuseppe Esposito classified as a member of the Sicilian Mafia, www.fbi.gov/about.us/investigate/organizedcrime/italian_mafia.

Dr. Hebner's information, including the location of the city he practiced medicine, was changed since the actual medical records of Paolo's doctor could not be accessed. Therefore, his treatment of Paolo could not be confirmed. Paolo had a very close relationship with his doctor according to his son. Dr. Hebner and his wife are fictional characters.

There is no way to verify the rationale behind the non-prosecution of Arthur Fry prior to 1966. Any statements or reasons are hearsay evidence.

"Fry Acquitted", article on the trial of Arthur Fry for the manslaughter of John Lomeo, The Washington Reporter, Washington, PA, page 14, December 1, 1966.

AFTERWORD

The following is an editorial from the Pittsburgh Post-Gazette, page 8, October 12, 1945.

What's the Use?

As Paul Lomeo gives up his losing fight and forks over $13 to the union he didn't want to join, the public which admired his spunk may as well join him in asking "What's the use?"

Owning his own little produce business and running it himself, Mr. Lomeo belongs to that diminishing group of men who are neither employers nor employes. As such, one might think he would have no connection with organized labor unless he was going to bargain with himself for himself. All he wanted to do was to earn his own living with his own hands and brains as he had been doing for a good many years.

But when the Commission House Drivers and Produce Workers renewed their drive to organize the small independent produce men in defiance of a court injunction, he discovered that courts and police departments as well were organized against him. A judge, to be sure, did grant him a writ to enable him to get his produce out of a warehouse but without any court protection. The police not only refused to defend his lawful business against unlawful interference but even revoked a permit for the gun with which he might have protected himself.

So a man who had the guts to buck a racket found himself up against something which apparently took the heart out of his fight. When the forces of law and order line up against the law-abiding citizen, it isn't surprising to find him saying, "What's the use?"

James Lomeo is an attorney in Monroeville, Pennsylvania. He graduated from Washington and Jefferson College and University of Pittsburgh School of Law.

Jim has developed a successful law office concentrating on real estate transactions.

As a member of his community, Jim has served in state, county and local appointed and elected offices. He is the former Mayor of Monroeville, Pennsylvania

On the personal front, Jim has been married to Susan since 1989 and they have three wonderful daughters, Natalie, Lucia and Juliet.

Made in the USA
Charleston, SC
01 November 2014